Praise for the Psychic Eye Mysteries

Better Read Than Dead

"This tense and suspenseful novel, based on a true story, sets a fast pace that never lags. And, in a perfectly designed conclusion, the pieces fall together in an utterly satisfying way."

—*Romantic Times*

"This catchy plot has it all—love, death, laughs, and action. Don't miss this terrific read."

—*Rendezvous*

"Victoria Laurie has done it again! This is a book that mystery fans will want to read over and over again. As with her first book, this one kept me guessing until the very end. Laurie is a very talented writer, with a knack for creating characters so real they practically jump off the page."

—BookReview.com

A Vision
of Murder

A Psychic Eye Mystery

Victoria Laurie

A SIGNET BOOK

SIGNET
Published by New American Library, a division of
Penguin Group (USA) Inc., 375 Hudson Street,
New York, New York 10014, USA
Penguin Group (Canada), 90 Eglinton Avenue East, Suite 700, Toronto,
Ontario M4P 2Y3, Canada (a division of Pearson Penguin Canada Inc.)
Penguin Books Ltd., 80 Strand, London WC2R 0RL, England
Penguin Ireland, 25 St. Stephen's Green, Dublin 2,
Ireland (a division of Penguin Books Ltd.)
Penguin Group (Australia), 250 Camberwell Road, Camberwell, Victoria 3124,
Australia (a division of Pearson Australia Group Pty. Ltd.)
Penguin Books India Pvt. Ltd., 11 Community Centre, Panchsheel Park,
New Delhi - 110 017, India
Penguin Group (NZ), cnr Airborne and Rosedale Roads, Albany,
Auckland 1310, New Zealand (a division of Pearson New Zealand Ltd.)
Penguin Books (South Africa) (Pty.) Ltd., 24 Sturdee Avenue,
Rosebank, Johannesburg 2196, South Africa

Penguin Books Ltd., Registered Offices:
80 Strand, London WC2R 0RL, England

First published by Signet, an imprint of New American Library,
a division of Penguin Group (USA) Inc.

First Printing, December 2005
10

Copyright © Victoria Laurie, 2005
All rights reserved

Ⓟ REGISTERED TRADEMARK—MARCA REGISTRADA

Printed in the United States of America

PUBLISHER'S NOTE
This is a work of fiction. Names, characters, places, and incidents either are
the product of the author's imagination or are used fictitiously, and any resemblance to actual persons, living or dead, business establishments, events, or
locales is entirely coincidental.

The publisher does not have any control over and does not assume any
responsibility for author or third-party Web sites or their content.

For Jim McCarthy and Martha Bushko.
Simply by saying yes, you changed my life and
made so many dreams come true.
I am forever grateful.

ACKNOWLEDGMENTS

More than any other manuscript I've written thus far, this one relied upon the help and generosity of so many people. In December of '04, while walking down three snowy steps, I slipped and broke my hand. At the time, I was one hundred pages into this very manuscript— with two hundred more due in less than thirty days.

I didn't make that deadline; in fact, had it not been for the understanding, kindness and assistance of so many dear friends and family, I'm not sure I would have finished at all. To that end, I can't tell you what it means to me that all of you offered so much time, advice, research, love, support and care. I'm so humbled by it all, and I hope that you're just as proud of this work as I am, because truly this is yours as much as it is mine.

So, I would like to thank the following people who stepped forward and gave of themselves so that this story could reach bookshelves on time:

My sister, Sandy, who cared for me after surgery with patience and love, and became my Google goddess! Thomas Robinson, you *amazing* man, you! Where would this story even be if not for all your efforts, knowledge and expertise? Dr. Stephen Pap, aka "Dr. Delicious," who mended my hand and got me through a very painful ten days with heavy doses of laughter and one *silky* accent. Martha Bushko, who went through a similar experience and understood exactly what I needed. I'm thankful for the fact that you put no pressure on me to finish and the amazing editing job you did means the world to me. Jim McCarthy, how do I even tell you how grateful I am for all your encouragement, support and enthusiasm? You're *so* one of my favorite people on earth! This one's for you, my friend.

Rebecca Rosen, merci for helping me to understand that connection between you and The Other Side, and making the character of Theresa come alive. Silas Hudson—I adore you, sugar. Thank you for checking in on me to see how I'm doing. You always boost my day. Dell Chase and Karen Orkney, my friends and cheering squad—I'm so grateful to you for your kindness, wisdom and laughter! Jon and Naoko Upham, my brother and sister-in-law, merci for your love and support. Lisa Madgwick . . . Liza, this is your story, sweetie—rest in peace my friend, I miss you so! And, of course, all of you out there who wrote letters and e-mailed me to tell me that you were enjoying the series. Your continued support and encouragement blow me away. I humbly thank you all.

Chapter One

I consider myself a professional; a psychic intuitive who is proud of how she makes a living; confident that the skills and abilities I innately possess give me a unique advantage to deal with just about any quirky, strange, bizarre or *unusual* situation that may crop up in my line of work.

Having said all that, however, I'll have to admit that I'm the first to say, "Eeeek!" and run screaming like a little girl when it comes to even the *thought* of a ghostly encounter. Hypocritical as that may sound, I'm a big fat yellowbelly when it comes to things that go bump in the night.

I'm so afraid of ghosts and the places they inhabit, in fact, that I can't even watch a *movie* about them, let alone hang out in a home they might occupy. That I would come to own a house haunted by a ghost trapped and reliving the night she was murdered over and over never even occurred to me on the day after Christmas as Cat—my sister—and I sat lazily in her living room sipping snifters of Grand Marnier and chewing the postholiday fat.

"I'm telling you, Abby, it's a great idea. I've always wanted to get into real estate, but—let's face it—the housing market here in Massachusetts is ridiculously overpriced. I understand that the market in Michigan is so much more affordable. I mean, look at your neighborhood. People are heading there in droves. This is a good idea, I just know it."

I sighed as I swirled the peachy amber liquid in the bottom of my snifter. I had no one to blame but myself for the current track of the conversation. After all, I'd brought the topic up myself when I'd casually mentioned that right before Christmas my handyman, Dave, had told me about an old house in my neighborhood that had been on the market for years, and was selling for a song. "What's wrong with it?" I'd asked him skeptically.

"Nothing a little TLC from yours truly couldn't fix," he'd answered, pumping his eyebrows up and down like he was all that and a bag of chips.

"So buy it," I'd said easily.

"I'd love to, but my credit wouldn't support the purchase."

"Oh? What's wrong with your credit?"

"I don't have any."

"Ah," I said flatly, already knowing where this was heading.

"See, that's why I'm talking to you about it. You're the one with the banking background. What would you say about going into business together? You and I could buy homes that need some work, then we could fix them up and sell them at a profit. You make the purchase and the payments, while I buy all the raw materials and supply the labor. After we're finished, we sell the house and split the profits, fifty-fifty."

Dave, of course, was hitting me at a vulnerable time.

I'd just closed on a new house, having financed the down payment with part of the check I'd received from the insurance agency for the settlement on my old home—which had recently burnt to the ground. There was still a substantial amount of money left and I'd been feeling pretty good about a bank account that now had a few more zeros in front of the decimal.

So I had the money to invest, but I wasn't so sure about the soundness of the idea. Besides, investment properties typically required a twenty percent down payment, which would effectively reduce the bank balance by a whole zero.

I took another sip from my snifter as Cat continued. "Really, Abby, I've seen the kind of work Dave does, and I trust him to do a terrific job. If I supply the down payment, you manage the mortgage payments, and Dave handles the construction—where's the risk?" she asked confidently.

I sighed and swirled the amber liquid around a few times mulling over the opportunity. After a moment I asked, "So how would this partnership work—specifically?"

"It's simple," she began, "The three of us should start a real estate investment firm. My lawyers can draw up the paperwork so that we are all equally represented, and as a group we can invest in properties that have potential. I can help identify the hottest neighborhoods and put up the down payment, you can arrange and manage the financing and Dave can work his construction magic."

I squirmed in my chair; it sounded like a lot of work.

Sensing my hesitancy, my sister offered, "Why don't we just try it on this first house, and see how it goes. We can always call it quits if it doesn't work out on this deal."

"Well . . ." I hemmed, "I'm just not sure, Cat. It's a big commitment."

"Oh, get over it," Cat said looking sternly at me. "This isn't charity, this is an investment. This could be very lucrative for all three of us."

Cat obviously thought I was hesitating because I was reluctant to take her money—which she had gobs and gobs of. But taking her money hadn't bothered me nearly as much as the thought of being her business partner.

Now, don't get me wrong, I love my sister dearly. But I also know her and know how she operates. Cat is a financial genius and single-handedly runs a multimillion-dollar corporation she built on little more than chutzpah, but she is also a tyrant when it comes to being the boss. It isn't just that my sister knows best . . . it's that Cat *knows* she knows best. By going into business with her I'd be saying yes to Patton.

"I don't know . . ." I hemmed again.

"Okay," she persisted, going for a different angle, "what does your intuition say?"

"I haven't checked with it yet," I answered sheepishly.

"Why not?"

"I don't know, it just didn't occur to me," I said, trying to dodge the bullet. The truth was that I hadn't checked with my intuition on the subject because I was afraid of the answer—namely, that I should go for it.

For once I wanted the decision to be a logical, rational choice and not one that I'd arrived at after pestering my spirit guides about it. They wouldn't steer me wrong of course, but sometimes it's just nice to be able to make a decision that is, for better or for worse, solely my own.

"So, why don't you ask now?" Cat persisted.

I scowled at her, "Not right now, honey, I'm tired—"

"Oh pish-posh!" she snapped. "God, Abby, sometimes you are *so* indecisive. Trust me, this is a good business opportunity, and if you don't take Dave and I up on this, then he and I will just do it together . . . without you."

My eyes grew large. "So, if I don't agree, then you'll just go around me to Dave?"

"In a heartbeat," she said firmly. "If for nothing else than to say 'I told you so' six months from now."

I scowled at her reply. I had little doubt that Cat would move forward with this idea if I didn't hop on board. She was like that; the moment her mind was made up it was made up, and I didn't think I could let Dave try to "manage" Cat on his own. He'd definitely need a buffer. *"Fine,"* I said with an exasperated sigh.

"Really?" she asked, leaning forward in the overstuffed chair she was sitting in. "Oh, Abby, that's great! See? Isn't this exciting?" She beamed.

"Thrilling," I said, my voice a monotone. "I'll call Dave tomorrow and get the ball rolling. We'll probably want to finance through my bank since I still have connections in the mortgage department and can probably get us a good deal on the closing costs." I was referring to the bank I used to work for before becoming a professional psychic.

Cat continued to smile hugely at me as she lifted her glass in a toasting gesture. "Good for you! See? That wasn't so hard, now was it?"

Later that night, as I was packing for my return home the next morning, the phone rang and in a few moments, Donna, Cat's housekeeper, came to my bedroom door. "The telephone is for you," she said stiffly.

"Did you bring the cordless up with you?" I asked, looking at her empty hands. Everyone knew that the phone in Cat's room had terrible reception.

"No," she answered, with a small smile that reminded me of a crocodile.

I didn't like Donna, and it bothered me that Cat wouldn't listen to my suggestion that she replace the woman. "After you then," I said tersely as I followed her out the door and down the stairs. As I walked behind her, I was troubled by the icky feeling I got every time the woman was within ten feet of me. I couldn't really put my finger on it, but this woman was up to something, and I didn't trust her as far as I could throw her, which, given her portly size, was one dislocated disc away from a millimeter.

At the bottom of the stairs I made a quick dash around her—the only person calling me at night here was my boyfriend, Dutch, and even though I'd see him in the morning when he picked me up from the airport I still looked forward to talking with my favorite baritone. Reaching the phone I snatched it up and said in the silkiest voice I could muster, "Hello, sexy, guess who's not wearing any underwear?"

"Excuse me?!" came a shocked and indignant female voice on the other end.

"Uh . . . uh . . . uh . . ." I sputtered, immediately recognizing that the voice belonged to my very own Mommy Dearest.

"Abigail, is that you?" my mother demanded.

"Uh . . . ha, ha . . . hello, Claire, merry Christmas!" I stammered as my face grew hot and my palms began to sweat.

"Yes . . . to you as well, dear," she replied, her tone clipped and cold just like always. "Is your sister there? I'd like to speak with her if I could."

"Of course, I'll get her for you, and tell Sam I said

merry Christmas too," I offered, still trying to collect myself.

When my mother didn't reply I set the phone down gently on the counter and looked around the kitchen. Donna was in the corner by the cupboard with a satisfied smirk on her face. I knew immediately that she had gotten revenge on me for an incident that happened Christmas Eve, when I'd been telling Cat she needed to keep a close eye on her housekeeper and Donna had walked into the room. From the look of death I'd gotten Christmas morning, it had been quite obvious she'd overheard the entire conversation.

And, it was no secret that my parents considered me the black sheep of the family, and that I'd only agreed to spend Christmas with my sister this year because my parents, who lived in South Carolina and had originally promised to visit over the holidays, had opted instead to visit my aunt in California.

"Where's Cat?" I demanded.

Donna turned toward me, her face a mocking angelic "O." "Was that for Mrs. Masters? I thought it was for you. Sorry," she sang. *Liar, liar . . . pants on fire . . .* my intuitive inboard lie detector sang in my head.

"I'll bet," I snipped. "My sister? Where is she?"

"I think she's in the family room with the boys. Would you like me to go get her?"

"No, Donna, I think you've done plenty for one night," and I stomped out of the room hearing her chuckle under her breath behind me.

I walked into the family room and found Cat playing with my two nephews, Mathew and Michael. "Hey," I said, getting Cat's attention. "Claire and Sam have called to wish us all a bah humbug."

Cat's head snapped up at the mention of my parents' names—which, by the way, they'd insisted we call them since our teens. My relationship with them was very different from the one my sister shared with them, and for the life of me I couldn't figure out how my sister and I could agree that my parents were one Trisket short of a party tray, and yet treat them so differently.

For me, it was easy: I simply ignored them. This of course was made considerably easier by the fact that they'd ignored me my whole life, so they probably hadn't even noticed when the Hallmark cards stopped coming to their mailbox.

Cat, however, was a completely different story. She bit her tongue, swallowed her pride and tried to be civil. It was a testament to her willpower that she'd managed it for so long, as Claire and Sam Cooper were about the most bigoted, obtuse, stuck-up people ever to utter the words, "Pat Buchanan for President!"

"They're on the phone?" she asked nervously, her hand reaching to twist the strand of pearls at her neck.

"Asking to speak to you," I answered, giving her a sympathetic look.

"Oh!" Cat said, jumping to her feet and squaring her shoulders. "Wish me luck," she whispered as she quickstepped past me and headed for kitchen.

She would need a lot more than luck, but I nodded at her and gave her a thumbs-up as she looked back one more time before rounding into the kitchen. Poor Cat. It was like watching the lamb trot into the slaughterhouse.

A little while later I was back upstairs packing a tissue-wrapped package in my suitcase, when my bedroom door burst open. "Eeeeek!" I squealed, startled by the movement.

"Sorry!" Cat said, stifling a giggle. "It's only me. Geez, you're a little jumpy tonight."

I realized then that I was still clutching the tissue-clad package to my chest. Discreetly I turned away from my sister as I tried to stuff it into my luggage without drawing her attention.

"What's that?" Cat asked, peeking over my shoulder.

"Oh, this? It's nothing." I said as I reached for the zipper to the suitcase. "How was your conversation with Claire and Sam?"

"Ugh! They're coming to visit," Cat said, still peeking over my shoulder trying to see inside the suitcase.

"What? I thought they were headed back home to South Carolina after visiting with Betty." I moved my body a little closer to the opening of the suitcase trying to block Cat's view.

"No, they've decided to pay a visit. Apparently, Aunt Betty made them feel guilty about not having any current pictures of the twins, so they're on their way out here to take a few photos—you know, so they can prove they're good grandparents after all."

"Ah," I said as I got the suitcase closed and began to lift it off the bed to the floor. "Remind me to nominate them for grandparents of the year."

"You'll have to beat me to it," Cat deadpanned. "What are you hiding?" she asked, watching me struggle with the suitcase.

"Nothing," I answered a little too quickly.

"Really?" she replied, her mouth forming a knowing smile. "Would it perhaps have anything to do with that little dart into Victoria's Secret I saw you take on your way to the restroom this afternoon at the mall?"

"So when are they coming to visit?" I asked, trying to change the subject.

"Oh, come on, Abby! Tell me what you bought!" Cat demanded, pointing to the suitcase.

I sighed at my nosy sister, and knew there was no

getting out of it. "It's just a little something I picked up." I said casually as I set the suitcase on the floor. "Really, it's nothing special."

"Then why won't you show it to me?"

"Well . . ." I said, searching for an excuse she would buy, "it's a little risqué, and I'm afraid you'd judge me."

"Why would I do that? Come on, what's the special occasion?"

I regarded her for a moment, then shrugged my shoulders and explained, "Dutch is taking me to Toronto for my birthday, and I just wanted something special—you know, something that puts a little 'voom' into the old 'va-va.' "

"Slut? . . . I mean 'what'?" Cat said, her eyes dancing with merriment. My sister really put the "T" in tact.

"And you wonder why I didn't show you sooner," I said while I watched Cat heave my luggage back onto the bed and tear it open. She retrieved the now crumpled tissue bundle and tore it open, revealing a black lace velvet teddy.

"Ooooo, Abby! This is gorgeous!"

"Yeah, thanks. Can we put it back in the suitcase now?" I asked, my cheeks feeling warm for the second time that evening.

"Let's see how it looks on!" Cat said, and threw the teddy on the floor by the bed. "Yep," she declared through another chuckle, "it fits *perfectly*."

"Ha, ha!" I said as I stooped to pick up the teddy. "You're *hilarious,* Cat. Really mining some *comic gold* here."

"Oh, lighten up," she said as she plopped onto the bed. There was no getting rid of her now. Her interest had been piqued. "So! Tell me about this little *excursion* you two lovebirds are taking."

I rolled my eyes and fought the urge to walk out of the room. "It's no big deal, just something nice Dutch is doing for my birthday." I was turning thirty-two in three days and this was the first birthday in a very long time I would be celebrating with a significant other.

"That's so romantic!" Cat said. "When are you going?"

"We're supposed to go tomorrow, but . . ."

"But?"

"Well, it's weird. I don't know why, but I just feel like Dutch is going to cancel on me. I mean, the plans are all set, and I talked to him yesterday and he's still gung ho, but something's telling me he's going to pull out at the last minute."

"Do you think he'll have to work?" Cat asked.

"I don't know. He's supposedly wrapping up a case right now, but with the FBI you never know."

Cat looked at me while she tapped a thoughtful finger against her lips. She'd known me long enough to trust that when my intuition said something was going to happen it nearly always did. After a moment she brightened and said, "All you can do is hope for the best. I'm sure it will all be fine. You're just nervous about your first night together."

"I don't even want to know how you know that," I said crossly.

"Oh please, Abby. You went all red faced and sweaty the moment I pulled out the teddy. What I don't understand is how you two have waited so long to consummate your relationship. I mean—don't you two have *urges*?"

"Can we talk about something else?" I asked, burying my face in my hands. This was humiliating. Dutch and I had been dating for several months now, and the fact that we hadn't spent the night together had been a combination of poor timing, injuries and cold feet. It seemed that every time one of us was ready, the other wasn't, and so the pressure of having put it off for so long was making my stomach bunch like a virgin on her wedding night.

"Hey," my sister offered, "I'm sure it will be great. You two really seem to like each other, and that's the important part. So many of my friends rushed the physical part of their relationships and they paid for it later when they realized they had never built a good foundation. You and Dutch have that connection, and I'm thinking that teddy or no teddy, it's going to be fine."

"You sure?" I asked, peeking through a crack in my hands.

"I'm positive," my sister answered, flashing me a reassuring smile.

Just then there was a quick knock on my door and Cat and I both looked up to see Donna in the doorway. "Yes?" Cat asked.

"There is another phone call for you, Miss Cooper," Donna said looking at me.

I'll bet, I thought. "Who is it?" I asked wary.

"It is a gentleman. He says it's urgent and to come quickly."

My boyfriend the prankster. Urgent was our code word for "turned on." I smiled at Cat, gave her a wink and bounded down the stairs to the kitchen phone. "Hello!" I said.

"Abby?" a male voice that wasn't my boyfriend's asked.

"Yes?" I replied, my brow frowning as my mind raced to put a name to the voice.

"It's Milo."

"Milo! Happy holidays, honey! Are you over at Dutch's?" I asked. Milo was Dutch's old police partner and best friend.

"No. Listen, I don't know how to tell you this . . ." Milo began and I suddenly realized how tense he sounded even as a chill swept up my spine and my intuitive phone began buzzing loudly in my head.

"Oh my God," I whispered. "Something's happened, hasn't it?"

"Yes, I'm afraid so. It's Dutch," Milo said as the world began to spin around me. "You need to come home tonight if you can, Abby. Dutch has been shot."

Chapter Two

"So are you just going to pout in the corner all day?" Dutch asked me.

I glanced up from my chair across the hospital room long enough to shoot him a look of death, then lowered my gaze back to my shoe as it bounced up and down, tapping out my irritation.

"Come on, Edgar," he said. Edgar was Dutch's favorite nickname for me. It was short for the great psychic of the 1920s, Edgar Casey. In his quest to understand his girlfriend and her abilities, Dutch had read up on Mr. Casey, and now considered himself something of a subject matter expert. "Give me a break, after all, I've been shot."

"In the ass," I added, my tone ice cold.

"Well, it still hurts," Dutch said, his baritone coming up an octave, searching for sympathy.

"Good. I'm glad it hurts!" I said getting up from my chair to stand over him as he lay on his side in the hospital bed. "Maybe next time you'll listen to me."

"Do you have to keep bringing that up?"

"Yes!" I snapped, crossing my arms and glaring down

at him. "I told you not to trust the dark-haired man with the parrot. That he was going to double-cross you and you shouldn't trust anything he said and that you needed to be especially careful near a warehouse. I don't know how much clearer I could be!"

Dutch had been shot in a warehouse by his own informant—a man with dark hair and an elaborate tattoo of a parrot on his arm. "What would you like me to tell my commander, Abby? That my girlfriend said I shouldn't finish out the assignment because a guy with a parrot might have it out for me?"

"Yes!" I wailed, as tears welled in my eyes. "That's exactly what I want you to do! Don't you get it? Don't you understand that you could have been *killed* out there?"

"Hey," he said, his voice low and soothing now that he saw the tears, "come on, Edgar, don't cry."

I was dribbling now, tears flowing freely down my cheeks. "Why don't you trust me?" I asked, wiping at the wetness.

"What are you talking about? Of course I trust you," he said as he reached out and grabbed my hand.

"No. No you don't. I have this gift for a reason. It's to help people. And if you don't trust *it,* then you don't trust *me.*"

"Abby," he said, drawing out my name with a sigh. "I do trust you, and I trust your gift. I know you think I ignored you, but the truth is that I did take your advice. I wore a vest—which I normally don't do when meeting an informant—and because I took precautions and was ready for trouble, the guy only managed to pop me in the rear. See? If I hadn't listened to you I'd probably be dead about now instead of enjoying your company in this *charming* setting."

"No," I argued moodily. "If you had listened to me, we'd be in Toronto by now."

With a grunt Dutch leaned over the side of his bed and worked the hinge to lower the metal bars. When they were down he reached over to me and pulled me to him, forcing me to sit down. From the beads of sweat on his forehead I could tell all that movement must have hurt so I didn't resist. "Listen to me," he said gently as he swept stray hair out of my eyes. "I will always listen to your spidey-sense, but I have a job to do, and I can't do that job effectively if I'm always worried about what might happen. The best I can do is listen to what you have to say and take some precautions. Anything more than that and I might as well quit the Bureau, which isn't something I'm prepared to do right now. Can you understand?"

I sighed heavily, and wiped again at the tears on my face. I knew he was right, but I didn't want to give in. I was still too emotional and I was using anger to cover up the intense fear I'd experienced ever since I'd heard he'd been shot. "So when are they bustin' you out of here?" I asked after a moment, wanting to change the subject.

Dutch sighed and squeezed my hand. He was smart enough to know when to quit while he was ahead. "Today."

"They're letting you go already?" I asked, worried again.

"Yeah. It's not like it's a critical wound. Besides, I told them my girlfriend would be playing nursemaid and the doc said that as long as I had someone to cook, clean and take care of my every whim, it'd be okay to check out this afternoon."

I narrowed my eyes at him, then looked around the room. "So where is this girlfriend anyway? We'd better get her over here pronto if she's going to be at your beck and call."

"Aww, come on, Abby. Play nice," he said, throwing me the puppy dog look.

"Maybe you should think about hiring a real nurse. I mean, I'm not really cut out for this type of thing, plus I've got a lot of work to do."

"I thought you took the month off?" Dutch challenged.

He had me there. I'd taken the supreme luxury of keeping the month of January all to myself. No readings were scheduled in my appointment book until February first, and I had planned to use the time to chill out, and decorate my new home. "I meant on the house. I have a lot of work to do on the house."

"Oh," he said and looked away from me toward the television. "Okay. I didn't realize it was such an inconvenience. I'll hire a nurse or something."

Crap. Why were relationships always so much easier in the movies? Finally I gave in and rolling my eyes asked, "So how long do you need me to change your diaper and warm your bottle?"

"Couple weeks."

"And I suppose you want me to stay with you while I'm playing nursemaid?"

"That's what I'm thinking."

I sighed heavily and shook my head. "*Fine*. But for the record? You owe me."

"I'd expect nothing less," he said, giving me a wink.

Several hours later I'd packed Eggy, my miniature dachshund, and me for a long visit and had returned to the hospital to pick up Dutch, who was then loaded carefully into my car and propped precariously on a doughnut-shaped pillow, wincing over every bump and pothole. "Why are you turning left here?" he asked as I took a slight detour.

"Dave and I are making an offer on an investment property and I wanted to drive by and see it."

"And you have to do that now?" he asked, squirming again in the seat as he tried to find a comfortable position.

"It'll only take a minute," I said, distracted as I looked from my directions to the road and back again. From the backseat Eggy gave an excited yap.

"See? Eggy wants to get home too. Can't you do this another time?" Dutch whined, squirming again.

"Relax," I said unsympathetically as I turned onto Fern Street and slowed the car as I looked for number 172. "It should be right down here . . ." I mumbled, counting down the addresses until I came to the last house on a dead-end street. Even before reading the number on the side of the house I could tell this was it.

"You're kidding, right?" Dutch said, gazing skeptically at the house in front of us.

"Unfortunately, I'm not." I answered, looking from my instructions to the house and back again. The place was awful. A one-story ranch with broken windows, hanging shutters, peeling siding and missing roof tiles, the scene looked like something right out of an Alfred Hitchcock movie. The front lawn was a mess of large holes; overgrown shrubbery and leaves piled high against the sides of the house. A rusty fence encircled the property and a squeaky gate swung back and forth as the wind blew, creaking out its annoyance.

"This place is a dump," Dutch said.

"Thanks for pointing out the obvious."

Just then, Eggy, who had been staring out the back window, moved over to the passenger side window and went haywire. As I looked back at my pooch I noticed the hair on his neck sticking straight up as his lips curled in a snarl and he began to growl, then bark in earnest in the direction of the house. The sound was piercing and I quickly tried to calm him by reaching over and giving him a pat on the back, but the longer we sat there the more upset he became. Finally I pulled away from the house and began driving away, but Eggy kept up his commotion until we were a few blocks away.

"What was *that* about?" Dutch asked when Eggy finally calmed down.

"I have no idea." I said, just as I noticed that the hair on my arms was also sticking straight up. I shuddered while a chill crept down my spine.

"You cold?" Dutch asked.

"Yeah, a little. Come on, Cowboy, let's get you home."

Later, after I'd made Dutch as comfortable as possible on his couch, I went into the study to call Dave.

"Hey, Abby!" he said jovially when he picked up the phone.

"Are you *kidding* me with this house, Dave?" I said, not wasting time on the niceties.

"Well Happy New Year to you, too," he said reproachfully.

"Sorry," I said, pulling in my horns. "But I had no idea the place was such a dump."

"That's why we're getting it for a song. Trust me, by the time I'm through with it, you won't even recognize it."

"Okay, okay," I said, remembering what a fantastic job Dave had done on my own home. "So I talked to Rick, my friend at the bank, and he says that he just got the paperwork for our LLC and we can close early next week if we want." Cat, Dave and I had just formed the investment firm of CO-MAS-MAC, which combined the first few letters of each of our last names. Not a very glamorous name, but hopefully a profitable

one. "Cat's providing the down payment," I continued, "and the house didn't appraise for much, so the
loan amount is fairly low. Have you talked with the
realtor?"

"Yeah, we're good to go on that. She said that she's
ready to do the closing whenever you are." I had been
named president and CEO of CO-MAS-MAC and
held the signing rights for all investments. Dave and
Cat weren't required to attend the closing. "The quicker
we get this thing buttoned up the sooner I can get
started on the repairs, so let me know the moment we
take possession, okay?" Dave said.

"It should be late next week, but I'll get back to
you with the official date in the next couple of days."

"Sounds good. I think I'll go to the Depot this week
and start preordering all the wood and supplies."

"Hey, what's the deal with that house anyway?" I
asked. "It looks like a bomb went off in it."

"From what I understand, no one's been living in
it for quite some time. The realtor says it's been aban-
doned for a while, and the owner has been trying to
sell it for a couple of years now."

"You would think they would have tried fixing it up
a little before putting it on the market," I remarked.

"Yeah, that would have been my plan, but the house
needs a ton of work and that costs money. The seller
might not have had the resources."

All of a sudden my intuition began to vibrate on
high. The way my intuition works is that when there's
a piece of information that I should know about, a
sensation much like a telephone ringing in another
room goes off in my head. If I want to know what the
message is, I simply answer the call. Automatically I
shifted my focus and tuned in to what my guides were
trying to tell me. An image of the house came to my

mind's eye and then the vision shifted to an emerald, a sapphire and a diamond sitting in a bird's nest. I shook my head not understanding the message, and got another vision of a swastika painted on the side of a tank. Confused, I tuned out Dave, who was still talking, and focused on the vision. I saw a small café that had a French flag waving from the doorway in my mind's eye. Odd. What did all of these images have to do with the house?

"Abby?" I heard Dave call from the receiver. "Abby, you there?"

"Uh, yeah, I'm here," I said, snapping out of my thoughts. "Say, do you know anything about the owner? Like, did they have a connection to Europe or something?"

"Sorry, I don't know anything about him other than the house originally belonged to a guy who died in the early nineties. I hear he willed it to his grandson who's the one trying to sell it to us."

Alarm bells were going off in my head. I had the distinct sensation that the house was bad news, but when I thought about pulling out of the sale, I intuitively felt that wasn't a good idea. Dave must have read my mind because he asked, "You thinking about canceling on me?"

I hesitated for just a moment, then said, "No, it's not that. I just hope you haven't bitten off more than you can chew here, with all the repairs this place needs."

"No sweat," he reassured me. "I've got everything under control." *Liar, liar . . . pants on fire . . .*

Great. Now I was really worried.

Ten days later, on January eighth, I scooted away from the closing table and stood up to shake my realtor's hand. The seller had not come to the closing, but had signed off earlier in the day leaving me to zip through the paperwork in record time.

"Congratulations," Kimber Relough, my realtor, said.

"Thanks, Kimber, but I'm not really sure I want to be congratulated yet."

"Oh, I know what you mean," she said with a wink. "You've really got your work cut out for you."

"Not me, my handyman." I whipped out my phone and speed-dialed Dave's number. "You can officially get to work, buddy," I said as he picked up.

"About time, I've been parked in the driveway for an hour."

"Patience isn't one of your virtues is it, Dave?"

"The quicker I get going, the sooner it gets done and the sooner we can collect our profit."

I chuckled as I thought about the change I'd seen in Dave since this whole thing began. When he'd worked for me on the renovation of my old house, he'd had one pace that I'd put somewhere just out of park and a little slower than snail, but suddenly, with the prospect of making a significant return on investment he was lit up and ready to go.

"Call me later with a progress report," I offered as I heard his truck door squeak open.

"You got it," he said and hung up.

I left the realty office and headed back to Dutch's, in no particular hurry to get back to playing nursemaid. I might be crazy about my boyfriend, but spending so much time together was beginning to wear on my last nerve. That, coupled with the fact that he had turned into a whiny four-year-old, was testing my patience. It seems that getting shot in the ass is far more debilitating an injury than I'd first suspected. The wound had made it difficult for Dutch to get up and maneuver, but apparently it had also made it difficult to reach the paper on the coffee table, change the channel even with the help of the remote, and brush one's teeth. In the past few days I'd seen a side of my boyfriend I wished I hadn't and I was beginning to rethink this whole "quality time" idea. I was thinking that when I got back to his place I should have a little chat with him about hiring a professional so I could go home.

When I walked through his front door, however, I was greeted with a pleasant surprise. A bathed and clean-shaven hunk stood in the living room leaning on a cane. "Hello, gorgeous," he said in greeting.

"Hey there, yourself," I answered. "What's all this?" I asked, waving at him.

"I guess I got tired of sitting around and complaining to you. It took me most of the morning but I managed a shower and got dressed all by myself," he said proudly.

"And you cleaned too," I said, noticing that the newspapers had been picked up off the floor then stacked on the coffee table, and the sheets on the couch had been folded into a neat little pile.

"Least I could do," Dutch said limping stiffly over to me. He'd been taking several steps a day around the living room, which was part of his physical therapy, and day by day it had grown a little easier for him. Today he managed to walk the ten steps over to me without grimacing.

"Way to go, Lightning," I chuckled.

"I have something for you," he sang.

"More dirty laundry?"

"That, *and* . . ." he said, pulling something out of his pocket, "this."

I leaned in to take a better look at the small red velvet box he was holding in his hand. "What's this?" I asked.

"It's a present."

"What's the occasion?"

"Your birthday."

"You missed it by a whole week there, Gimpy." I said, the hurt finally showing on my face. The day of my birthday had come and gone with nary a word from Dutch. I had convinced myself that in his injured delirium he had simply overlooked the date, but now that he'd finally remembered, it brought the sting right back.

"I know. I'm sorry. I don't know what I was thinking. You should have reminded me," he said, looking chagrined.

"You're a big boy," I suggested. "You're old enough to remember the important stuff on your own."

"Just open it," he coaxed and nudged the box at me.

I smiled, taking the box then pulled up the lid, and there, inside, was the most gorgeous pendant I'd ever seen. It was gold, in the shape of a triangle, and in the center was a fiery red opal with brilliant specks of orange, purple and green. "It's gorgeous," I said breathlessly.

"Just like the girl it was meant for," he said and caressed my cheek.

Just then my cell phone chirped loudly from my purse. I looked toward my purse then back at Dutch who was giving me a look like, "You gonna answer that?"

I smirked back and ignored the phone as I took a step closer to him, intending to kiss his socks off but just as I was about to make my move the house phone rang and Dutch and I both looked at the phone in the kitchen then back to each other. We seemed to both be tempted to answer the line, but we also didn't want to ruin the spontaneous romantic moment building between us. So we compromised and waited for the machine to pick up the call.

From the kitchen we could hear the answering machine announce that Dutch was unable to come to the phone and to leave a message. The moment the answering machine bleeped, a panicked voice shouted out from the machine, "Abby?! Dutch?! If you're there, *pick up*!"

I darted around Dutch and dashed into the kitchen, grabbed the phone and clicked the ON button. "Dave? I'm here, what's wrong?!"

"You guys gotta get over here right away!" Dave said, the anxiety in his voice making his voice spike.

"Why? What's happened?" I asked just as Dutch reached my side.

"I . . . I . . . I don't really know," he stammered. "You're gonna have to see it for yourselves."

"We're on our way," I said, and hung up the phone.

"Let's go," Dutch said, grabbing his coat off the chair.

Ten minutes later we had pulled up in front of the dilapidated house. As we got out of the car and headed up the driveway, we stopped in front of Dave's truck, where I noticed him inside, pale, shaking and staring blankly at the house. I knocked on the glass because he didn't seem to notice that we'd arrived. Without getting out of the truck, Dave lowered the window a fraction and spoke through the crack. "In there," he said, pointing to the house.

"What's in there?" Dutch asked.

"Oh man . . . I don't *know*!" Dave said, his eyes wide and frightened, and his hand shaking as he ran it through his long hair. "All I know is that I was in there working on the walls, when all of a sudden stuff started flying through the air."

"Excuse me?" I said as Dutch and I glanced at each other.

"I know it sounds crazy!" Dave said, his voice shrill. "But it happened, okay? I was pulling off the old drywall, and all of a sudden my drill came flying through the air, right at me, and if I hadn't ducked it would have nailed me in the head! And then my circular saw started up all by itself and chased me around the room! I'm telling you it was like some kind of Amityville horror in there!"

Dutch leaned in just a little closer to the crack in the window. I saw him discreetly sniff at the crack, and I knew he was checking for alcohol on Dave's breath. "What'd you have for lunch today, buddy?" he asked, his voice calm and soothing.

"A ham sandwich—with a side of 7-Up. I'm not drunk, Rivers," Dave said, clearly angered by the insinuation.

"He's telling the truth, Dutch," I said. Throughout Dave's panicked speech my inboard lie detector hadn't gone off once.

Dutch looked at me, a rather perplexed expression on his face. "You two stay here, I'm going in to check it out."

"That's a good plan there, Gimpy," I said pointing to the cane clutched in his hand. "You can barely hobble, much less run. What if someone's in there and they attack you?"

"I came prepared," he said, patting his breast pocket.

"Oh please," I replied. "I'm going with you and that's final." And with that I began walking toward the house. Behind me I could hear grumbling as Dutch forced himself to keep up with me.

"Will you slow down!" he hissed.

With a sigh I slowed down just enough for him to catch up, but not slow enough for him to overtake me. I could just imagine him handcuffing me to the front railing to keep me from going inside the house. My thought was that it was probably a bunch of kids or some kind of practical joke, but I'd never known Dave to lie or even exaggerate, and I couldn't imagine what had scared him so badly.

We reached the front porch and I stopped, suddenly unsure about going in. Dutch rounded me there and pulled me behind him, a move that made him wince, and my heart went out to the guy. He was sweating from the exertion of moving so quickly and I suddenly felt like a schmuck.

"Stay close behind me, and don't talk until I give the all clear," he said. With a jolt I suddenly realized he had already drawn his gun. Slowly, Dutch nudged the door open with his cane and after listening for a moment, moved to the doorway and took a very quick peek inside.

The house was silent. There was no clanging, or banging or rustling of chains. No eerie voice calling, "Get out!" and yet, the silence seemed more menacing. Dutch took a step forward, and I followed right on his heels, hanging on to his blazer as much to steady him as to reassure myself. He carefully moved into the front room of the house, his eyes darting around the interior.

I took in the front room and couldn't believe the sight. The house was a mess. The walls were so riddled with holes that it looked as if they had been attacked with a sledgehammer. The carpet was dotted with rips and tears and I couldn't even ascertain what its original color had been. Some shade of either blue or green by my estimate. There were no light fixtures but Dave had obviously rigged a bulb in the center of what used to be the living room, and even though it was midday on a sunny afternoon the interior seemed dark and foreboding. Shadows played off the walls as Dutch and I inched into the room, making the place look even spookier. To the right of us I spotted Dave's drill, poking straight out of the wall as if it had been thrown like a dart.

I pointed this out to Dutch and he nodded, his eyes focused and intent as we moved further into the room. We crossed the living room to the entrance of the kitchen and almost tripped over Dave's circular saw, which was resting peacefully just inside the doorway.

Just then a scent drifted under my nostrils. Alarmed I yanked on Dutch's blazer, the movement pulling him into me butt first. He winced, stifling a moan. I shrugged my shoulders in apology, then quickly pointed to my nose and gave a sniff. There it was. Cigarette smoke.

Dutch sniffed too, but shrugged his shoulders. He couldn't smell it. I sniffed again, moving my head in the direction of the kitchen. Dutch took another whiff, but shook his head "no." He still couldn't smell it. I nodded again toward the kitchen and we moved slowly into its interior. And as soon as we did so, the smell vanished. I came up short and continued to inhale through my nose hoping I could catch the pungent odor again, but to no avail. I left Dutch's side and moved about the kitchen looking for the scent, but I couldn't find it.

After a few beats he motioned for me to follow him again, and we moved into the other rooms—the living room, down the hallway to the two bedrooms and the bathroom—but we could find no trace of anyone or anything amiss, apart from the already demolished interior. Finally we came back to the kitchen. "What do you make of it?" he asked me.

"Hell if I know," I said, letting my arms slap at my sides. "I've known Dave for a year and I've never known the guy to be off his rocker. And did you see that drill in there? I mean, that puppy's really nailed into the wall!"

"What did you smell earlier?" Dutch said.

"I can't believe you couldn't smell it. I swear someone was chain-smoking in here."

"Cigarette smoke?"

"Yeah. It was really clear, like someone was smoking in the next room, but I couldn't see the smoke. You didn't smell anything?" I asked.

"Not a whiff."

"Weird."

"Very."

Just then I caught it again, the distinct smell of cigarette smoke and excitedly I whispered, "There! There it is, Dutch! Do you smell it?" I asked, taking several long sniffs.

"I don't smell anything," Dutch complained smelling the air just like me.

"It's coming from over there!" I said pointing over Dutch's shoulder toward a door that looked like it led to the basement.

We moved to the door, and Dutch stepped to one side and moved me behind him again. Leaning his cane against the wall, he grabbed the door handle in one hand, his gun in the other and pulled the door open. I tensed as the door swung wide, but nothing happened. After a moment I peeked around his shoulder into the dark interior where only the first several steps were visible. Nothing moved and no one said "Boo!" so I began to relax a little.

Just then, Dutch reached for the light switch and flooded the narrow staircase with light. I came around him to get a better view when a sudden burst of fluttering movement came straight at us up the staircase, and began to flap its wings over my head. Scared out of my mind I dropped to the ground and covered my head, screaming. A moment later I felt Dutch's hands on my arms as he shook me and yelled, "Abby! Abby, stop it!"

I stopped screaming and looked up into midnight blues that were dancing with merriment. "It's only a bird. Just a swallow that got trapped in the basement."

"A . . . a . . . bird?" I stammered as I got to my feet. Sure enough a small sparrow was flapping anxiously at the back sliding glass door, desperate to get out. "Oh! Yeah. Right," I said, laughing now. For some reason the comedy of the situation relieved all of the tension that I had felt when we entered the house and the two of us began to laugh. Dutch imitated my reaction covering his head with his hands and calling out, *"Ahhhhhhh!"* and that made the both of us bend over with laughter. When I calmed down long enough to remember there was a trapped bird in the house, I walked slowly over to the sliding glass door where the bird was still fluttering, unlocked it and let the little guy out. As it flew away I said, "Now we know what scared Dave."

Silence.

I pulled the door closed and said again, "What I mean is, Dave must have seen or heard the bird and thrown his own drill at the wall."

Silence.

"Dutch?" I asked over my shoulder as I watched the little bird flutter to a birdhouse out back.

"Abby!" he barked from behind me, his voice completely void of humor. "Call nine one one!"

"What?" I asked, turning around just in time to catch Dutch's cell phone, which he tossed at me from across the room.

"Call nine one one!" he shouted and dashed down the basement steps.

Alarmed, I tore across the kitchen to the top of the stairs to see whom he was chasing after, but as I reached the landing I came to an abrupt halt and sucked in a breath of surprise. At the bottom of the stairwell lay the crumpled form of a woman with beautiful blond hair dressed in a white nightgown and matching silk robe. Her skin was very pale, and her face stared up at me with lifeless eyes. About her head was a thick pool of red and I knew she had not survived her fall. Dutch was moving quickly down the stairs toward her, mindless of his own injury. "Ohmigod!" I gasped as I flipped open the phone and began punching in the three digits to emergency.

But even before I reached the final digit I heard Dutch say, "What the hell . . . ?!" And as I looked up quickly I sucked in another breath. Dutch stood stock still at the bottom of the stairwell, a look of shock and surprise plastered onto his face as he looked up at me as if to ask for an explanation. That's when I realized he was alone, and the woman in the nightgown had vanished into thin air.

Chapter Three

"So then what happened?" Milo asked as we sat in the ER. Dutch lay on his stomach with his butt in the air as an intern restitched all the sutures he'd pulled out of his wound on his flight down the stairs. I sat in a chair nearby trying not to squirm as I watched the attending doctor's needle dip up and down on my boyfriend's beautiful derriere.

"We saw this bird—" Dutch said.

"What kind of bird?" Milo interrupted.

Dutch looked a question at me and I shrugged. "I don't know, I never really got a good look at it. I think it was a swallow or something close to a swallow."

"Okay, go on." Milo said as he penciled the detail into his notebook.

"Well, then Abby went to let the bird out and I turned toward the basement stairs and there she was."

"There who was?" Milo asked, his pencil pausing on his pad.

"I don't know exactly. There was a young woman lying at the bottom of the steps, and she was hurt."

"Describe her," Milo said, back to scribbling.

"She was white, blond, petite . . . I'd say about five feet to five two in height. Age was late twenties, early thirties, roughly ninety to a hundred pounds. She was wearing a white dress—"

"Negligee," I supplied.

"What?" Milo asked, turning to me.

"She was wearing a white negligee, and a matching robe. And she was barefoot."

"Uh-huh, got it. Okay, so then what happened?"

Dutch and I looked at each other, still completely perplexed by what had happened at the house. The truth was, we really didn't know what we'd seen. One minute we'd been rushing to the rescue of some poor woman lying in a pool of blood at the bottom of a stairwell, and the next we were staring at an empty space and looking around as if we'd just entered the twilight zone. I had rushed down the stairs to see for myself that she'd really vanished and confirm that it wasn't just some strange trick of the eye, and that's when I'd noticed Dutch was bleeding.

We'd come here as quickly as we could to get Dutch cleaned up and restitched and on an impulse Dutch had called Milo, thinking that filling out a police report was the sort of thing one should do in this type of situation—whatever that meant.

"Well . . ." Dutch stammered, "I'm not really sure." He looked to me to supply the answer.

I dealt with weird on a daily basis, so I didn't hesitate to say, "She disappeared."

"Excuse me?" Milo asked, his pencil paused again on the top of the pad.

"Vanished. Into thin air," I said, allowing a little drama to creep into my voice.

"I don't understand." Milo said and turned to Dutch for explanation.

"Join the club, buddy," Dutch said and scratched his head.

"Okay, you're all set, Agent Rivers." The doctor said from behind Dutch as he peeled off his rubber gloves and came around the gurney. "Now, I recommend that you avoid taking any more stairs and rest for a few days before starting your physical therapy."

"Will do," Dutch said as he carefully squirmed back into his boxers.

I got up from my seat and went to help Dutch roll off the gurney and get his pants buttoned. "Thanks," he said sheepishly as I carefully pulled the back of his pants up over his new bandage.

"You're welcome, and you still owe me," I said, smiling at him.

"Can we get back to the vanishing chick?" Milo asked, watching us with a bit of skepticism.

"Milo," Dutch began as he reached carefully for his cane, "I don't know what to tell you, buddy. One minute I'm looking at a woman with a head trauma and the next thing I know she just isn't there. I don't know where she went and I don't know how it happened but I swear, I saw what I saw."

"Okay, okay," Milo said, holding up a hand of concession. "So, just to humor me, what kind of pain meds have you been taking for that war wound?"

"I saw it too, Milo," I said before Dutch had a chance to snap at his former partner.

"You saw her disappear?"

"Well, not exactly. I mean, I glanced away to dial nine one one, but when I looked back she was definitely gone."

"So you're positive you saw her lying at the bottom of the stairs?"

"Absolutely," I said, nodding.

"Okay," Milo shrugged and closed his notebook. "Maybe this one's better for you guys, Dutch."

"What do you mean?"

"Well, if this doesn't sound like something out of the *X-Files* I don't know what does. Come on," he said, looking at us with a big grin on his face. "You guys are playin' me, right?"

Dutch shot an angry look at his former partner, then turned and began to limp out of the curtained area.

"What'd I say?" Milo asked as Dutch swung back the curtain and limped over to the checkout desk.

"We're not making it up, Milo. It really happened."

"Okay." Milo said after a moment. "So you explain it, Abby. How the hell do both of you see a woman who's lying at the bottom of a stairwell, and in front of your eyes she disappears?"

"I have an idea how, but I'll need an hour to check it out."

"What?"

"Can you take Dutch home?"

Milo looked skeptically at the back of his old partner. "I'm willing," he said, "but he's a different story."

"I'll tell him you're taking him home. I have to check something out, and I'll be back with you guys in about an hour."

"Uh-huh . . ." Milo said doubtfully.

"Oh, Milo," I said reproachfully. "Order him some stinking pizza and he'll forgive you. I gotta fly. See ya later," I called and dashed out of the hospital, pausing for only a moment to let Dutch know that Milo would be his escort home.

An hour later I was back at Dutch's, the smell of warm pizza filling the room. "Where'd you go?" Dutch asked from the couch, a large piece of the meat-lover's special folded slightly and about to enter his mouth.

"I had to get this," I said holding up a thick reference text that I'd had to go to two bookstores to find.

"Haunted America," Dutch read from the title. "Spooky."

"Yes, but in here, gentlemen, is the answer to what we saw in that house today."

"I'm all ears," Milo said, his mouth full of pizza.

Quickly I shrugged out of my coat and reached over to open the lid of one of the boxes of pizza on the coffee table. "Awww, Hawaiian! You remembered," I said happily to Dutch, who gave me a wink and a smile as I scooped out a large piece and carefully laid it on the empty plate that had been set out for me.

"So here's the drill," I said when I was comfortably seated, the plate in my lap. "I think what we saw in that house is what's known as an imprint."

Both Dutch and Milo blinked at me, their faces suggesting they hadn't a clue what I was talking about. "Say what?" Milo asked me.

"An imprint," I repeated, my own mouth now full of crust and cheese. After swallowing I explained. "Six months ago I had a client tell me that her house was haunted. I did some research back then and I remembered this book and something about what we saw tonight clicked with something I read in this book." I set my plate down and reached for the text. Flipping it open to the section I'd marked I read, " 'There are places all over the United States marred by events so terrible that they have left their images forever imprinted on that physical space. The battle of Gettysburg is one such example where every night gunfire can be heard and wounded soldiers still call out for help.' "

"Say *what*?" Dutch asked me, looking at me like I'd grown four heads.

"I think what we saw today was the imprint of a murder," I said slowly, making my words ring with importance. "The woman at the bottom of the stairs was the ghost of someone who was murdered in that house."

"Murdered?" Milo asked, leaning forward with a skeptical look. "How do you know she didn't just slip and fall?"

I tapped my forehead and said, "My spidey-sense is saying she was the victim of foul play. Something awful happened to her—I think she was thrown down those stairs, and left to die."

"So you're saying we saw this woman's ghost?" Dutch asked, doubt creeping into his eyes.

"Yes, that's exactly what I'm saying."

"I don't believe in ghosts," he replied.

"Tell that to the woman at the bottom of the stairs," I said.

"She's got a point there, buddy."

"Shut up, Milo."

"I'm just sayin' . . ."

"This is crazy!" Dutch said, throwing down his pizza. "Abby, there's got to be another explanation."

"I'm all ears," I challenged, leaning back in my chair and giving him a "come on" motion with my hands.

There was a very long moment of hesitation as we stared each other down before Dutch finally scratched his head and said, "Give me that book, would ya?"

Milo and Dutch pawed through the text for about an hour, pausing at photos and drawings and reading out loud small snippets of interesting factoids from the text. While the boys examined the book, I finished my pizza, then went to call Dave. No one answered at his home phone, so I called his cell and waited while it rang.

"Hello?" Dave said when he finally picked up the line, his voice muffled and weird.

"Dave?" I asked, concerned. "What's wrong?"

"Nuffin . . ." he said. "I'm fffffine."

"You're drunk."

"NawI'mnot!" he slurred.

"Where are you?" I demanded. I was worried that he might try and drive in his condition.

"Home sweet hommme," Dave sang, and burped loudly. "Just watchin' the boob tube an' drinkin' some beer."

"Okay. I just wanted to check on you and make sure you weren't too shaken up by today."

"Don't want ta talk about it, Abby," Dave said.

"Okay. Go back to your show. I'll call you tomorrow afternoon," I said and hung up. Apparently Dave dealt with the unexplained by attempting to pickle himself.

I came back into the living room and took my seat again as Dutch and Milo closed the ghost text. "Okay. So what's the next step?" Milo asked us.

"I think we should try and find out who our mysterious woman was," I said. "Milo, can you check old police reports and find out if there are any records of a woman being murdered there?"

"How far back do you want me to go?" Milo said.

"From what I remember about what she looked like, it seemed to me that her hair style and clothing should have been twentieth century at least. Try going back fifty years and see what you come up with."

"Fifty?" Milo gasped. "Do you know how much time that will take me?"

"Okay, then try twenty-five and see if that reveals

anything. I'll go to the library and see if I can find anything with that address from the newspaper clippings. Something's gotta show up."

"What are we supposed to do once we find out who was murdered there?" Dutch asked, and for a moment that really stumped me.

"Good question." I said as I thought about it. "I don't know offhand, but I can put a call in to Theresa and see if she has any ideas."

"Theresa?" Milo asked.

"My best friend. She lives in California and she's a fantastic medium."

"I'm a large myself," Milo deadpanned.

"Funny!" I said with a forced laugh. "And that's the *first* time I've heard that joke."

"Okay. Sorry. What's a medium?"

"Psychic mediums act as a conduit for uniting the living with the dead," I explained.

"In English?" Dutch asked.

"They talk to dead people."

"Well, why didn't you say so in the first place? Why can't you just call this Theresa and have her talk to the woman at the bottom of the stairs and we can all get on with our lives?" Dutch asked.

"Because it, unfortunately, doesn't work that way."

"What way?" Milo said.

"The easy way. See, Theresa's expertise isn't talking to ghosts. It's talking to people who already know they're dead and have reached The Other Side."

Milo looked at Dutch. "Does she always talk like this?"

"All the time," Dutch said, rolling his eyes.

"Man! You got some translation book around here or something?"

"Mostly I just wing it and nod. It keeps things simple."

"Simpleminded," I snapped, losing patience with them. "Fine. I will dumb it down for the both of you. A ghost is the spirit of a person who does not realize they have died. They are stuck between two worlds. Ours, and The Other Side."

"You mean heaven?" Milo said.

"Well . . . yes. I prefer 'The Other Side' but it's really the same thing. Anyway, as I was saying, when most people die they go straight to The Other Side, and they are fully conscious of the fact that they are now dead. Ghosts, however, are people whose deaths were so unexpected that they can't digest the fact that they've been killed. So when the opportunity comes to move to The Other Side they hesitate, and consequently, they get stuck between the two worlds. From what I understand about ghosts—which is very little— they typically relive the moment of their death, or the moments leading up to their death, over and over again. And they may be aware that they've experienced something terrible, but they are unwilling to acknowledge this so they continue to replay the incident time and time again, without fully accepting their fate. Meanwhile, time on this plane marches on, and these poor souls are unaware of this because they are so consumed with their own tragedies."

"So why can't Theresa talk to them?"

"I'm getting to that," I said. "Theresa communicates with people who have crossed over. She can only communicate with spirits who make the connection willingly. She hasn't had a lot of luck with ghosts, because as I said, they are unaware that they're dead and that time is moving forward without them. They often don't notice the living at all. This makes it very difficult to talk to them, because they don't usually acknowledge someone trying to start up a conversation. There's also the fact that Theresa lives in California, and if we're going to have someone confront this ghost, I'm pretty sure they're going to have to do it in person. So, it's not like she can just drive right over to help us out."

"How come I knew this wasn't going to be easy?" Dutch asked, wiggling on the couch in an attempt to find a more comfortable sitting position.

"What I can do," I said, ignoring him, "is give her a call anyway, and see if by chance she can help us out in some way. Sometimes she's able to pick up names and dates that could be relevant."

"Sounds good, but I have one question for you, Abby," Milo said.

"Shoot."

"Why do we need to find out who the ghost is to get rid of it?"

"If we can find out how this woman died, and even better, if we can find out her name, I think we can then shock her into leaving."

"Shock a ghost?" Dutch asked, one eyebrow raised skeptically.

"Yes. As I said, these spirits are hard to communicate with, but if we can yell her name out she might recognize it, and then it's just a matter of telling her that she fell down some stairs, or was murdered or whatever. Get her to realize that she's dead. Once they understand they've been killed, they usually move on to The Other Side."

"Sounds easy enough," Milo said agreeably.

"I can't believe I'm having this conversation," Dutch said, shaking his head.

"Who's going to talk to this ghost when we find out her name and how she died?" Milo asked.

The three of us looked around the room at each other, no one volunteering. Finally, Dutch said, "Isn't this right up your alley, Edgar?"

"Just because I'm psychic I'm also a ghost buster?"

"Well, aren't you?" Milo asked.

I thought about that for a minute. The truth was I was scared to go near that house. I'd had a few rough experiences with ghosts in my youth, and didn't relish having a fresh encounter. "Tell you what," I said, trying to bargain, "I'll ask Theresa if she knows of anyone local who can help us out. I mean, I've only read up on the subject, I haven't exactly helped a ghost cross over."

Dutch looked at Milo and winked, "Somebody's *scared*," he sang.

"You know what, Dutch?" I said, getting snippy. "I couldn't help noticing how fast you bolted out of that basement the moment that woman disappeared today. Since she obviously likes you, maybe you should be the one to help her cross over."

"What the hell do I know about it?" he complained a little too quickly.

Milo and I chuckled, and I said, "So maybe calling in an expert is the right way to go?"

"Yeah, that might be best," he said, as Milo and I laughed again.

Later that night after I'd helped Dutch get settled on his couch, I crawled upstairs and called Theresa from Dutch's bedroom. "Hello?" a male voice answered.

"Brett!" I said, excited to hear Theresa's husband's voice.

"Abby? Hey! How the heck are ya?"

"I'm great pal, Happy New Year to you," I said, suddenly realizing how much I missed my old friends.

"And to you. You looking for Theresa?"

"Yeah. Is she around?"

"No, sorry. She's at the studio doing some of the

promos for the show." Theresa had been lured to California with the promise of a television career. Currently she was in preproduction for a local cable show based on her amazing talent, with the promise that the show could be picked up nationally if local response was positive.

"Would you pass along a message for me?" I asked.

"Sure."

"Can you tell her to call me the moment she gets a chance? I have something kind of urgent I need to talk to her about."

"Is everything okay?" he asked, sounding worried.

"Oh, sure. Everything's fine." *Liar, liar . . . pants on fire . . .* "I just need her expertise for something."

"Good to know. I'll make sure she gets the message. She won't be home until about ten our time, is that going to be too late for you?"

I looked at the clock and thought about how tired I was. "Yeah, I'm afraid that might be. Ask her if she has any time over the next day or so to give me a call on my cell."

"Will do. It was good to hear your voice, Abby," he said, his own voice kind. "We miss you."

"Ditto, Brett. On all counts. I'll talk to you soon."

We hung up and I sat back on the bed, melancholy settling into my tired bones. Theresa and I had been best friends and business partners for four years before she moved out to California. It had been a big adjustment getting used to her not being around. And with a three-hour time difference between us and our busy schedules there seemed to be little time for phone calls. The sad truth was that we talked less and less.

Just as my eyelids began to feel heavy the phone rang. "Hello?" I answered, picking up the line.

"How's your boyfriend?" my sister said.

"Hey there, Cat," I said perking up. "He's recovering well, thanks for asking."

"Least I could do. And how's our little investment coming along? I'm assuming the closing went smoothly?"

Uh-oh. I'd forgotten to bring her up to speed on the haunted house. "Uhhh . . ." I began. "We've run into a tiny snafu."

"What kind of snafu?" she asked, tension creeping into her voice.

"It's nothing huge," I said, trying to reassure her. "Nothing we can't overcome."

"Abby what are you talking about?" she demanded.

"The thing of it is," I said, pausing to think how best to explain this weird development concerning our investment property, "it appears the house is haunted."

"Oh, is that all?" she laughed, relief filling the airwaves. "God! For a minute there I thought you were going to tell me something awful, like we couldn't get the work permits or something."

Only my sister would think not getting a work permit was worse than dealing with a haunted house. "Yeah, well it scared the hell out of Dave," I said, trying to impart the seriousness of the situation.

"Oh, pish-posh," she said dismissively. "You tell him I said get back to work and stop acting like a sissy-girl!"

"Gee, Cat. That's so sensitive of you," I said woodenly.

"Oh, come on, Abby! You cannot seriously expect me to be sympathetic to a little ghost sighting! What harm can one little Casper do? After all, it's dead!"

I didn't want to argue with her anymore so I simply said, "Listen, I'm beat, so I'll talk to you later, okay?"

"Fine," Cat replied. "But you tell Dave to quit being a baby and get back to work."

"I hear ya, gotta go, good night," I said.

We hung up and again I lay back on the bed. No sooner had I closed my eyes than the phone rang again. "Hello?" I asked tentatively.

"Hey sweethot," my favorite baritone said in his best Humphrey Bogart voice. "What'cha wearing?"

"Dutch?" I said sitting up in bed. "Where're you calling from?"

"Downstairs. I'm calling from my business line."

"What's up?" I asked.

"What'cha wearing?" he repeated, his voice a husky whisper.

I giggled and said, "My new necklace."

"Anything else?" he asked playfully.

"Nope . . . I'm *naked*."

"Oooo," he said, his voice growing thicker. "Want to come down here and give me a fashion show?"

"What are you doing?" I asked, in a tone that was just a smidgen more serious.

"Lying on the couch talkin' to my girl."

"No," I said patiently. "I meant that the doctor told you to take it easy for the next several weeks. That precludes any hanky-panky."

"Can't I just have some hanky?" he asked.

"I'm hanging up."

"Okay, okay," he said, "but if you get scared and need someone to hold you in the middle of the night, you'd better be naked."

"Good night," I sang and hung up the phone.

As I curled myself around Eggy and finally closed my eyes, I couldn't help but wonder about the woman we'd seen at the bottom of the stairs. What was her story and how had she come to such a tragic end? I shivered as I thought about the prospect of having to deal with a ghost. I'm really scared of them. But if I wanted to get out of this mess I'd have to figure out a way to un-haunt my investment so that I could get my handyman to finish the job. I was the one stuck making the payments, so unless we solved the mystery and got back to work, I'd be paying for it for the next thirty years. And, I had a little less than a month to take care of it before I'd have to head back to the office and my busy reading schedule, so I didn't have any time to waste. I made the decision right then to head down to the library first thing in the morning and search through the papers to see if I could find a news story about the tragedy. Something was telling me though, that this wasn't going to be as simple as that. If I'd only known then that that wasn't even the half of it.

Chapter Four

"Excuse me," I said to the woman behind the counter at the Royal Oak Library's information desk.

She looked up and focused her attention on me. "May I help you?"

"Can you tell me if you know of any local newspapers other than the ones listed here?" I'd been at the library since it opened and for the past three hours I'd been going over reel after reel of microfilm from every local paper I could think of, trying to find any mention or note of 172 Fern Street.

"Hmm," she said as she looked over my list. "Let me just double-check." She began typing on her computer. After a moment she squinted at her computer screen, then quickly scanned over my list again. "Nope. You have them all here."

"I was afraid of that," I said, my shoulders slumping in disappointment.

"Can't find a particular article?" she asked.

"Yeah. See, I just bought this house in town and I wanted to research its history, but I'm not finding anything on it."

"I see." She squinted again in concentration. "Have you checked the county's title registry?"

"The what?"

"Sometimes there are interesting things to be found on the property's title. You can research who the property belonged to and if there were any significant liens on the title."

"Hmmm," I said, silently slapping my forehead. "Now why didn't I think of that?"

"Happy to help," she said as she returned to sorting some periodicals.

"I'm happy you helped too, and by the way, congratulations," I added, feeling a particular buzz in her energy.

"Congratulations?" she repeated. "For what?"

"Your engagement."

"Excuse me?"

"You're engaged, right?"

"No."

"But you have a steady boyfriend, correct?" I persisted, convinced I wasn't wrong.

"Yes, but—"

"And your boyfriend has a connection to Canada, right?"

"Yes, he's Canadian, but how—"

"And he's into cars, like he fixes up cars that have dents in them, right?"

"Uh . . . yes, he owns an auto body repair shop . . . how do you know all this?" she demanded, clearly spooked.

I smiled wisely at her, then reached into my purse and pulled out my card, which I handed over to her. "He's going to pop the question any minute, and he's just waiting for the perfect moment. There's some sort of family reunion or birthday party or something coming up, and my guess is that's when he's going to make the announcement."

"Ohmigod!" she squealed. "We're headed to Windsor this weekend for his mother's birthday, and he's been acting all weird lately! I thought he was getting ready to break up with me!"

"Nope. He just doesn't want you to guess what he's up to." I suddenly felt sheepish for spoiling the surprise. "Sorry I spilled the beans."

"Oh, that's wonderful!" she said, coming around the counter to give me an impromptu hug. "I would have been completely caught off guard if I hadn't known, and I probably would have made a fool of myself in front of his family. Thank you so much!"

"Happy to help."

As I walked out of the library the back pocket of my jeans began to vibrate. Reaching behind I pulled out my cell phone and flipped it open. "Abby Cooper," I announced brusquely.

"Hey, girlfriend!"

"Theresa!" I exclaimed, hurrying down the steps of the library as a brisk January wind whipped my hair wildly about my head.

"I got your message yesterday, but this is the first chance I've had to call you back. It sounded urgent, what's up?"

"Something freaky—even for us," I explained as I got into my car, relieved to be out of the cold.

"Do tell," she said. I mentally pictured her sweeping her curly chestnut hair behind her ear as she focused on our conversation. Although I hadn't seen my best friend in six months, I knew her well enough to remember every small habit.

"It appears I've just purchased my very own haunted house."

"The one you mentioned in your last e-mail?"

"Yep. And this ghost appears to have a violent streak."

"Are you okay? What happened?" she asked, sounding worried.

"I'm fine," I assured her, and then went on to explain the strange events of the day before.

When I was done, Theresa said, "You're right, that is freaky, even for us. Do you want my help?"

I smiled broadly. "Thought you'd never ask. Do you have time now?" Theresa was offering to attempt to connect with the deceased energy inhabiting my investment property.

"Sure do. Got something to write with?"

I reached into my glove compartment and extracted a pen and a notepad, "Check. Fire when ready, Captain."

Theresa giggled. "Great, give me just a minute here . . ." I waited patiently for her to collect herself and get into mode. "Okay, I've got your grandmother, Margaret, here. I'm asking her about this new house and the first thing I'm picking up is that there's something about a French connection here."

"French?" I repeated, remembering my vision of the café and the French flag waving from the doorway.

"Yes, did you already pick up on that? Because Margaret is giving me the feeling that this isn't news to you."

I laughed and said, "Yeah, when we first bought the house I had a vision of a little café with a French flag waving from the doorway."

"Cool! So we're definitely in sync. The next thing I'm getting is that there's a World War II connection here. And I feel like you also got this already too."

"Right on the money, girlfriend," I confirmed.

"Great. Now I'm getting the name John . . . no . . .

wait . . . Paul. Abby, do you know if there was someone living there named John or Paul?"

"Unfortunately, I haven't snooped around that far
yet. I was on my way over to the county clerk to
research the property's title, but I'll make a note of
the names."

"Good. It's weird because I keep hearing a 'J' for
John and then a 'P' for Paul. Maybe they were
brothers?"

"Hmmm. That could be. Dave told me that the
house was owned by a man whose grandfather had
willed it to him. Maybe he has a brother."

"Okay, I'm also getting an 'L', like Lisa, but this is
weird. In my head it sounds like 'lie' and then 'sa,' so
I believe there's a Lisa or Liza connection."

"Got it," I said writing down both names.

"I'm going to try and reach out to this Liza woman.
I think she's the one you and Dutch saw at the bottom
of the stairwell."

"Can you do that?"

"I can try, hang on a minute."

I sat still as a statue, waiting excitedly to hear if Theresa could make a connection to the woman. Maybe
we'd get lucky and she would tell us what happened to
her. After a few minutes Theresa said into the silence,
"Damn. Abby, I'm sorry, but this energy just won't
come forward. I can feel her hovering there, and your
grandmother is working really hard to bring her
through, but this woman doesn't trust us. All I get is
that there's some sort of a connection to World War
II. There's also some theft or someone stole something
really valuable and that's what is keeping her trapped
between the two planes. I feel like she tried to take
back something that belonged to her but wasn't suc-
cessful, and she won't leave it, whatever it is. She's
watching over it and won't move on until she knows

it's safe. There's also something more sinister here, and I want you to be very careful in that house because whoever stole this thing of value is still in there."

"You mean, someone's coming in when we aren't there?"

"No. This person isn't alive. There's a very dark energy connected to the house. Whenever I try and reach out to it, this energy sends some seriously negative vibrations. I would venture to say there's someone evil still prowling that house. It's definitely male, and there's a connection to John or Paul and he's also looking for this thing of value. I get the feeling he's hunting it and trying to protect it too."

"Bizarre!"

"Extremely."

"So what's the connection between these two energies?" I asked.

"All I keep getting is this reference to World War II."

"This gets stranger by the minute," I said, leaning back in my seat.

"I know. Listen, they're all pulling their energies back, so I'm going to cut the connection . . . wait . . . your grandmother has one more message for you." Theresa paused while she listened intently. After a moment she said, "Abby, you need to be very careful of the twins."

"Twins?"

"Yes. The twins. She is insisting that you be careful of the twins."

"My nephews?" I asked, not getting what she meant and coming up with the only twins I knew.

"No, definitely not them. But that's all I get. She keeps repeating it, 'Be very careful of the twins.'"

"Okay," I said, shaking my head not knowing what else to say.

"That's it. She's pulled her energy back."

"Wow! Now I have more questions than I did before I called you," I said, trying to make light of the tension that had suddenly entered the conversation.

"I'll bet. So, you're going to take Margaret's advice, right? You'll be careful?"

"I'd love to take her advice, but until I meet John and Paul, who I'm guessing are the twins she was talking about, I don't know how cautious I can be."

"I could try again for you later on if you'd like?" Theresa offered.

I smiled. I knew what it cost Theresa every time she reached out her antennae to an energy that had crossed over. As a medium, she tends to tire far more easily than I do, and I knew that thanks to her private sessions and the taping of her local television show she must be doing a lot of readings. "No, that's okay, honey. You've already done more than your share. But I do have a question. Do you know any ghost busters?"

Theresa laughed. "As in, 'Who ya gonna call?' "

"Something like that."

"You're still scared of the dark, aren't you, Abby?"

"Terrified."

"Well, as a matter of fact I do. I got this woman's name from a client of mine. I hear she's pretty pricey, but you may want to check her out."

"Cool, how do I reach her?"

"Hold on a sec while I get my address book out . . ." Theresa said as I listened to paper shuffling. After a moment Theresa said, "Here it is. Her name is M. J. Holliday, and her cell number is five-five-five, six-two-g-h-o-s-t."

I snickered as I jotted down the information, "Ten bucks says she's got a dog named Buster."

Theresa laughed as well. "I wouldn't be surprised. Good luck Abs, and please be careful, 'kay?"

"Yeah, yeah," I said as I shrugged off my own reservations. "I'll call you next week, T, thanks again."

After Theresa and I disconnected I went back over the notes I'd taken during our quick minisession. Nothing in particular seemed to ring any bells, so with a sigh I started the car and pointed my Mazda in the direction of the county clerk's office.

Ten minutes into the drive my cell phone chirped and grabbing it off the seat I flipped it open. "Abby Cooper," I said, keeping my eyes on the road.

"I'm hungry," purred a familiar baritone.

"There's soup in the fridge," I suggested.

"I'm not that kind of hungry."

"Dutch . . ." I admonished.

"Where are you?"

"Telegraph and Square Lake Road."

"Why so far from home?"

"I'm headed to the county clerk to research the title on Fern Street."

"Good idea," he praised. "Looking for anything in particular?"

"I'm not sure, but I just had an interesting conversation with Theresa, and I'm hoping a clue in the chain of title will back me up. I'll tell you all about it when I get home."

"Sounds good. Milo's coming over around two. Think you'll be back by then?"

I glanced at the clock on the dashboard just as I felt a light and airy feeling on my right side—my sign for yes. "Count me in."

"Hey, on your way back can you stop by Spago's and pick me up the usual?"

Rolling my eyes I asked, "And do you think Milo will want his usual too?"

"Do you really need me to answer that?"

"See you later, mooch," I said, and clicked off.

An hour and a half later I arrived back at Dutch's with two full bags of Coney dogs, chili fries and a folder full of notes. I'd hit pay dirt at the clerk's office, and I was anxious to share my findings with Dutch and Milo.

"Hey, Abby!" Milo said jovially as he greeted me at the door.

"Here," I said, giving him one of the bags. "No onions, extra mustard, right?"

"On the money, honey," he said, taking the bag and trotting into the living room.

I closed the door with my foot and followed him, then set the other bag and my folder on the coffee table while I shrugged out of my coat and took a seat next to Dutch on the couch. As I was unloading the second bag for Dutch and me, I got an unexpected smooch on the cheek and an impromptu hug from him, which made me turn and look a question mark at him.

"What?" he asked.

"What's that for?" I asked, smiling a little. Dutch and I hadn't exactly been . . . uh . . . *familiar* with each other recently. Since his injury we'd been acting more like Nurse Ratched and her whiny, irritating and annoying patient, so the PDA was a pleasant surprise.

"I'll tell you later," he whispered, ignoring Milo's probing eyes.

"You mean after two weeks of sponge baths, cooking, doing your laundry, cleaning up after you, and taking care of your cat all I get is a peck and an I'll tell you later?"

Milo stopped munching on his Coney dog and leaned in, smirking at Dutch's obvious discomfort.

Dutch paused for a moment then turned to me,

"You know, Abby? When you're right, you're right. You've been great. As in exceptional. And the moment these stitches come out, you and I are heading to Toronto, because I've missed you." And with that he leaned in and gave me one of those long, lingering kisses that make your hair curl.

It was now my turn to blush. "Thanks," I said after the smooch, then reached for my Coke, taking a long sip and resisting the urge to fan myself. Milo chuckled softly and shook his head, while Dutch grabbed a chili dog and flashed me a toothy grin.

When I'd had a moment to compose myself, Milo asked me, "I hear you talked to your friend, what's her name? The one that sees dead people?"

"Theresa. And she doesn't actually *see* them," I explained. "It's more like she gets a name or an initial and references to places and events."

"And what's the difference between you two again?" he said.

"For one thing, Theresa is able to hit on names, and that's not something I'm particularly adept at," I said, as I nibbled on a chili-covered fry. "For another, Theresa is able to distinguish individual energies and their connection to the client a whole lot better than me."

Milo gave me a quizzical look and said, "Huh?"

"Maybe it'd be better if I gave you an analogy?"

"That might help."

I paused for a moment to collect my thoughts, then said, "Think of it like this: if Theresa and I were each going to tell you about a movie, she would describe it in terms of the actors, who their characters were and their relationship to each other. I, on the other hand, would tell you all about the plot line and the special effects. You'd get the same general information, but in two completely different formats."

Milo nodded his head. "So she focuses on the people, you focus on the events."

"Exactly," I said beaming at him. Milo had a charming curiosity about all things psychic and I liked the fact that from the first time I'd met him he had regarded my gifts with an open mind and lack of judgment. Which is more than I could say for my boyfriend, who continued to harbor a heavy dose of skepticism for all things metaphysical. Secretly, I was happy Dutch had tasted a bit of something at the house on Fern that he couldn't readily explain.

"So what'd Theresa say?" Dutch asked, wiping his hands on his napkin after polishing off his first hot dog.

"She confirmed a few of the clues I'd already hit on—"

"Excuse me?" Dutch interrupted. "What clues? And when did you get them?"

I smiled sheepishly at him. I hadn't shared any of my intuitive thoughts about the house with him because I wasn't sure what to make of them. "I know, I know," I said, waving my hand. "I should have said something earlier, but when I first talked to Dave about the house I got a couple of hits right away, only I didn't know how they fit until now."

"What'd you see?" Milo asked.

"For starters there was this connection to World War II and a café with a French flag above a doorway. Theresa picked up almost exactly the same thing."

"What else?" Dutch prompted.

I reached over to my folder and pulled out my notes, rearranged some pages and gave the men the highlights. "Theresa picked up the name John-Paul, although she thought it might be John or Paul. However, as it turns out, the house was owned by Avril and Jean-Paul Carlier from 1946 to 1968 when a death certificate for Avril was recorded. Jean-Paul held title solely from 1968 to 1990, when his death certificate was recorded and the house was inherited by his grandsons, James and Jean-Luke Carlier. Title then transferred from Jean-Luke to his brother through a power of attorney in 2002 where it remained until two days ago when it was sold to me."

"So Jean-Paul must be your French connection and quite possibly your World War II reference," Milo said.

I nodded at him. "Yep. We are definitely on the right track. I gotta believe with an energy as powerful as the one we encountered, that someone living in that house had to know it."

"So what did you turn up, Milo?" Dutch asked, switching gears.

Milo sighed and said, "Bubkes."

"Nothing?" Dutch and I said together.

" 'Fraid so. I pooled through about a hundred years of police records, and the only thing I turned up were some complaints from neighbors in the late nineties about the house being an eyesore. The department logged the complaints but no follow-up was ever recorded. It looks like the neighbors all gave up after a while and put up privacy fences to block out the view."

"But that's not possible!" I insisted. "Dutch and I saw a woman lying at the bottom of the stairs—she had to have died in that house to still be inhabiting it. There *must* be a police record of it. Even if she slipped and fell there should be some sort of police report or something, right?"

"Not if it wasn't a slip and fall," Dutch said ominously.

I gave him a quizzical look. "What do you mean?"

"Well, if she were murdered, and it was never reported, then there would be no record of it. The other obvious question to ask is, where's the body?"

We all pondered that for a long moment until Milo asked, "Did Theresa pick up anything else, Abby?"

I paused, thinking for a minute before I remembered the female energy T had touched on. "Actually," I said, shuffling through my notes again, "she mentioned the woman on the landing. She kept getting the name Liza, but I couldn't find any reference to her in the chain of title. I really don't think Liza is short for Avril, so I gotta believe they're two different people."

"Maybe she was a sister or daughter?" Milo suggested.

My left side felt thick and heavy. "My spidey-sense says no."

Dutch began to pile up all of the trash from lunch and as he smunched wrappers and napkins together into one big pile he said, "Let me run Jean-Paul's name through the national index and see what I can come up with. Sometimes the FBI has more on a local name that the police files do."

"And now that I have a name to go on, I'll head back to the library and look through old newspaper articles for anything on Jean-Paul and his grandsons."

"Good idea," Milo said as he stood up to go. "You two let me know if there's anything else you need on my end."

"Thanks, buddy," Dutch said, as he pushed himself up off the couch, wincing the whole way. "We'll keep you posted."

Later that night as Dutch and I were watching television, his phone rang. He looked at the caller ID and promptly handed it to me. "It's your sister."

Frowning a little at the prospect of having to tell

Cat we couldn't work on the house until we solved the mystery of our ghost, I took the phone into the kitchen. "Hey, Cat!" I said brightly.

"You have *got* to help me!" she squealed into my ear.

"What's the matter?"

"Our parents," she said flatly. "I'm now convinced that you and I were adopted." I had forgotten that Claire and Sam were due to make a pit stop at Cat's on their way back to South Carolina. They must have just landed and I was now getting my first of many painful phone calls from Dysfunctionville, USA.

"That bad?" I asked, already knowing it was likely worse than even I expected.

"Claire is refusing to stay in the guest house! And Sam won't do anything without Claire's approval—so that means that I'm stuck! What am I going to do if they won't stay in the guest house?!" Last summer my sister had begun construction on a two-thousand square foot guest house on the very edge of her property in anticipation of my parents' visit. During construction, Cat had spared no expense knowing full well our mother's natural inclination to be unhappy with anything less than spectacular. And so she'd gone to great lengths to ensure that Claire would be comfortable under a roof half an acre away.

"But I thought you furnished it with all of Mommy Dearest's favorites. Why wouldn't she want to stay there?"

"She doesn't like the wall color."

I blinked a few times in confusion. "Didn't you go with off-white?" Our mother detested bright colors, and knowing this, Cat had gone as neutral as possible.

"Yes, but *apparently* it is not 'off' enough!"

"Oh, you poor thing," I offered, feeling her pain. "What are you going to do?"

"After I take a Xanax?" Cat said, with a heavy sigh.

"I'm going to call the painter and pay him any amount of money it takes to repaint all the walls in twenty-four hours."

"So, where'd you put her in the meantime?" I asked, privately chuckling at the messes my sister got herself into.

Cat groaned and said, "She took our room."

"Claire and Sam are actually going to stay in your room?" Cat had the most luxurious, truly gorgeous bedroom suite I'd ever seen. It was as large as Dutch's entire downstairs and besides accommodating a California king-sized bed, sitting area, separate office space and huge plasma TV, with individual his and her bathrooms, it also had the largest walk-in closet in New England.

"No," my sister said tersely, "Claire is staying in our room. Sam has decided he wants to stay in the downstairs guest room."

The guest room Cat mentioned was the second-largest room in the house and it was built to accommodate many of Tommy's golfing buddies when they came into town. It too was a complete testament to luxury. "So where does that leave you, Tommy and the boys?"

"At the Four Seasons."

I laughed, thinking she was making a joke, but when she didn't join me, I asked, "You're kidding, right?"

"Nope. I'm having our luggage loaded as we speak. I just wanted to call you and tell you where I'd be in case you needed me."

"Wow. Well, have fun at the Four Seasons," I said.

"Thanks, Abby. By the way, how's our investment coming along?"

"Uh . . . we're definitely making progress," I hemmed.

"Good. At least one of us is. I'll talk to you tomorrow. Say hello to your man for me."

"Will do. Good night, Cat."

After hanging up the phone, I walked back into the living room and sat down next to Dutch, who wrapped his arm around me and pulled me in close. Kissing me on the forehead, he asked, "So did you tell her?"

"Not really."

"How do you mean, 'Not really'?"

"Not at all."

Dutch began to cluck like a chicken and I flashed him a warning eyebrow. He smiled ruefully and asked, "What's the worst that could happen?"

"My sister could show up here with a demolition crew and plow down the house."

"Really?"

"Sugar, when it comes to making money, Cat is *all* about time. She doesn't believe in waiting. The longer we take to figure out what the hell happened in that house, the more Cat's profit gets postponed."

"Maybe we'll turn up something tomorrow in the FBI database or in the newspaper articles."

With relief I felt my right side go light and airy. "Maybe we will."

Chapter Five

"Holliday," I heard a woman's crisp voice announce through my cell phone as I pulled into a parking space near the Birmingham Public Library.

"Good morning, Miss Holliday. My name is Abigail Cooper and I got your name from a friend of mine who suggested you might be able to help me get rid of a certain unwelcome guest."

"Hello, Abigail, please call me M.J."

"Then please call me Abby," I said, liking this woman immediately.

"Now talk to me about your problem," she said, getting right to the point.

"It seems that I've purchased an investment property with a rather checkered past."

"How so?"

I told her the story about purchasing the home with the hopes of fixing it up when my handyman encountered a violent energy that tossed his tools around like paper, and finished by describing what Dutch and I had seen. I also revealed what I did for a living and that her name had come to me by way of Theresa and what her own insights had been.

"Sounds like you've got yourself a doozy," M.J. said when I was done. "What are you interested in having me do for you?"

"To be honest, I'm not sure what you can offer me—I mean, the only thing I know about ghost busters is what I learned from Bill Murray."

M.J. laughed politely and replied, "Just don't mention marshmallows and we'll get along fine. I can offer you a couple of different options. The first, and most expensive, is to uncover what happened in the house, confront the entity with that event and help them to cross over. Your investment property sounds like a pretty typical scenario, where a ghost is reliving the night of their death because they haven't fully accepted their demise. In order for us to convince your ghost, we need to uncover what happened to cause their death, and force them to accept the truth."

"As it happens, I'm already working that angle, but just for curiosity's sake, what would that run me?"

"Two grand."

I gulped. "Gee, that's just *slightly* higher than I'd wanted to pay. Do you have anything more in the bargain basement category?"

M.J. chuckled. "I know I'm on the expensive side, but it's more work than people realize. I suppose if you were willing to do your own detective work, and just needed me to confront the energy and help it cross over, I could cut you a deal for—say—five hundred?"

Five hundred bucks to avoid encountering a violent nasty poltergeist? "Sold," I said without hesitation.

"Great. I'm in the middle of another case right now, but I should be finished in a week or two. Why don't you call me when you've finished your research and I'll hop a flight."

"Where are you now?" I asked.

"Georgetown, D.C."

"Cool. I'll call you when I've figured things out. Thanks, M.J."

"Good luck, Abby."

We disconnected and I got out to shove a couple of quarters into the meter. I'd decided to head to the neighboring town of Birmingham to check out their records because it was a bigger and better funded library, and I figured it might have a few more resources than the one in my hometown. As I got out of the car I heard someone call my name, and turning, I saw one of my regular clients come trotting over. "Hey, Miriam," I said when she drew close.

"Abby! I'm so happy I ran into you! I called your office yesterday, and your message said you were out for the month of January. I really, *really* need some advice."

Back in September I'd gotten my own intuitive message to block out the entire month of January and take a nice long vacation. I hadn't had more than a few days off for lollygagging since the previous February, and I'd trusted the message and not booked a single reading. This was a rather risky endeavor at the time, because even good psychics can see a sharp decline in income once they start ignoring their clientele.

Still, I'd taken the chance and, as usual, everything had worked out for the best as Dutch's injury and my new investment property were now taking up all of my time. "What's wrong, Miriam?" I asked, willing to give an impromptu minisession for one of my favorite clients.

"Well, as you predicted, my company downsized right before Thanksgiving and I lost my job."

I read for so many clients that all my readings tend to blend together, and even though I didn't remember the details Miriam was bringing up now, that didn't mean I couldn't empathize. "Oh, I'm so sorry. How've you been holding up?"

"Well, thanks to your insight, I was able to prepare myself for it, so I've actually been doing pretty good. And I've been interviewing all over town. You also predicted I'd be very popular with headhunters and prospective employers and that's why I wanted to see if you could just answer me one question."

"Shoot," I said, already turning on the antennae.

"Well, I've been offered a job with two different companies and I don't know which one I should take. They both pay about the same, but I'm just not sure which one I'll be happier at."

"Hmmm," I said while I focused on the messages already blipping through my mind. "I can tell you that both choices feel right, and that you won't make a bad decision at either of them. However, does one company have a woman in a position of power with dark brown or black hair?"

"Yes! I interviewed with a woman who would be my boss at Endicorp, and she does have black hair."

"Uh-huh, now that I know I'm on the right track I can tell you that this woman is heavy on the micromanagement side, and if that drives you crazy you may want to go with the other company."

"How much of a micromanager?"

"Bordering on obsessive," I said frowning. "She's also just a bit cuckoo," I added, making little circular motions by my head with my finger.

"Cuckoo?"

"Yep. She's a nut, and my feeling is that the company didn't know what to do with her so they just kept promoting her. If you take the job you may love the salary but you also may have your hands full trying to deal with her."

"You know," Miriam said thoughtfully, "I thought she was rather odd when I sat down with her, but she seemed to like my credentials so much that I overlooked it."

"It's always best to go with your own gut, especially when you'll be working with someone."

"Do you see anything for the other job?"

"What's with all the flowers?"

Miriam laughed heartily and said, "You are *so* good! I'd be the new marketing manager of Blumer-ang Flowers."

"Wow! They're huge! Go for it, Miriam!"

"Thanks, Abby, I'm going to call them right now and accept the position. What do I owe you?" she asked, reaching for her checkbook.

"This one's on me. And congratulations on the new job!"

I walked into the library feeling rather proud of myself. There was a time not too long ago when, if a client had approached me about tuning in on something small, I wouldn't have complied. I used to have a stringent policy about not extending myself for fear of being taken advantage of. However, I'd learned a very powerful lesson the previous summer when one of my clients wound up dead because I'd been so rigid. Never again, I vowed, and I was proud of the fact that I was holding up to my promise.

I rounded the corner of the front lobby and headed to the information desk where I asked a librarian for help finding newspaper articles about Jean-Paul Carlier. She led me to a row of computers and explained, "If there's anything of note for that name you'll find it using the library's central index, which is on this computer here."

"What, no microfilm to paw through? What will I do with all the extra time I'll save?" I deadpanned.

The librarian laughed politely and said, "I know, isn't modern technology fabulous? I mean, to think I spent years in school wasting so much time on those god-awful machines, getting dizzy while searching through all the data. Now we simply receive a digital copy of each day's paper and save it to the file. It takes seconds instead of hours. Amazing stuff."

"Thanks for your help," I said, taking my seat.

"No problem. If you have any more questions, let me know."

As the librarian walked away I pulled the mouse toward me and clicked on the search field typing in Jean-Paul's name and then clicking the GO button. A few seconds later, and to my immense relief, a list of articles appeared, beginning with the most recent one from the obituary column listing Jean-Paul's death on August 19, 1990. I read the article, which posted the cause of death as heart failure and noted only two surviving relatives, James and Jean-Luke Carlier, Jean-Paul's grandsons.

I closed that article and went down a few to November 11, 1960. This article turned out to be a wedding announcement mentioning Jean-Paul as the proud father of Paul Carlier who was set to marry Karen Pedigood the following April. Scanning up a few articles I discovered another obituary, this one for both Paul and Karen who were killed in a car accident while visiting Karen's family in Atlanta, and this was dated January 10, 1975. Sad that James and Jean-Luke had lost both parents so young.

Scanning the headings of the articles a little further I came across something interesting from May 14, 1946. The article had a picture of a young Jean-Paul leaning against the side of a storefront and the head-line read FRENCH WAR HERO SETS UP SHOP.

The article was rather short and sketchy on the de-tails, but described Jean-Paul as a recent emigrant from France who "had been a key resource in the fight for French liberation and liked Americans so much that he wanted to bring his family's jewelry business over to America." He'd named the shop "Essence" and by all accounts it was set to be a smashing success. The reporter covering the story was most impressed by the quality of the jewels being offered for sale. "Europe's finest gems set in fantastic settings," the article claimed and went on to embellish, "Just what every GI needs to capture the heart of his favorite lady." Jean-Paul seemed to have a genius for marketing too, as his shop offered monthly payment plans for re-turning GIs rushing to propose to their faithful girlfriends.

As I looked at the shadowy picture of Jean-Paul leaning against the side of the shop, a cigarette dan-gling from his fingertips, I got the smallest shiver up my spine. I didn't care how swell the guy was; I in-stantly disliked him.

I read a few more of the articles, which were mainly small mentions at charity functions and local events. Nothing else of interest caught my attention. I printed out all of the articles anyway, thinking there might be something I could connect the dots with later, then clicked out of my selections and vacated the chair. As I was walking out of the library, something occurred to me and I headed back in.

A few minutes later I was flipping through one of the library's local phone books until I found the jewel-ers section. I scanned the alphabetized list looking for

Essence. No such shop existed yet my intuition was insisting that the shop was still in business. I grabbed the newspaper article, found the store's address and began to search using that. I hit paydirt under the Os. "Opalescence" was listed at the same address on Brown Street in Birmingham. "Worth a visit," I mumbled under my breath as I put the yellow pages back on the shelf and again headed toward the exit.

A few minutes later I was back in the car cruising the main drag of downtown Birmingham, a place that can darken my mood no matter how bright the day. Birmingham is the town I grew up in and couldn't wait to move out of. I have no love for the place, with its snooty residents looking down their noses at anything that isn't name-brand and real estate priced somewhere up in the stratosphere. I tend to glower my way through its downtown whenever an errand requires me to take a tour.

Today was no different as a fat man in a gigantic SUV of the Hummer variety pulled out of his parking space right in front of me, causing me to slam on my brakes, then he had the nerve to dial his cell phone before putting the car into a forward gear. I ground my teeth as I followed him and consoled myself by thinking the Hummer was clearly an attempt to compensate for something . . . like a teeny weenie.

Luckily, he turned left down Maple and I continued down Old Woodward Avenue, then rounded onto Brown and began looking in earnest at the shop signs, finally locating Opalescence midway down on the left. It took me another block to find a parking space, and after doing a mediocre job of parallel parking I trotted down the street clutching at my coat as a cold wind sent it flapping.

I paused for a moment when I reached the shop and took in the opulent signage made of brushed metal.

There were no windows, just a flat paneled wood exterior, and large glass front door with a huge and very ornate door pull. The effect was enticing and if I were honest with myself, I'd have to admit I liked it. I pulled at the giant glass door and it opened more easily than I would have thought. I stepped through the doorway and was immediately dazzled.

In front of me was an enormous rock the size of a small boulder resting on a pedestal poised to chest level, that dominated the room. Embedded within the stone were thousands of small opal clusters. I walked forward and stood mesmerized for a moment as I looked at all the beautiful gems, glittering their rainbow colors and making my senses hum.

Like many psychics I'm pretty sensitive to crystals and gemstones. The opals gave me a feeling of bubbling energy, like a slow hum beginning in my solar plexus and subtly radiating out along my limbs and fingertips.

"May I help you?" someone asked off to my right.

"Oh! Hello," I said, a little startled as I looked up at a tall man with thick dark brown hair, beard and mustache, tortoiseshell glasses and a ready smile. "I was just enjoying this beautiful display. These clusters are amazing."

"Yes, it's very special. I had that rock shipped in from India where this particular brand of opal is mined and it took a crew of ten just to get it on the pedestal."

"I'll bet. It looks like it weighs a ton."

"Just under, actually. And that looks like it's one of ours," he said, pointing to my neck.

Reflexively I reached up to twirl my birthday present that I'd been wearing since the night Dutch had given it to me and I chuckled. "Yes, this was a gift from my boyfriend and I love it so much that I had to come here and check the place out." Inside my head I was only slightly surprised at the coincidence—stuff like this happens to me all the time.

"Wonderful. My name is James," the salesman said, extending his hand out to me.

"I'm Abby, pleased to meet you."

"Is there something in particular that I could help you with today?"

Uh-oh. I hadn't really thought this whole thing through. What should I say? Should I pose as a buyer? Or should I tell this man that I needed answers to questions about the shop's former owner? After a beat, I decided to play it noncommittal.

"I'm looking for a gift for my sister's birthday. She's fond of pearls. Do you have any suggestions?"

The man smiled kindly while his eyes gave an apology. "I'm sorry, but I only deal in opals. I could, however, show you some nice items for your sister. Did you have a price range in mind?"

Weird. Mentally I scratched my head that a jeweler would limit himself to just one gemstone. That seemed risky to me. "Why do you only deal in opals? I mean, wouldn't you want to offer a wider range of gemstones for the general public?" I asked.

James smiled confidently and replied, "Have you *seen* my selection?"

"Uh, no," I admitted.

"Come with me," he said and led me over to a display case off to my right. I approached the counter and peered down at row upon row of some of the most beautiful jewelry I'd ever seen. Opals in every size and color of the rainbow were beautifully assembled in gold, silver and platinum. There were bracelets of unique design and shape, rings for men and women that ranged from simple classic designs to very contemporary ornate creations. Pendants, similar to the one around my neck, sparkled in brilliant blues, greens, purples, reds and oranges, and opal-inlaid earrings twinkled under the lights of the display case like stars.

"Wow . . ." I whispered in awe. "I see what you mean. Your stuff is breathtaking."

"Thank you," he said. "Are you still sold on pearls for your sister?"

I snickered and smiled back at this clever salesman. Next to this stuff pearls seemed so blah. "I'll bet you convert a lot of people this way, huh?"

James chuckled. "Oodles. Now, does your sister have pierced ears? Because this set over here," he said, pointing to a pair to my left, "are a particularly nice arrangement."

I nodded as I surveyed the menagerie, while thinking about how I should play this all out. What I needed was information, and I needed it without tipping my hand as to my real purpose. It wasn't that I got any kind of malicious feeling from James, whom I was pretty sure was the grandson of Jean-Paul. His energy suggested that he was sincere and harmless. Still, I wanted to proceed cautiously until I knew more. I'd have to gain James's trust and ease my way into pumping him for information. I decided to play into the ruse I'd created. At the very least I'd come away with a spectacular gift for my sister. "Those are amazing," I said leaning in over the counter to get a better look. "How much?"

"One seventy-five," he said without looking at the tag.

"Hmmm, that sounds reasonable. What else do you have?"

James proceeded to pull out individual sets of earrings, each just as gorgeous as the previous, and I continued to play it interested, but noncommittal, while in my head I looked for ways to segue into the house on Fern. In the end James provided the perfect opportunity when he suggested, "And if none of these are tickling your fancy we could always help you design an original piece for your sister."

"Really?" I asked.

"Yes, if you'd like to step back into my office, I could show you some examples of what some of my other clients have produced for their loved ones, and take you through some common molds that people like to use as a starting point."

"Lead the way," I said as my intuition buzzed a thumbs-up in my head.

We proceeded to the back of the store where a short corridor led to a large and comfortable office. James offered me a seat in one of two plush leather chairs he had positioned in front of a gorgeous glass desk. James took his seat and I glanced around the office, which was painted a light mocha and adorned with a few tasteful paintings. On one massive oak credenza set against the wall I noticed frame upon frame of personal photos. Ahhh, opportunity at last! Jumping up from my seat I took note of the photos. "Wow! Look at all of these pictures! Is this your family?" I asked, picking up one of the frames and studying the images of a man and a woman seated on the beach, each holding a smiling young boy in their arms.

"Yes, that's my mother, father and my brother, Luke, and I," James said with a hint of sadness in his voice.

Belatedly, I noticed that the man and woman both smiled out from the photo in a rather flat and plastic way—my way of knowing that these two people had passed away.

"It was taken when I was seven, the year before my parents were killed," he added.

"Oh, I'm sorry to hear that," I said, setting the photo down. "It must have been difficult losing your parents so young. Who ended up raising you?" A bold question for me to ask, but I was hoping James wouldn't notice.

"My grandfather took us in and raised us. He put my brother and I through college, taught us the jewelry business and left us this store when he passed away."

"Sounds like a good man," I said as I set down the frame.

"Yes," James said with a sigh, "yes, he was." *Liar, liar . . . pants on fire . . .*

I cocked my head slightly, hearing my inner lie detector go off, and I gazed off for a moment trying to put his comment and my lie detector into context.

"What's the matter?" he asked, looking at me curiously.

"Oh, nothing," I said, quickly shaking my head, "I just thought I heard the front door open. Is there anyone up front to cover for you while you're back here with me?"

James got up quickly from behind the desk and walked to the office doorway peering out at the store. "Nope, no one's there. My other two employees should be returning from lunch any minute, so I think we'll be fine until they get back."

"Okay," I said, taking one last look at the photos on the credenza. One other picture caught my eye and I couldn't help but smile when I saw it. Feeling playful I picked up the frame and waved it at James. "Spelling bee champ, huh?" The photo was of a young James, his smiling mouth full of braces as he hugged his smaller brother with one arm and held up a large trophy in the other. A banner behind the boys spelled out OAKLAND COUNTY SPELLING CHAMPION.

James turned bright red and came over to where I was holding the photo. Taking it from me, he smiled sheepishly. "This was taken when I was thirteen. I thought I was king of the world that day, and my brother really helped me out by quizzing me and making sure I was prepared for the competition."

My intuition buzzed and Theresa's warning came back to me. "Are you two twins?" I asked, looking at the photo. James was clearly the taller of the two, but perhaps they were fraternal.

James chuckled and set the photo down again. "No, he's two years my junior, although we became as close as twins after my parents died."

"Does he help you run the shop?" I asked, taking my seat again.

James turned away from me as he headed back to his own chair and without meeting my eyes he replied, "No. Sadly we parted ways a few years ago. One of those sibling rivalry things that just about every family has, I guess."

"Ahh," I answered, not knowing what else to say. Deciding to take it one step further I focused my radar at him and took an assessment. After a moment I blurted out, "So, how's the new puppy?"

James's face snapped up. "She's fine. How did you know I got a puppy?"

I shot him a broad smile and replied, "What I haven't told you is that along with needing a really good birthday present for my sister, I'm also a professional psychic. Your puppy's a golden retriever, right?"

James laughed, his eyes wide, "Close, she's a golden Labrador. Her name is Chloe and I just brought her home from the breeder a week ago."

My intuition kicked in again and I puzzled over the message before saying what came to me next. "Are you sure you're adjusting well to the dog?"

"I think so, I mean she's still not house trained but that's to be expected."

"Hmmm," I said. I didn't understand the message, so I just blurted out what was in my head. "James, this is so weird because I get the feeling that you're getting rid of the dog, but there's great regret here."

"No, that's got to be wrong. I'm telling you, Abby, I've already bonded with her. I could never give her away," James insisted.

"Yeah, maybe I'm wrong. It happens," I said, throwing up my hands, ready to change the subject. Just then a pretty twenty-something redheaded woman poked her nose around the doorway and announced, "We're back, James."

"Hey, Marie, is Josh with you?"

"Yeah, he's going to work on that set for Mrs. McDonald so that he can get it done in time for her five o'clock pickup."

"Great. I'm with a customer right now," he said, gesturing at me. "So can you just watch the store until we're through?"

"You got it, chief," she said and trotted off.

"She's a cutie," I said after she left.

James blushed again and looked down at the molds on his desk, rearranging them and selecting two to show to me. I smiled at his obvious change of subject but didn't press. He seemed the shy type. "Now," he announced, holding up the two wax molds. "Would you say your sister is a traditionalist, or has more modern taste?"

An hour later James and I had designed the perfect pair of opal earrings for Cat, made out of white gold and blue opals that caught the light with brilliant flecks of yellow, purple and green. Cat was impossible to shop for, so I congratulated myself at finding something specially made for her birthday, which was a mere six weeks away.

"I will have Josh begin work on them later this

week, and they should be finished by the end of next week or the following week if we get backed up."

"Sounds great," I said as I scrawled my name across the bottom of the check I was writing. "By the way, and please don't think that I'm prying, but are you going on a diet soon?"

James wasn't skinny, but not someone I would call overweight either, and I had the sense that he was about to embark on some crazy plan to shed several pounds by starving himself.

James cocked his head at me slightly and replied, "I was looking at that South Beach Diet. It's supposed to be really safe and effective."

"That's what I've heard too," I said, handing him the check. "Just don't go overboard by skipping meals or anything, okay?"

"No sweat. And thank you for all the insights, this was fun."

"No trouble at all, it was great talking to you," I agreed, smiling.

"I'll call you in a week and give you a status on the earrings. But if you get anything else on your radar that I should know about, give me a call," he said, handing me a business card.

I took the opportunity to change the course of the conversation to discreetly inquire about Fern Street. "The only other thing my radar is buzzing about is a recent real estate transaction. Did you just sell some property?"

James's jaw dropped a millimeter, and for the first time since I'd met him his expression turned nervous. "Yes. I just closed on the sale of my grandfather's house. It'd been on the market for a while and we finally sold it."

"Must be a relief to be rid of it, huh?" I asked, meeting his eyes.

"Why would you say that?" he asked, sweating now.

"Oh, nothing," I said. "Just that you said it had been on the market for a while. I'm sure the current owners are going to love it."

"Well, we managed to sell it to a development company. The house needed a little work," he confessed.

That's not all it needs, I thought as I smiled and took my leave. "Thanks so much for your time, James. Call me when the earrings are ready and I'll swing by."

I left the jewelry store feeling slightly regretful. I had wanted to pry a little more about the house and reveal to James that I was one of the purchasers, but my intuition held me in check. For whatever reason I wasn't supposed to let him know that I was involved with Fern Street just yet. The irritating thing was that I didn't know why.

I headed back to my car and jumped in just as the first few flecks of snow, predicted to plaster our city with five to ten inches by early the next morning, began to fall. "Great," I said into the silence of the car. Throwing on my seat belt, I turned the ignition and pointed my car in the direction of my house. I was almost out of dog food for Eggy and I wanted to pick some up from the reserves at my house before heading back to Dutch's. On the drive over I decided to touch base with Dave to see how he was recovering from his bender the other night.

"Hey there, woman," he said when he picked up my call.

"How you doin'?" I asked, smiling because he sounded like his old self again.

"Hanging in there. What's the word?"

"I'm working on evicting our unwanted tenant, and if worse comes to worst I will hire a bona-fide ghost buster so you can get back to making that place livable."

"I'm not setting foot back in that house, Abby," Dave said heatedly.

I sighed. This was going to be harder than I thought. "Dave, if we get this ghost to leave the premises, then there's no reason to be scared . . ."

"I'm not scared! I'm just sayin' that I'm busy . . . with other projects and stuff." *Liar, liar . . . pants on fire . . .*

"Did you forget about my inboard lie detector?" I asked, calling his bluff.

"I've got stuff to do!" he insisted. *Liar, liar . . . pants on fire . . .* "And I'm not going back into that house!"

"Dave, you are a damn stubborn mule," I said crossly. "If you don't do the labor, how the hell are we supposed to get our return on investment? I mean, I can *assure* you that I will not be stuck paying the mortgage on that house for the next thirty years."

"I'm working on it," Dave replied. "I think I got an angle that could work for everyone." *Liar, liar . . . pants on fire . . .*

I sighed as I pulled down my street. I wasn't going to win this argument with him right now. "Listen," I said patiently, "how about we talk about this a little later. I'm headed to my house to pick up some dog food, and then I gotta go to the grocery store to get some people food before the snow starts to get thick. I'll give you a call tonight from Dutch's and we'll talk a little more then, okay?"

"Fine, call me later," he said grudgingly, and hung up just as I pulled into my driveway. I parked and from inside the car I took a moment to take in the view, smiling the way I always did when I came home to this place. The one-story ranch had been a godsend and it was actually Dave who had first brought me here. A few months back after my former home and all my belongings had burnt to the ground, my handyman had been working a job on this house and knew the owner needed to sell. When Dave first led me inside I'd immediately fallen in love with it. The house had a terrific open floor plan, large rooms and all it needed after Dave finished was some furniture to make it warm and cozy.

The month of January had been set aside just for that function, but everything had been put on hold due to Dutch's injury and the Fern Street mystery. I was hoping that I could wrap things up within the next week, which would still leave me two weeks to shop for furniture and decorate before I had to go back to my busy workload.

Sighing, I got out of the car and walked up the front walkway with a smile, but as I was about to step up to the front steps my intuition went haywire and I stopped dead in my tracks. Something was wrong—very, *very* wrong. I paused with my foot hovering just above the front step and listened intently to the warning bells clanging in my head. Swiveling to my right I set my foot back on the ground and began to walk away from the front door and over to the side of the house, where my spidey-sense was pulling furiously at me.

When I rounded the corner my breath caught in my throat. My side living room window had been completely smashed in. Broken glass lay strewn all over the stone walkway. Quickly I retraced my steps as a sense of rage overtook me. Someone had broken into my house! I ignored the warning bells and headed up the front steps. I had my key out and placed it quietly into the keyhole. My blood was racing and my heart pounded furiously in my chest.

I slowly opened the front door and peeked in with just my head. I saw no one in the living room, and stepped inside keeping my back to the wall. My eyes roved over the living and dining rooms, and saw nothing out of place. Of course, these two rooms were completely void of furniture, so there wasn't really anything that could be messed with anyway. I stood there for several seconds, while I listened intently for the sound of the intruder, but heard nothing. Maybe they hadn't actually entered. Maybe the broken window was just the result of some kid looking for his jollies and finding great satisfaction in pounding in my side window. Left side, heavy feeling—my sign for no way José. *Great.*

I stepped forward on tiptoe and headed in the direction of the kitchen, which had a swing door that I always perched open, but today was closed. Someone had definitely been in my house.

With infinite care I carefully pushed on the door a millimeter at a time until I was able to peek into the kitchen's interior. Nothing moved, thank God. Slowly I inched my way through the door and looked around. All of my cabinets had been opened, and most of my brand new dinnerware lay shattered and strewn upon the countertops and floor. Adding to the mess were all of the contents of my kitchen drawers and cabinets. Food, silverware, pots, pans and Tupperware were mixed within the shards of porcelain.

My shoulders slumped as I looked at the mess. "Son of a bitch!" I hissed under my breath as I took a careful step. My foot stepped on a shard of dinnerware, which made a small crunching sound. This would take forever to clean up, not to mention all the broken dishes and glassware I'd have to replace.

Just then I heard what could only be described as a shuffling sound coming from my bedroom. Freezing in place I listened intently, and a moment later I heard it again. *Uh-oh!*

Careful not to make any further noise I reached into

my back pocket and pulled out my cell phone. Flipping it open I pressed the NINE key and at the same time took a very careful step back toward the kitchen door. I'd have to get out of site and hearing distance before I could call for help. My foot again connected with a shard of porcelain and made a rather loud crunching noise, and the moment the sound seemed to reverberate against the walls of the kitchen I heard the shuffling in the bedroom pause. *Shit!* I froze for a moment, then I heard more movement, but this was much quicker, and headed in my direction.

No longer trying to be quiet I took two long running steps in the direction of the swinging door. As I was about to push through it, the door came back at me with tremendous force pushed by someone crashing through from the other side. In an instant my forward motion stopped with a dramatic *THWAK!* as I collided with the door and the force of the blow sent me flying backward. When I hit the ground, intense and immediate pain ignited along my back as dozens of tiny shards embedded themselves into my skin. My mouth curled up in pain as I struggled to roll off the painful shards, but just as I was rolling up onto my shoulder, a large shape towered above me and before I even had a chance to put up a defensive arm, a boot-laden foot connected hard with my stomach. I doubled forward into the fetal position by the force of the blow, the wind completely knocked out of me, and the pain of rolling around on shards of glass was suddenly forgotten.

Stars swam before my eyes, and my vision clouded. I didn't pass out but I came damn close, as I worked to regain my breath and not puke my guts out. After five long, agonizing minutes I finally sat up carefully and looked around. The intruder was gone, and, thankfully, I was still alive.

With slow careful movements, I lifted the cell phone, still clutched in my hand and looked at the indicator, which still held the NINE on the display. With ragged breath and shaking fingers I managed to depress a ONE to join the NINE but just as I was about to press the other ONE the outgoing number disappeared as "Incoming Call" overrode it and my cell phone chirped. It took my beleaguered mind a moment to switch from calling out to picking up, but after a pause I pressed the ON button and said a breathless, "Yeah?"

"Abby?!" Dave shouted into the earpiece, "Abby, is that you?"

"Yes . . ." I said with a breath, relieved that help was just moments away. All I had to do was tell Dave that I'd been attacked, and he'd come running.

Before I could get the words out, however, he cut me off with, "I just came home and my house has been broken into! The place is totaled! And I think it's got something to do with that house on Fern! Whatever you do, don't go home alone!"

"Too late . . ." I said as stars danced around my eyes again and another wave of nausea overtook me.

"What? Where are you?"

"Send the cavalry to my house, Dave . . . I'm down for the count." And with that I lost the battle against puking my guts out.

Chapter Six

"Yee-ouch!" I squealed as one more glass splinter was pulled out of my back.

"Almost done," the ER doc said patiently.

I wanted to sock him—he'd made that same comment a half hour before. "Can we hurry this along?" I snipped. I had spent my fair share of time in hospitals in recent months.

"Let the doctor work, Abby," Dutch said sternly. He was mad at me, but I had yet to figure out why.

Milo, who was standing next to Dutch, flipped back several pages in his small notebook to the beginning of my statement, rereading certain sections, his mouth set in a grim line.

"So what do you make of it?" Dutch asked his old partner.

"For starters I think Dave was right, the two break-ins definitely seem related. I'll know more when the crime scene tech compares the fingerprints he retrieves from each scene—assuming he can find some left behind by our perp, but both break-ins had the same style of forced entry, breaking out a side window, same chaotic ransack to each place, and the only thing Dave can officially say is missing is the file with all the paperwork from your investment company. The question is why?"

I sucked in a quick breath as one more splinter was set free, and after a moment I said, "Someone didn't want us to buy that house."

"How do you know?" Dutch asked. I tapped my temple and winked. "Oh," he said, nodding. "So why would he be so messy about it?"

"What do you mean?" I asked as, blissfully, the last shard was dropped into a pan with a small "ting" and the last bandage was applied to my back.

"You can get dressed now," the doctor said, stepping around from my back and beginning to scribble notes on my file.

"If the guy who attacked you is the same guy who broke into Dave's house, and he got a hold of the file from Dave, why go into your house and destroy the place?" Dutch asked.

"Because he was looking for something." I said as I gingerly got off the gurney I'd been sitting on and walked over to the chair where my clothes were.

"What?" Milo and Dutch both said together.

"That's the sixty-four-million-dollar question, fellas," I said as I motioned for Dutch and Milo to turn their backs while I dressed.

Milo turned away immediately, but Dutch only smiled and winked at me, refusing to turn around. Rolling my eyes at him I carefully shrugged out of my hospital gown and slowly pulled on my shirt, forgoing my bra, then gingerly slid into my heavy sweatshirt, wincing as I stretched into the sleeve.

"All right, Miss Cooper, you are free to go," the doctor said as he finished his scribbling and handed me a small piece of paper. "Here is your prescription for the antibiotic and I would recommend taking Tylenol or ibuprofen for any discomfort you might have. You will most likely be very sore for a few days, especially with that rib. The bone is not bruised or broken but likely to be sore for a week or two."

"Thanks, Doc," I said, accepting the prescription. "I'll take it easy."

"You bet your ass you will," Dutch growled.

Crap, he was mad again. This would be a fun ride home. The three of us left my curtained gurney and walked, hobbled and limped out to the reception room, where an anxious Dave bounced up to greet us. "You okay?" he asked me, his eyes searching for anything still bleeding.

"I'm fine," I said, laying a reassuring hand on his arm. "Just some cuts and bruises. Nothing life threatening."

Dave let out a sigh of relief and grinned at me. "You want me to take you and Dutch back to his place?"

"Thanks, Dave, but Milo's got us," Dutch said quickly.

I stifled a chuckle. Dave drove an ancient truck with a hundred eighty on the odometer, while Milo drove a brand new BMW 750i with plush heated leather seats and a kick-ass sound system. It wasn't even a contest.

"Oh, okay. I guess I better get home," he said, sounding a little dejected.

I glared reproachfully at Dutch. "Hey, you can come over if you want. We're getting Thai from Pi's, Dutch's treat, if you want to join us."

Dave smiled again at me and said, "That's okay, Abby, my old lady's probably pissed that I'm not helping her clean up the mess. I better get back before she blows a gasket."

To this day I have no idea what Dave's common-law wife's real name was; his nickname for her had always been "old lady." Even though it wasn't flattering, I knew he was completely devoted to her. "Sure thing, buddy," I said as we walked toward the exit. "I'll give you a call tomorrow and see how you're doing, all right?"

"Cool," he said and punched the automatic door button on the big front doors opening them wide for us to all walk through.

When we got outside we all came up short. The snow was coming down in huge flakes that coated everything in sight with alarming speed. "We better get going," Milo said, eyeing his car and the snowy roads nervously.

Without further conversation the three of us piled into Milo's Beemer and headed to Dutch's, stopping at Pi's on the way for four orders of pad thai. A short time later Milo dropped Dutch and me off, then headed home to have dinner with his wife, Noelle.

Dutch and I shuffled into the house and I carefully helped him off with his coat, then he helped me with my sweatshirt, both mindful of the other's injuries. "We're quite a pair, huh?" I said as we moved into the living room.

"Mmm-hmm."

"Want a beer?" I asked after setting our dinner on the coffee table and heading toward the kitchen.

"Mmm-hmm."

"It'd be good to check out the news and see how much snow we're going to get," I said from the kitchen as I pulled two Sam Adamses from the fridge and heard the TV click on.

"Mmmm."

"Here you go," I said, taking my seat again next to Dutch.

"Grmmph," he said and opened the Styrofoam lid to reveal his extra-spicy dinner.

"Looks like the Red Wings are going to have another great year," I said as a sportscaster came on screen and led with a recent Motor City victory.

Head nod.

"Okay, what the *hell* is wrong with you?" I asked, snatching the fork out of Dutch's hand as it hovered above his rice noodles.

To his credit, he looked slightly taken aback for all of two heartbeats. Then his brow lowered, his mouth became a firm line and he growled, "I just don't understand how you could be so stupid."

"Excuse me?"

Dutch didn't respond. Instead he snatched the fork back and jammed it into his food.

I angrily grabbed it right back and said, "You've got a hell of a lot of nerve there, pal!"

Dutch reached for the fork and I pulled it away with a sneer. When he reached for it again, I threw it into the kitchen. "Explain yourself!" I demanded, glaring at him with the full force of my anger.

Dutch clenched his jaw a few times, his eyes becoming small, his anger building, but instead of talking to me he got up and limped into the kitchen where he pulled a clean fork from the utensil drawer and hobbled back to the couch. Continuing the silent treatment, he gingerly sat down again and, holding his fork tight, he aimed it toward his food.

Without hesitation I snatched up his dinner and walked into the kitchen where I hovered it over the trash can. "Start talking," I demanded.

Dutch glared at me for a long moment, his face turning red until finally he got up and came slowly over to me. He moved close enough to invade my personal space as we had ourselves a staring match, all the while he refused to speak. "You're an ass!" I said finally and began to turn the Styrofoam container end up.

With amazing speed Dutch caught my arm, freezing the motion, and bellowed, "Stupid! Dumb! Idiotic! Obtuse! Moronic! As in walking into a house where you know a crazy, drugged-out psychopath could be waiting for you!"

My mouth opened at the force of his voice, a booming thunderous sound that reverberated off the walls. I had never seen him so angry, and it shocked me to the core. "I . . . I . . . I . . ." I stammered.

"Don't you get it?" he continued, undaunted by my reaction. "That guy could have broken your pretty little neck like that!" he said, snapping his fingers an inch from my face. "You told Milo that you knew someone had broken into that house before you entered, and you *still* went in before calling me, or Milo, or the police or . . . *anyone* else!"

"But . . ." I managed.

"*But* what, Abby? *But* you didn't know he was still in there? Bullshit! You're the best damn psychic I've ever met, and *I know* that *you knew* that guy was still there."

Tears sprang to my eyes as the truth of his words echoed in my ears. He was right. In the back of my mind, as I'd entered my house, I'd known I wasn't alone. I'd been so angry at the violation that, foolishly, I thought I could exact some revenge by jumping the intruder and kicking his ass. Instead, I'd been the one who'd gotten kicked, and I was damn lucky that nothing worse had happened to me. "Okay," I said lowering my gaze, totally ashamed of myself. "You're right, I'm sorry."

And in that moment, Dutch took me completely by

surprise again. Letting go of my wrist he took the Thai food out of my hand, set it on the counter, grabbed me around the waist and pulled me to him, crushing me in a bear hug that hurt my back and battered ribcage something fierce—but I wasn't about to complain. "I couldn't handle it if something happened to you again," he whispered into my hair. "I can't take any more calls like the one I got from Dave today. You're just gonna have to trust me on this one, Edgar, I need you around, okay?"

I nodded against his shirt, soaking up the smell of him, finally understanding how much he cared about me. It scared and thrilled me at the same time, and I didn't want his hug to end.

Finally, though, Dutch let go of me, and took my face in his hands, lifting my chin for a soft kiss. "Want some cold Thai food?" he asked, back to his old charming self.

"Lead the way." I smiled and he took my hand and we ambled back to the couch for warm beer and cold Thai. It was one of the best meals I ever ate.

Later that night Dutch followed me upstairs. It took him almost ten minutes to climb twelve steps, but eventually he made it. We crawled under the covers together and held onto each other all night long.

In the morning I was up first, and headed downstairs to feed Virgil, Dutch's cat, and Eggy. I had only one can of dog food left, and really needed to go out for more but looking outside I knew I wasn't going to get very far. It had snowed about seven inches during the night, and although the road had been plowed, Dutch's car was buried from view in the driveway. Sighing, I headed into the kitchen where I threw on a pot of coffee, and tossed a few eggs in the pan for Eggy. I'd have to stretch the dog food until I could get to the store, which by the looks of it wouldn't be until tomorrow.

As I was tossing a few more eggs into the pan for Dutch and me, the house phone rang and just as I reached for it, I heard him get the upstairs line. I went on with my cooking, aware of a mumbled conversation happening upstairs, and wondered who could be calling Dutch so early in the morning.

While I was setting the table he came gingerly into the kitchen, his limp always more pronounced in the morning.

"How's it feel this morning?" I asked.

"A little tender. I didn't think to take the doughnut when Dave swung by to pick me up on the way to your house."

I winced. "Sorry 'bout that."

"Peace," Dutch said, indicating it wasn't a topic we needed to revisit. "Coffee?" he asked as he scratched his rumpled head and stifled a yawn.

"Already on the table," I said as I moved past him on the way to the counter to retrieve the eggs and hash browns.

Dutch swung an arm around my middle catching me before I could move all the way past. "Where's my kiss?"

"Also at the table," I giggled.

"Next to the sugar?" he answered playfully, not letting me go.

"Go," I said, laughing as I gently pried myself out of his grasp. "I'll be there in a minute."

Dutch sighed and ambled over to take his seat, where I heard him take a big slurp of his coffee. I grabbed the bowl of eggs, hash browns and juice and juggled them to the table. As I set them down I asked, "Who was calling you so early in the morning?"

"Kiss first," Dutch demanded with a playful grin.

I rolled my eyes and leaned forward, giving him a nice wet one before sitting down and looking expectantly at him for an answer.

"Well?"

"That was an old friend of mine, Peter Satch," he said as he scooped a huge mound of eggs onto his plate "We were buddies at U of M when I was in graduate school, and we were both in the same MBA program together."

"Criminal justice?" I asked as I too spooned a portion of eggs onto my plate.

"Yeah. Anyway, we've kept in touch off and on over the years, and I'd heard that he had taken a job at Interpol. On a hunch I thought maybe he could help us out with Jean-Paul. I don't care what the newspaper reports say—I got a funny feeling that guy was no war hero."

I smiled at my boyfriend. Apparently my sixth sense was rubbing off on him, because a few months ago a statement that began with, "I got a funny feeling," would have been reserved only for the doctor's office. "I couldn't agree with you more," I said. "There's some really bad energy in that house, and I know it's male. It's got to be Jean-Paul's."

Dutch chewed his food for a minute, then looking at me curiously, asked, "How can you tell it's male versus female?"

"Male energy feels heavier, thicker, more . . . pronounced," I said, trying to put into words what was so hard to describe. "Female energy feels lighter, softer, less . . . I don't know, *there,* I guess."

"Huh," he said, nodding as if he understood exactly what I'd said.

"So what did Peter have to say about Jean-Paul?" I asked.

"Oh, he was just returning my call. I told him that I had a friend who'd purchased a house from a guy whose origins were a little suspicious. I gave him Jean-Paul's vitals and he said he'd do some research and get back to me."

"Sounds good," I said, feeling like that was a step in the right direction. Just then Dutch and I heard a rumbling sound outside and we both got up to investigate at the same time. I beat him to the window and laughed when I saw the source of the noise. Dave was busy rumbling up and down the driveway with a snowplow attached to the front of his truck, clearing out a path for Dutch's car. I went to the front door, opened it and waved at him. He waved back and made one more push with the plow making a clear path from the garage to the street.

He lowered the window then and called, "Morning, honey!"

"Hey, Dave!" I called back and waved at him to come in, "I've got hot coffee, eggs and hash browns. Can I tempt you?"

"I'll be right in," he yelled back, smiling broadly. Dave never turned down food.

A few minutes later, as I was making a place for him at the table, we heard him come through the front door stomping off the snow and removing his boots. "That was some storm we got last night," he called from the foyer.

"Thanks for the shovel, buddy," Dutch called back.

"Sure thing. I didn't want Abby trying to tunnel out after what she went through yesterday," Dave said as he rounded into the kitchen.

I grinned at him as I gave him a steaming cup of hot coffee. "Always looking out for me, aren't you?"

"Well, since you manage to get yourself into more

trouble than anyone else I know, I figure between me and Dutch it's at least a two-person job."

Dutch and Dave laughed and nodded at each other while I gave them each a dark look and took my seat. "Ha, ha," I said, snapping my napkin into my lap.

"This looks great," Dave said as he settled into an empty chair.

"Glad I made extra," I said, only now realizing that I'd had the thought to make a lot more than I normally would for two people.

"So what's on your agenda?" Dave asked me as he took up his fork.

"Well, there's not much I can do without my car."

"I figured," Dave said. "That's why I wanted to come over and see if I could give you a lift to your place to get it. While I'm there I can also cover up that window."

"Oh, crap!" I said, only now realizing that with my window smashed out snow had probably piled up in my living room.

"Yeah, we'll need to get that taken care of today," Dave said, noting my anxiety.

"I'll get ready," I said bolting out of my chair and depositing my dishes in the sink. I wanted to get to my house as soon as possible.

As I headed out of the kitchen I heard Dutch say to Dave, "Don't let her out of your sight today, got it?"

"Way ahead of you, partner," Dave replied.

I rolled my eyes. Men have such little faith.

Twenty minutes later Dave was happily plowing out my driveway while I sat shotgun. We zoomed back and forth about ten times until he was satisfied I had a clear path out to the street, then we parked and trudged up the front walkway to the door. I unlocked the door and we stepped inside. My anxiety eased a little when we entered as I saw that only a little snow had made its way in. Luckily, the window was shielded from the heavy snowfall by a fir tree, which was why my intruder had obviously selected it from all the others in the house.

"I'll get the wood," Dave said, and darted back through the door. I walked to the kitchen and pushed open the swinging door, noticing the black splotches of powder left behind by Milo's fingerprint crew. I sighed when I walked into the kitchen and looked around at all the mess. Shrugging my shoulders I got the broom and a paper bag from the pantry and began sweeping up. While I worked, I heard Dave in the other room pounding nails into my window frame. I'd have to order a new window, which would probably take a week or two to come in. The wood wouldn't look pretty, but since I was already staying at Dutch's, it hardly mattered.

I finished in the kitchen and moved into my bedroom, investigating what damage my attacker had exacted there. I groaned as I entered the room, which was a total wreck. Clothes and bedding were strewn everywhere. It seemed the entire contents of my closet had been pulled from their hangers and thrown about in a windstorm. Something curious struck me as my eyes roamed the space, however. Two large holes had been torn in the drywall on the far side of the room. It reminded me of the condition of the house on Fern Street and I moved to the other side to investigate. Just then my intuition began to buzz loudly, and as I kneeled down to take a closer look at the holes I turned on my radar and focused on the message buzzing in my head. *Look in the floor . . .*

I cocked my head slightly as the thought swirled in my mind. *Look on the floor?* I asked as my eyes darted around, searching the clutter for some kind of clue.

As I asked that question my left side felt thick and heavy, my sign for no. Something was off. Crouching again by the holes in the wall I put my hand on one of them and completely opened up my intuition. I needed to concentrate on what my guides were trying to tell me. *Look in the floor* . . . came the thought, and in my mind's eye I saw the living room of the house on Fern and a small swallow dart around in a circle, then land on the floor. The bird then began to peck at the carpet like a woodpecker.

"Oh!" I said aloud. "I get it!"

"Get what?" Dave asked from the doorway as he looked at me curiously.

I jumped when he spoke; I'd been so focused on my intuitive message that I hadn't heard him come in. "Jesus!" I exclaimed, and put a hand to my heart.

"Sorry," he said sounding sheepish, "Didn't mean to scare you."

"No," I said taking a deep breath, "I didn't hear you come in. Listen, Dave, I gotta go somewhere, are you done?"

"Yeah, I'm all set. Where do you need to go?"

"I've got to go back to Fern Street. Can you cover for me and call Dutch, just tell him that I'm still here cleaning up and I'll be home in a little while?"

Dave's eyes had gotten huge at the mention of Fern Street, and got even larger when I asked him to lie to my boyfriend. "Are you out of your friggin' mind, Abby?"

"Nope," I said coming around to the other side of the room to move past him. "There's just something that I have to check out. I'll be okay, really."

"Whoa, whoa, *whoa*!" Dave said stepping in my path, barring my escape. "You're not going anywhere.

I promised your boyfriend I'd keep an eye on you, and given his considerable connections to the FBI and local law enforcement, something tells me I'd be looking at nothing less than three to ten if I let anything happen to you."

"Fine, then come with me."

Dave's eyes bugged even larger. "Again, I gotta ask you, are you *out of your friggin' mind?*"

"Dave, I *am* going to that house on Fern," I said sternly. "You can either come with me, or you can stay here and cover for me. Those are your choices. Pick one you can live with."

As Dave stared down at me with considerable frustration, the muscles in his jaw working through the dilemma, I did feel a little sorry for him. He knew I could outrun him, and wouldn't think twice about doing so. My driveway was now snow free and that meant I could zip right out with nary a backward glance. If I wanted to go somewhere, most likely he wouldn't be able to stop me. That meant he'd have to cover for me and hope for the best. Apparently, that was one gamble he wasn't willing to bet the farm on. After a minute he took a deep breath. Letting it out slowly he moved his hand to his chin and gave a good tug on his beard, then said, "*Fine!* I will go with you to Fern. But we have to make a few stops first, and I'm driving just so you don't get any ideas."

I smiled broadly at him and said, "Smart man, Dave."

An hour and forty-five minutes later we were finally headed in the right direction. I'd had to wait while Dave made several pit stops. The first to a grocery store where he purchased a bottle of water, a spray bottle, some string and several cloves of garlic. Next, I'd bitten my tongue as he'd driven to a nearby church and we'd waited twenty minutes for a priest to bless the water that Dave then poured into the spray bottle. After that, I'd opted to stay in Dave's truck while he drove to a small gift shop and bought a holy Bible, a crucifix and about ten rosaries. He'd then gotten back in the truck and threaded the cloves of garlic and three strands of string into a smelly necklace, looped the rosaries through the cloves and string and secured the crucifix to his coat.

"Are you ready yet?" I finally complained, holding my nose at the overwhelming scent of garlic. This was getting ridiculous.

"It's best to come prepared," he answered, and it was then that I noticed how shaky his voice was.

"Oh, brother," I said and rolled my eyes again. "Dave, we're not up against vampires."

"Who knows what we're up against, Abby? I mean, *something* really bad is in that house. It could be a vampire, it could be the devil. Who really knows?"

I stared at him and saw he was serious. "It's neither of those two things."

"Yeah, well I'm not taking any chances. My mother always said that garlic was the best way to ward off evil spirits, and I figure it can't hurt to take some precautions."

I scowled at him even though my own nerves were starting to get a little frayed now that I thought about what might be waiting for us in that house. Still, I figured we could just dart in, and dart out again. I knew where to look and it was still daylight out.

Plus, on our way out after seeing Liza disappear in the stairwell, Dutch and I had thought to grab Dave's drill and circular saw. Good thing too, because now nothing could be used as a projectile. So, what could possibly happen?

We drove the rest of the way in silence, Dave's knuckles white as they gripped the steering wheel, and

my own resolve dwindling. I perked up, however, when
the house came into view. With all the snow covering
the worst parts of it, the house seemed much less
threatening.

Dave did his shovel thing in the driveway, zipping
back and forth a few extra times as a stall tactic, until
I finally put my hand on his arm and said, "How about
we just get it over with already?"

He nodded gravely and cut the engine. We got out
of the truck and trudged up the walkway to the house,
Dave's rosaries clinking with every step. I moved to
the door and unlocked it, allowing it to swing open as
we stood outside for a moment to make sure nothing
jumped out at us. Dave stepped forward and raised
the spray bottle. *Sprrrrrt,* went the sprayer. As the
moisture fell to floor he looked at me and nodded.

Slowly we entered the house and flipped on the living room light. Even though there was still plenty of
daylight, the interior seemed oppressive and dark. Inching our way into the living room neither one of us
spoke, the silence was cut only by the *sprrrt* sound
of Dave and his holy water. After giving the room a
good dousing he finally turned to me and whispered,
"Okay, chief, what did you want to check out?"

I took a deep breath to compose myself and stepped
into the middle of the room, closing my eyes and focusing my attention on my intuition. In my mind's eye
I visualized the room and saw the swallow that had
been part of my earlier vision enter the room. The bird
circled around before coming to rest in the center of
the room. I opened my eyes and looked where the
bird had landed. Dave was standing right on the spot.
"There," I said and pointed at his feet.

"What?" he asked, picking up his foot to examine
it. He thought I was pointing to his shoes.

"Under your feet. We need to get this carpet up,

Dave. There's something underneath the carpet I need to see."

Dave cocked his head at me looking puzzled. "Under the carpet?"

"Yeah, right where you're standing as a matter of fact. Do you have anything on you that could cut a hole in this carpet?"

"Uh, sure . . . out in my truck. Here," he said, handing me the spray bottle, "I'll be right back."

As Dave bolted out of the house, I moved to where he had been standing and got down on bended knee to more closely examine the carpet. There were no seams or tears in the fabric, just worn fibers and a few stains. Then, without warning, I suddenly smelled the distinct scent of cigarette smoke. "Shit!" I said jumping to my feet and holding the spray bottle up in front of me, ready to squirt the daylights out of anything that moved. "Dave!" I called in a voice that shook.

"Right here," he said from behind me. "What's the matter?" he asked, looking around as he saw my anxious expression.

"Do you smell anything?" I asked as I sniffed the air. It was still there, and growing more pungent.

Dave took a whiff of air. "Nope, not a thing. Why? What are you getting?"

"Nothing," I said as I eyed the crowbar Dave had brought back in with him. "But let's get this over with. I don't want to be here any longer than necessary."

Dave nodded, walked over to me and got down on one knee. "Right about here?" he asked.

"Yep. That's the spot," I said, ignoring the even thicker smell of smoke. I could have sworn I was standing right next to someone exhaling great puffs of tar into my face.

Dave reached into his back pocket, pulled out a box cutter, and clicking the blade into place sliced a small hole into the carpet. As I watched him a chill began to spread up my spine. Something was in this house with us, and it was angry. "Do you want some help?" I asked, anxious to get the heck out of there as soon as possible.

"Nope, I got it," Dave said as he tucked the box cutter back into his pocket and picked up the crowbar. It was then that we noticed the mist.

"What the . . . ?" Dave asked as he paused and looked around the room that had begun to fill with a smoky fog that had materialized out of nowhere.

"Hurry up," I whispered, the hairs on my arms and neck now standing up on end.

Dave quickly plunged the crowbar into the carpet, and tugged at it. "Spray the bottle!" he called to me as he pushed the crowbar through the thick fabric.

"What?" I asked him as I glanced around the foggy room. The mist was getting thicker, and the temperature seemed suddenly frigid.

"Spray the holy water!" Dave yelled, grunting as he pushed at the carpet, which thankfully, began to tear.

Sprrrrt, I sprayed. *Sprrrrrt, sprrrrrt, sprrrrrrrrrrt!* Still the mist was getting thicker. It was getting hard to see the floor, and Dave had to wave his hand over the hole in the carpet to see his progress. Finally he had a large hole and he then tore through the thick padding, tearing with his hands to reveal the floorboards underneath.

"Hurry!" I said, continuing to spray from the bottle.

"This is crazy! Abby, we need to get the hell out of here right now . . . *holy crap*!" he exclaimed, bending low over the floorboard and waving his hand at the mist.

"What?" I asked, bowing to get a better view.

"Look!" Dave said, pointing to the floor. As I squinted I could see what he was so excited about.

There was a small trapdoor in the floorboard, still partially covered by the carpet. I dropped the spray bottle and knelt down next to him, grabbing at a corner of the carpet and pulling with all my might. We had to get that door open and get at whatever was underneath, and we had to do that now!

Dave took my cue and tugged from his end, pulling the hole larger between us. Just as we were clearing away the padding to reveal the rest of the trapdoor we heard a horrible noise that turned my blood cold. It was a cross between a moan and an angry growl, and it came from the direction of the kitchen. "Hurry!" I said, my hands shaking as Dave clutched at the handle to the trapdoor, a cord forming in his neck muscles as he yanked at the opening.

It was then that I felt something coming into the room, and my spidey-sense said that it wasn't happy with our discovery. It slithered into the room like a snake, and it coiled itself around my energy as it overpowered me and overtook my sense of reality. From somewhere deep inside myself I was aware that I had stopped pulling on the carpet. I heard noises, but I wasn't able to comprehend them, and all I could see, sense, feel and touch was a memory that wasn't mine.

I saw a man. He was older and he was very angry. He clutched my throat tightly and yelled obscenities at me as he shook me so hard my teeth rattled. I couldn't breathe and I knew I was doomed, still I clutched at the hands that circled my neck, trying to form the words that he demanded me to speak, but his anger overtook him and he heaved me with all his might into a wall. I felt my collarbone snap, the pain was excruciating, and still he would not relent. Suddenly, the man let go of my neck and I was able to take one, ragged, painful breath before he grabbed a fistful of my hair and pulled my head forward, then slammed it back against the wall with such force that my ears rang and darkness threatened to overtake me. The next thing I knew I was lifted off the ground and tossed like a sack of potatoes backward, the stairwell walls slipping past me as I fell through the air and slammed against the pavement in the basement. Then I knew nothing more.

Chapter Seven

"Abby!" Dave shouted from someplace that sounded like a tunnel. "Abby!" he yelled again, and I felt small slaps against my cheek. "Abby, *come on*!"

"Stop . . ." I managed as the slapping continued.

"Oh, thank Christ!" he said, the relief evident in his voice. "Damn, girl! You scared the *shit* outta me!"

My eyes fluttered as my senses returned. I became aware that the air seemed crisp and cool, and my bum was wet and growing numb. "Where . . . ?" I asked as I managed to open my eyes.

"You're okay," Dave said. "But man! I thought I was gonna have to take you back to the hospital, and Dutch woulda had my ass!"

I focused on Dave's face, hovering above me. I was lying across his lap out in the driveway of Fern Street, and I had no memory at all of what had happened beyond the angry man who had killed me. I shook my head a little and sat up, relieved to discover that I wasn't dizzy or nauseous. "What happened in there?"

"Hell if I know, lady. All I remember is you saying, 'hurry' and I get that door open and look up and you've gone all blank on me. I kept yelling at you, but you wouldn't even blink, and then you just fell backward in a dead faint. I had a hell of a time getting you outside, you know. You were all dead weight."

"No pun intended," I said as I pushed off from the ground to give my wet butt and sore back a break. It was then that I noticed the box. "What's that?"

"That's what was in that trapdoor," Dave said like I should have known.

I reached over and picked up the box. At first glance it looked like a jewelry box, delicately carved out of fine wood. It was dusty, but otherwise unmarred and I noticed an ornate crest engraved in the shape of an eagle flanked by a shield engraved on the top of the box. In one foot the eagle clutched a sword, in the other a small nest with three eggs. I ran my fingers over the crest, feeling the grooves in the wood and taking in the fine craftsmanship. I turned the box over a few times, but couldn't find a catch or a lid. The box was too light to be solid, but still, there was no obvious way to get inside.

"So what happened to you in there?" Dave asked, pulling my attention away from the box.

I looked at him for a long moment, not sure how to answer. The truth was that I had no idea. On a psychic level, it felt like my identity had been overtaken and I'd been forced to witness a horrible crime through the victim's eyes. I knew the man I'd been looking at was Jean-Paul, because even though he'd been older than any of his newspaper pictures, his facial features had been the same. And, I also knew that the woman he'd killed was Liza, the same woman at the bottom of the stairs. But why? Why had he killed her? What had sparked such anger, and why had I been forced to witness it?

My intuition buzzed and my attention went back to

the box. "I don't really know, Dave," I said finally. "But, whatever's in this box is sure going to help me find out."

"Well, you'd better hope so, Abby, 'cuz I'm never setting foot in that house again."

I got up and said, "I'm right there with you, pal. Come on, let's get back to Dutch's and see if we can't figure out how to open this thing. Oh, and no mention of my fainting spell or any of the scary stuff to Dutch, 'kay?"

"Like you had to ask," Dave said, gingerly getting to his feet. "He'd have my ass in a sling if he knew we hadn't bolted at the first sign of that smoky stuff. Say, is that what you smelled in there? Smoke?"

"Yeah, but it was cigarette smoke. It appears that I'm the only one who smells it—and it always seems to be right before all the weird stuff starts happening."

"Well, the *really* weird thing is that right after you fainted, all the mist just disappeared."

"What?"

"Yep, it was there one second and then you plop backward and it's gone, like it was never there."

"Come on, Dave," I said, heading for the truck. "I've got a phone call to make."

"Holliday," came a crisp female voice through the phone line.

"Hey, M.J. It's Abby Cooper calling," I said, relieved that I hadn't gotten voice mail.

"Hey, Abby, how's the ghost busting coming?" she asked amiably.

"Funny you should ask," I began, then I filled her in on what happened at the Fern Street house. I had to lower my voice as I talked to her, because Dutch was downstairs with Dave and the two were trying to figure out how to open the mysterious box we'd discovered, and I didn't want Dutch to hear the additional details around unearthing the thing.

"That's quite a tale, Abby," M.J. said when I'd finished.

"What do you make of it?"

"Well, for starters you definitely have one nasty poltergeist on your hands."

"Thanks for the news flash," I said flatly.

M.J. laughed and replied, "You'd be surprised how many people I help who simply want to hear that they're not crazy when they see stuff fly through the air and have all kinds of strange encounters. But let's talk through the sequence and see if I can't give you a feel for what happened. First, you smelled smoke, but no one else did, is that right?"

"Yes. I first smelled it the other day when my boyfriend and I were in the house together and we saw the woman at the bottom of the stairs, the one who was murdered in the house. Dutch, my boyfriend, swears he never smelled anything unusual, but I know I got a good whiff. Then, today, when Dave and I were there, the minute we started digging at the carpet I smelled it again, only this time it was like someone was standing right next to me, puffing on a cigarette and blowing the smoke right in my face."

"I see. . . ." M.J. said. "One of the little oddities of ghost hunting is that not everyone attracts them."

"I'm sorry?" I asked, not understanding. "What do you mean, attracts them?"

"Well, there's a theory out there that I tend to believe myself, and it says that human beings emit individually unique electromagnetic wavelengths, similar to how no two humans have identical fingerprints. Some people emit low wavelengths, and others emit high ones. It's no coincidence, Abby, that you're a psychic and are attractive to the spirit world. I'll bet you can sense when your spirit guides are around, huh?"

She'd hit that one on the head. "Yes, yes I can," I said, "but what does that have to do with being attractive to ghosts?"

"It's the same type of thing, really. Your energy is easy for those in the spirit world to be around. They can get near enough to you to be sensed or seen and this makes you more sensitive to their presence. Ghosts are no different than people really, they love attention. In fact, they're starved for it. This man, Jean-Paul you said?"

"Yes?"

"Do you know if he was a smoker?"

I instantly remembered the photograph I'd seen in the library of a young Jean-Paul holding a cigarette between his fingers as he leaned against the brick wall of his jewelry shop. "Yes, he was," I confirmed.

"So it's a pretty safe bet that he's the one who's been giving you grief. Now, the mist that you saw come into the room, that is a phenomena we like to call ghost juice but you may have heard it by its more proper name, ectoplasm."

"Ectoplasm is real?" I asked. I'd heard the term from Bill Murray in the movie *Ghostbusters*, but thought it was a made-up word.

"It sure is. Now it is rare for it to show up to the degree that you and your friend saw it. That takes a lot of energy, so the other thing we need to be aware of is that this Jean-Paul dude is feistier than most. It's also not unusual for you to see ectoplasm one minute and have it disappear the next, that's actually a common occurrence and why a lot of my clients think they're one step away from the loo-loo farm."

I chuckled as I listened. I liked this woman and her

very practical, down-to-earth approach. It helped that she didn't seem rattled, scared or suspicious of my story. It made me feel a lot better about what I'd experienced. "So I'm attractive to this Jean-Paul guy, and that's why he tried to . . . what? Kill me?"

"Not necessarily," M.J. said quickly, "even though I'm sure it felt like that. I think what happened was that you discovered something that he'd been protecting for years when he was alive, something so precious to him that even in death he couldn't let go and so continues to guard it. When you guys started digging he must have been very angry and that's why there was so much energy swirling around, giving off the ghost juice. You must have really worked him into a good lather. Then, when that didn't scare you off, he showed you what happened to the last woman who got too close to his little treasure, and he took you through her experience. Very frightening for you, I'm sure, but again, you must hum at an electromagnetic frequency that allows him to jump into your energy and shake things up. Are you sure you're not a medium too?"

I thought about what M.J. was saying to me, and squirmed in my chair. Years ago Theresa had tried to teach me how to open up to spirits who had crossed over. My experience hadn't been fun, because unlike her I couldn't get names, I could only identify the energies I came in contact with through a physical sensation. The way these spirits identified themselves was typically by the last physical sensation they had experienced, like a heart attack or awful sickness. The last time I'd physically experienced this kind of thing had been when I'd opened up to a young man who'd overdosed on drugs, and had died of asphyxiation when his lungs filled with vomit. It had been awful and I'd never opened up again. "I'm not a medium in the traditional sense," I finally said, "but, to answer your question, yes, I can open up to energies who have crossed over. This was a similar experience, but far more visual and violent than I'm used to, and it also happened without my permission."

"Yeah, I'm sure Jean-Paul likes the fact that he practically highjacked you. But now you know his tricks, and if you protect yourself it shouldn't happen again."

"How can I do that?" If there was a way not to have to go through that again, I was all for it.

"The answer is so easy you're gonna laugh," M.J. said.

"Tell me," I begged.

"Magnets."

"What?"

"Magnets," she repeated. "As in what's probably hanging on your refrigerator at this very moment."

"I don't get it," I said, mentally scratching my head. "How could a refrigerator magnet ward off evil spirits?"

"It's simple," M.J. continued. "Magnets screw with the electromagnetic frequencies we all emit and it's like the ghost doesn't want to be in the same room with one. It's the equivalent of having a smoke alarm blaring in a small room, all you want to do is get away from the noise. Now, determined ghosts like Jean-Paul may be able to take it for a minute or two, but after that they want no part of it. It's very uncomfortable for them and they tend to recede as far away from the magnets as they can get. So, if you need to go back to your haunted house before you solve your mystery, take plenty of magnets, and place them in the four corners of each room. I guarantee you won't see much of Jean-Paul after that."

"Why didn't you tell me that in the beginning?" I asked, more than a little annoyed. If M.J. had simply shared that little tidbit with me, we could have gotten rid of Jean-Paul and Dave could have had the house fixed up and ready to go by now.

"Because the right thing to do is not to lock your ghost down with a bunch of magnets, Abby," M.J. explained patiently. "It's to discover the reason they're in pain, and help them cross over. Even if Jean-Paul did commit murder, he deserves to cross over and face his own judgment day, wouldn't you agree?"

I sighed heavily and gave in. "Yeah, I suppose. Still, that would have been good to know," I said stubbornly.

"Well, now you do, and you also know a lot more about what specifically happened to Liza. You're ahead of the game even though it wasn't the most pleasant experience. Don't worry, you'll figure out what triggered Jean-Paul's rage and solve the mystery, and once you know that you can leave the rest up to me. Now, I gotta fly, but call me when you're ready for me to come to town, okay?"

"Sure, sure," I said and we disconnected. I sat on the edge of Dutch's bed for a few moments considering everything M.J. had said and knowing she was right. Even so, magnets were going to be at the very top of my shopping list this week.

"Abby?" I heard Dutch call from downstairs. "You still on the phone?"

"Nope," I said, getting up and heading for the stairs. When I reached the bottom I noticed Dutch and Dave still seated on the couch, both eyeing the wooden box with interest. "No luck opening it, huh?"

"Oh, I can open it," Dave said as he leaned back against the sofa cushions. "It's just a question of how many pieces you'll have after I do that's the question."

"No!" I said sternly. "You promised not to damage

it, Dave." My guides had insisted that the box remain intact.

"Then I don't have a friggin' clue how you expect to find out what's inside it, Abby. There are no moving parts, no latches, or seams, or hinges for that matter, and the only way I know that it opens is that it's too light to be solid and when you shake it you can hear something shuffling around inside."

I looked questioningly at Dutch to get his input and he shrugged his shoulders agreeing with Dave. "Sorry, Edgar, I'm with him. I say we get a saw and cut this baby open . . ."

"No!" I said and bent forward, retrieving the box. "No one is sawing open anything!"

"Why not?" Dutch asked me, surprised by my outburst. "I mean, you could be holding the key to this entire little mystery. Why be stubborn about an old wooden box?"

I cradled the box defensively in my arms. "I don't know, Dutch, but trust me, it's important that this thing remain intact."

"Important to whom?" he said, still perplexed.

"Liza," I said without hesitation.

"The dead girl?" he asked.

"Yes. This was hers, and she doesn't want it ruined."

"How do you know?" Dave asked me.

I paused for a long moment and thought about that. The truth was, I didn't know how I knew. The only thing I could think of was that when Jean-Paul had taken me through Liza's death, some of her energy must have imprinted itself on me. I knew what I knew as if it were something I'd lived through, but couldn't remember. "I don't know how, Dave, but I just do. Okay?"

Dave threw up his hands and said, "Have it your

way, honey, but I don't think you're going to get that thing open without a good hammer."

My intuition buzzed, and my guides assured me they would help me find a way. "Give me some time and I'll figure it out," I said, and left it at that.

The next day I took Dutch to get his stitches removed and then dropped him off for his first physical therapy appointment. His physical therapist was a pretty brunette named Lori, and she promised not to be too hard on him. Given that he'd just had two-dozen little black threads pulled out of his butt and was in one hell of a mood, I could only hope that he'd return the favor.

While Dutch was put through his paces, I took advantage of the time and location of the physical therapist's office and scooted two streets over to Opalescence. I managed to find a parking spot just down the street, and extracted the wooden box from the back seat of my SUV, where I'd hidden it when Dutch's back was turned. Given the watchful eye he'd been scrutinizing me with lately, I didn't want to give too much away about what I was up to.

Coming into the store I spotted James right way behind one of the counters munching on a freshly opened bag of peanut M&M's. Being a true chocoholic I trotted over to him, hoping for morsel.

"Hi, Abby!" he said happily when he saw me.

"How's it going?" I asked as I stopped in front of him, placing the box on the counter.

"What'cha got there?" he asked as he extended the bag my way.

I gratefully nodded my head at the bag and he poured a generous portion into my outstretched palm. "This is a riddle, wrapped in a mystery inside an enigma," I said as I popped a blue M&M into my mouth.

"Hmmm," James said as he picked up the box. "Well, Mr. Churchill, I doubt Stalin could actually fit in here, but I guess anything's possible."

I laughed. "Actually, I don't know what's inside. That's why I thought of you. I found this box hidden in a crawl space at my house, and I think there's something inside, but I don't know how to open it." I watched James's face carefully for any sign of recognition of the box on his counter. It was a huge gamble, I knew, but I had to know if he knew about the box hidden by his grandfather.

"You know," he said, his expression inquisitive, "I've seen one of these before at a trade show. There's a trick to opening them, but the last time I saw one was years ago, and I don't remember how to get inside. If you'd like, I can do some research for you, and maybe track down someone who could help?"

"Normally, I'd take you up on that, James, thank you. But there's one more source I think I'll try before I give up and leave it with anyone." *Liar, liar . . . pants on fire . . .* The truth was there was no other source, but there was no way in hell I could risk leaving it with James and have him open it to discover what his grandfather had hidden so long ago, and how that was connected to Liza.

"Okay," he said, shrugging his shoulders. "Say, your earrings are coming along really nicely. We should have them ready for you by the end of the week."

"Sounds great. My sister's going to love them," I said as I picked the box back up preparing to leave, when my intuition buzzed loudly in my ear. "Say, James," I said, pausing for a moment. "Do you have an old friend or something coming for a visit? A family member or something?"

James cocked his head slightly at my question. "No, not that I know of."

"You sure?" I asked, as my intuition insisted that this was the case. "A cousin or a really close friend or something?"

"Nope," James said, shaking his head slowly back and forth, looking perplexed, "no one is planning a visit as far as I know."

"Hmmm," I said, scratching my own head. The thought continued to swirl in my mind so I went with it and explained, "Sometimes I get stuff that isn't on the agenda yet, but let me just say that if you end up inviting a relative, or close friend over to your house, look out. Whoever this guy is isn't the best of house-guests and he could take advantage of you. It feels like he's a pest or a nuisance or something, and you'll end up regretting having him over."

James's face turned from confused to thoughtful, then, to something that for a moment looked very much like fear. It was gone as quickly as it came, however, and after he'd recovered himself he said, "Thanks, Abby, I'll keep that in mind."

"No sweat. Say how's the puppy?"

James smiled. "She's terrific, thanks for asking, almost house trained and, so far, she's only chewed up a few pair of shoes."

"Yeah, my puppy went through that stage, too. It'll pass eventually and you can go back to wearing something other than ratty old sneakers."

"Good to know," James chuckled. "I'll be sure and give you a call when your earrings are done. Let me know if you want me to help figure out how to open that box."

"Sure thing," I said and took my leave. I walked back to the car, and stowed the box back in the trunk, then headed back over to pick up Dutch. When I got to the PT's office he was waiting for me in the lobby, leaning heavily on the cane.

"Did you get your errands done?" he asked, looking at me with a suspicious eye.

"Yep. Ready to go?" I didn't want to have to explain myself.

"Abby . . ." He said in a tone that meant he knew I'd been up to something.

"I've got the car nice and toasty for you. . . ."

"Tell me what you did," he demanded, refusing to budge.

"Why does everything have to have an ulterior motive?" I asked him.

"Because I know you."

"Well, maybe you don't know me as well as you think you do," I shot back.

"Oh, trust me," he said chuckling, "I know you well enough to understand when you've been up to something, now tell me or it's going to be a mighty long ride home."

"Fine, but let's talk about it in the car," I coaxed. I figured if he got upset at me while I was driving I could always run over a pothole to take his mind off it.

Once we were settled and on our way Dutch asked, "So?"

"Okay, I'll tell you, but first you have to promise me you won't get mad."

Dutch sighed audibly and rubbed a tired hand over his face. I had to hand it to him; he was really working hard to hang on to his patience. "I knew it," he said finally, "I knew you were up to no good."

I gave him a look and said, "It's no big deal, see? I'm safe and sound."

"So who did you go see?"

"James Carlier."

Dutch's lips thinned a bit at the mention of Jean-Paul's grandson. "And what did he have to say?"

"Not a lot. See, I went to his jewelry store a few

days ago to check it out, and he seems like a perfectly harmless guy. He doesn't know I'm the one who purchased his grandfather's house. As far as he knows the house was bought by a real estate investment firm."

"So why did you go back to see him today?"

"I took the box to him to see what his reaction would be."

Dutch gave me a cold hard look as his face turned flush, his lips formed a thin line and I began to frantically look for a pothole. I found a little one and swerved slightly to hit it. "Hey!" he yelled as the car bumped. "Cut that out!"

"Sorry, tough road," I said and nonchalantly turned on the radio.

Dutch snapped the radio off. "Abby, stop it."

I gave him a Bo Peep smile and small shrug, that said, "Who, me?"

"I mean it," he demanded crossly. "Now keep your eyes on the road and don't you dare hit any more potholes, got it?"

I saluted smartly, but stopped short of promising until he calmed down a little. "It was no big deal," I mumbled after a minute of silence while Dutch worked to rein in his horns.

"You don't know that," he said sharply. "All you do know is that you found a mysterious box in a house where a woman was murdered. You don't know who the killer was . . ."

"Actually, I do. I witnessed the whole thing at the house yesterday."

"Excuse me?" he said in a tone that meant business.

"Uh . . . I mean . . . uh . . ." *Crap!* I'd let the cat out of the bag.

"Lucy," Dutch said in a great Ricky Ricardo impression, "you got some 'splainin' to do."

I sighed, looking for a way out. We were stopped

at a stoplight and I looked around for distractions. Spotting Spago's Coney Island I offered, "Okay, I'll tell you all of it, but how about we do it over lunch? I'm starved." Dutch was always more agreeable when he had food in his stomach, and Spago's was a particular favorite of his.

As our waitress hurried away from the table to place our order, I took a long pull on my Coke and began telling Dutch what happened at the house on Fern the day before. He interrupted once or twice to clarify about what the mist that had surrounded Dave and I looked like, and why we didn't just get the hell out of there before things got too dicey. Mostly, though, he just listened as I told him about what I'd seen through Liza's eyes in the moments leading up to her murder.

"So Jean-Paul killed her, you're certain?" he asked when I was through with my story.

"Yes, it was definitely him. I recognized him from the photo in the newspaper, but he was considerably older at the time."

"How old?"

"I'd guess somewhere between sixty and seventy."

"Pretty strong for a guy in his midsixties to hurl a woman down a flight of stairs."

I thought about that for moment and said, "I can tell you that I saw and felt everything through Liza's perspective. I know that sounds weird but her thoughts were my thoughts and her feelings were mine. I obviously didn't retain her memories, or her history, and I don't know her last name, but I can tell you that she was tiny, she was much smaller than Jean-Paul and probably didn't weigh over a hundred pounds soaking wet. I remember clutching at the hands around my neck, and they were so big compared to mine. James is fairly tall, so his grandfather probably had some height on him as well."

"Speaking of which," Dutch said, eyeing me critically, "what were you thinking taking that box to him, anyway? He could be just as evil as his grandfather, Abby. And if his granddaddy was willing to kill for the thing, the apple might not fall far from the tree."

"I know, that's what logic would say, but I don't think he's like that. I opened up my spidey sense when I asked him about the box, and he didn't recognize it, I'm sure of it. He'd never seen it before."

"So did he know how to open it?"

"No, unfortunately he didn't."

"I see," Dutch said, giving me his best "told you so" look. "Listen, I may know of someone who can help," he offered.

"Really?"

"Yeah. I know a guy at the Bureau who's a crack safe opener. If there's a way to open that box, he'll figure it out. But," he said, looking meaningfully at me, "the condition for my help is that you promise to behave yourself."

I made a face to show him what I thought of his condition. "You act like I look for stuff to happen to me," I said, crossing my arms.

Dutch's mood softened and he said, "I figure that's the only way someone could get into as much trouble as you do, sweethot."

I sighed at him and said, "Come on, Mr. Bogart, let's get you home."

Later that night as I was putting clean sheets on the bed, Dutch's phone rang. A minute later I heard him call, "Abby? Your sister's on the phone."

"I'll get it up here," I yelled back and picked up

the receiver. "Hey, Cat!" I said happily. It'd been a few days since we'd talked and I was anxious to catch up.

"You have *got* to help me!" she said.

Uh-oh. This sounded bad. "Don't tell me, Claire and Sam are still unhappy?"

"That isn't even the half of it, Abby. You just wouldn't *believe* what I've been through!"

"Dish," I said, relaxing down onto the bed. This sounded like a long one.

"As you know, I went to *extensive* expense to repaint the entire guesthouse all over again."

"Paint still not neutral enough for Claire?" I asked.

"Oh, no. She was fine with the *color;* it's now the *smell* that bothers her. So to accommodate our Mommy Dearest I opened every window and door, airing it out but good, and in the middle of winter no less."

"Did it help?"

"Yeah, the smell is now tolerable, however, because the windows were open the house became cold, and a pipe burst, causing *major* water damage."

"No!"

"Yes! So, I've had a repair crew over there for two days fixing everything up nice and tidy."

"And, it's ready to go now?"

"Oh, you're funny," Cat said, the absence of humor in her own voice telling me she was close to the edge. "No, Claire stepped one foot in the door ten minutes ago, and pulled it right back out again. *Apparently,* the carpet is still damp and is giving off a musty odor."

I shook my head back and forth. Poor Cat, she was one sharp cookie, but our mother had a lot more experience manipulating people into granting her every whim. After all, she'd been at it for considerably longer. "When are you going to send them packing?" I asked. I had no problem telling my parents what flight they could take on their way out of town.

"I can't," Cat said tiredly as she let out an exasperated sigh. "I know I should stand up to her, Abby, but every time I get near that woman I turn into a five-year-old."

There was a pause before I asked, "When do the carpet guys show up?"

"First thing tomorrow morning."

I chuckled in spite of myself. "Cat, when are you gonna *learn*?"

"I know, I know," she said and I could hear the tension in her voice. "Can't you talk to her for me?"

I barked a laugh into the phone and said, "No friggin' way, my friend. You got yourself into this mess, and I'm not going to do your homework for you. You'll never learn until you stand up to her, and I wouldn't be helping you if I stepped in. Call her right now— I'm assuming you're still at the Four Seasons?"

"Yes . . ." Cat groused.

"Okay, so get off the line with me, ring her up and tell her flat out to pack up her crap and hit the road, Jack!"

"I'll think about it," Cat whispered.

I backed off a little and offered, "She can't stay there forever, honey. Eventually she'll get bored and want to go back home."

"One would hope so."

"Call me tomorrow and give me an update, okay?"

"Oh! Speaking of updates, how's our project coming?"

Ugh! I'd almost gotten away without having to talk about Fern Street. "Still haunted," I confessed. "But we're looking to resolve it soon and then Dave can head back to work."

"He's not working on it?" Cat asked sharply. "You

mean to tell me it's just sitting there soaking up mortgage interest and he's not even working on it?"

"Uh . . . well . . . see . . . the thing of it is . . ."
How could I tell my sister that because of two very
harrowing experiences my handyman was now wearing
garlic as an accessory and sleeping with the lights on.

"Abby, you tell that man to get his butt in gear and
get to work. I have put some considerable resources
together to purchase that property, and my money can't
turn a profit if it's just sitting there, stalled."

"Let me handle it," I said sternly. I had no doubt
that if we didn't get rid of our ghostly tenants soon,
my sister would take matters into her own hands, and
I wanted to avoid that at all costs.

"I mean it, Abby, time is money."

"Don't you have a call to make?" I threw back,
wanting to end this conversation.

There was a sound like a growl on the other end of
the phone line as I pictured my sister's eyebrows lowering. "Don't be mean," she scolded. "I'll call you
tomorrow."

" 'Night, Cat," I said and we disconnected.

Later that night as Dutch and I lay in bed together
he said, "I'm supposed to work in the pool tomorrow
for my physical therapy. My PT said it should take a
couple of hours. Why don't you go furniture shopping
while I'm working out?"

I smiled in the dark as I stroked Dutch's hand and
snuggled closer to him, relishing the feel of his warm
skin against mine. "Trying to keep me distracted and
out of trouble, huh?"

"I noticed Englander's Furniture is having a sale,"
he coaxed.

"Okay, okay," I said as I gave his shoulder a kiss.
"I'll go furniture shopping. But in return you have to

help me with that box and call your friend at the Bureau."

"I'm already on it," Dutch said, pulling me on top of him and kissing my neck.

"Hey," I said in mild protest. "This is the sort of thing that can get us into trouble." Secretly I didn't want him to stop, but I knew his injury wouldn't allow anything more than a good tease, and we were sexually tense enough as it was. I felt like I was going to explode if he didn't hurry up and get well soon.

"This?" he asked as he moved to my ear.

"Cowboy . . ." I said breathlessly. *Oh, God that felt good!*

"How about this?" he asked and moved to my lips.

"You're rotten," I said after he'd melted me like butter.

"I never claimed to be otherwise, sweethot," he chuckled and kissed me some more.

Chapter Eight

The next day found me happily bouncing my bum from couch to couch on the Englander's Furniture showroom floor. I was torn between an easy-to-clean mocha-colored microfiber suede loveseat with matching chair and ottoman, or an overstuffed, fabric cream-colored couch. Unable to decide I let the crew weigh in; they went with the microfiber, which was a smart move considering my penchant for eating ravioli in the living room.

While I was following my salesman to the front checkout I passed a living room display with a familiar fixture. "Hold it!" I said and darted over to get a closer look. There, on one of the bookshelves, was a box very similar to the one still hidden in my backseat. "Ohmigod!" I said to my startled salesclerk. "How do you open this?"

My salesman paused to gape at me for a moment as I shook the box to hear if anything rattled inside. Finally he indulged me by flipping it upside down and sliding his finger along a thin panel of wood. The panel moved easily, then he slid his finger along another panel and it moved as well. One more panel was slipped to the side and abruptly there was the smallest of popping sounds. The salesman flipped the box right up and gently removed the top of the box. "Voila!" he announced proudly. "These are Japanese puzzle boxes. They were all the rage years ago and they're making a comeback now," he explained.

"Awesome!" I said, bouncing on the balls of my feet.

"Would you like to add this to your purchases today?" he asked me, holding up the box, dollar signs dancing in his eyes.

"Nope. But I need to hurry with my other stuff. There's something I gotta do."

I paid for my new furniture and set up delivery for the following week, then bolted out of the store and flew to my car. My hand shook as I pushed the button on my key ring releasing the SUV's locks and retrieved the box from the backseat. I then scurried into the front seat, anxious to see what treasures lay hidden after all these years. This was the key to Liza's murder, I was sure of it.

I got settled and flipped the box over, searching for a similar panel on the bottom of the box. I found one panel that was so subtly off color from the others as to not be distinguishable unless one was looking for it. Nervously I ran my finger down it and to my complete joy it moved. I slid it out of the way and then felt for the next panel. In two more moves I had the box open. "Eureka!" I said into the silence. Slowly I removed the lid, mindful of anything that might slip out. I discovered that the box contained a little book, about the size of a small notebook, bound in leather and looking very worn. I carefully reached in and extracted the item, then looked back inside the box one more time to see if there might be something else.

Could this be all there was? Just this little notebook? *This* was worth killing for? I set the box aside and held the book in my hands. I turned it around and around but couldn't see any writing on the cover or the back. Gingerly, I opened the cover trying not to tear the worn leather. Inside were pages and pages of columns with names, notations, abbreviations and numbers all written with a precise hand. I looked at the notations, but couldn't make sense of them; they seemed to be in a foreign language.

The names all had a foreign ring to them as well, and I scratched my head as my finger slid down the second to last column of abbreviations that listed "dmt" regularly but also included the occasional "sr" or "ém" and sometimes to the side of these was written "or" and "agt." The last column simply contained a number, but there seemed to be no sequential order, and often the same numbers would repeat for many rows. I continued to flip carefully through each page, there were only about twenty-five or so, but nothing seemed to make sense.

Finally, I shrugged my shoulders and placed the notebook carefully back in the box, setting it on the seat as I flipped on the engine. Maybe Dutch would have better luck with the hieroglyphics.

I pulled into the PT's office and saw him already waiting for me out front, his hair wet and a rather pained expression on his face. "Tough session?" I asked when he got into the car.

"That woman's relentless," he said, referring to his physical therapist.

"Well, you said yourself you wanted to be back to the Bureau as soon as possible. I'm sure she's just working on the agenda you set for her."

Dutch scowled at me and leaned forward to scoop up the box, which I'd set on the floor of the car while he got in. "You handing this over?" he asked me.

"Oh! Guess what! I figured out how to open it!" I said excitedly as I pulled into a parking space and snatched the box out of his hand. Flipping it over I moved the panels, then flipped the box over and pulled up the top as I said, "Ta da!"

"You figured this out all by yourself?" he asked me.

"Well, not exactly. Turns out Englander's sells these by the dozen, and my sales clerk was only too happy to demonstrate."

"Was this the only thing inside?" Dutch asked, taking out the book.

"Yeah, and I was hoping you could help me figure out what the heck it means, 'cuz I can't make heads or tails out of it."

"It's written in French," he said.

"Can you read it?" I asked, about to be impressed.

"Only a little. I'm better at Dutch and German but I got another friend of mine that might be able to help us decipher this."

"You know, for a guy who sits around on weekends watching old movies with his girlfriend, you sure got a lot of friends I've never heard of."

"I know people," he said with a wink.

"Apparently," I said and pulled back out of the space.

"I'll make a call when we get home," he offered. "This might be a good time to catch T.J., anyway."

"T.J.?"

"Yeah, he was another roommate of mine back in the day."

"What's T.J. do these days that makes him an expert on French scribbles?"

"He's a professor at U of M. He teaches fourteenth-century French literature."

"Impressive," I said.

"Yeah, he's one smart guy. I haven't seen him in

years. . . ." Dutch said thoughtfully, then chuckled as he remembered something.

"What?" I asked, as we drove.

Dutch laughed again. "Nothing, just that T.J. and I used to have some wild times together."

"How wild?" I asked giving him a sideways glance.

"*Kowabunga* wild."

"Hmmm," I said, feeling uncomfortable. Already I was getting too much information. "That's nice." Thankfully, we pulled into Dutch's driveway right about then and made a hasty shuffle into the house. The temperature had dipped and it was frigid outside.

"Why don't you go make us some lunch, and I'll call T.J.?" Dutch said when we got in the door.

"Kowabunga," I retorted and trotted off to the kitchen.

Dutch joined me about fifteen minutes later and announced, "I got a hold of him and he said he'd be very interested in helping us out. Do you want to take a road trip right after lunch?"

"I'm game," I said as I pushed a plate at him.

We ate quickly then got back in the car and headed west toward Ann Arbor. The trip took about forty minutes and in that time, Dutch recounted just about every sordid, wild and crazy adventure he and T.J. ever had. Most of them involved booze and loose women, so I feigned interest and discreetly kept turning up the radio volume.

Finally we reached U of M's campus and spent another twenty minutes circling the block in front of T.J.'s building to find a decent parking spot. While Dutch took his time getting out of the car, I retrieved the box from the backseat and came around to his side. "Still sore?" I asked, noticing an exaggerated wince as he pivoted to shut the car door.

"It's always worse after therapy," he said, closing

the door. He turned back to me and wrapped a loose arm across my shoulder as we headed toward T.J.'s building.

When we got inside Dutch walked over to an information board, and scrolled his finger down the list of names. "Here he is," he said after a moment. "Professor Thomas J. Robins. Come on, Edgar, he's on the third floor."

We took the elevator up and were able to find T.J.'s office without much trouble. Dutch walked through the open door first, trying to tuck his cane behind him in a manner that suggested he was suddenly self-conscious. "T!" he said jovially to a man standing up and coming around the desk to greet him.

Dutch and T.J. gave each other one of those big bear hugs manly men exchange and I took that moment to study Dutch's old friend. T.J. looked about the same age as Dutch and was similar in build with strawberry blond hair and smart wire-rimmed glasses. As the two men slapped each other on the back I cocked my head a bit. My intuition said something was off about the scene, but I couldn't pinpoint what it was.

After a moment Dutch backed away and turned to me, "Buddy, I'd like you to meet my girl. This is Abby Cooper. Abby, T. J. Robins."

"Nice to meet you," I said, leaning in to shake T.J.'s hand.

"Likewise," T.J. said. *Liar, liar . . . pants on fire . . .*

I shook my head slightly hearing the sing-song chant in my mind. *That* was weird.

"So, Dutch, what do you have for me?" T.J. asked, indicating two leather chairs for us to sit in while he took his own seat behind a metal desk piled high with books and papers.

"Like I started to explain to you on the phone, Abby found this box in a house she just bought. It was hidden under some floorboards, and had likely been there for a couple dozen years. Anyway, we figured out how to open the thing, and inside was this little booklet . . ." Dutch paused and turned to me expectantly, and quickly I flipped the box on its end and popped the top. I extracted the booklet and handed it to Dutch who handed it over to T.J.

"Hmmm," T.J. said as he opened to the first page. "Do you know if there was a jeweler connected to the house you purchased?" He looked up at me.

"Yes!" I said excitedly. Finally, someone who could help us. "Does it mention his business in there?"

"Well, not exactly," T.J. said, turning the pages and scanning the notations.

"What does it mention?" Dutch asked.

"For starters, it talks about gemstones, like diamonds, rubies and emeralds. See these notations?" he said, holding the book open to point at the column I'd been most confused about. " 'dmt' is a French acronym for diamant, or diamond; 'or' is French for gold and 'agt' is for argent or silver. Most of these appear to be about diamonds, but there are enough of the others mixed in here to be significant. The numbers to the right of the gemstones appear to be carat weights. Like this first line where it says, dmt one point five. He must be talking about a one-point-five carat weight diamond. The person who wrote this kept it like an inventory of some kind, and there are other notations of interest here . . . Straus . . . Videlburg . . . Brencht. Curious." T.J. said.

"What do you think it means?" I asked.

"Off the cuff, I'm not sure. But I love a good mystery. Why don't you two allow me to hold on to this for a few days and let me see if I can't make more sense of it?"

"Sounds good," I said smiling at him, grateful for

the help. "Why don't you call me if you get anything good," I offered as I reached for one of my cards.

"I have Dutch's number," T.J. said shooing my efforts away with a flip of his hand. "I'll just call him if I come up with something."

My intuition buzzed loudly in my ear just then and I cocked my head as T.J. set the book down and turned his attention to my boyfriend. Discreetly I shot my intuitive arrow at T.J. and after a moment I had to work at stifling a laugh as I realized what my guides were trying to tell me. Now that I looked, it was so obvious I couldn't believe I hadn't noticed it right off the bat.

Dutch and T.J. caught up for another half hour, both men laughing at the good times they'd shared with their booze and loose women. I grew bored after about fifteen minutes and waited patiently for the two men to talk themselves out. Finally, as the afternoon sun began to wane, Dutch got up to take his leave. T.J. leaned in for another bear hug and said, "It has been way too long, buddy. You need to call me more than once in a blue moon."

"I know, I know," Dutch said apologetically. "I promise, as soon as the old keister's mended, we'll hang out, maybe catch a Red Wings game or something?"

"Sounds like a plan," T.J. said happily. Turning to me, he politely shook my hand again and said, "It was a pleasure to meet you, Abby." *Liar, liar . . . pants on fire . . .*

"Likewise," I said with a grin.

Dutch and I left T.J.'s office and headed back down the hallway. "He seems nice," I began.

"Yeah. He's the greatest," Dutch said.

"And he thinks the world of you," I said, working to stifle a giggle.

"He's a good friend."

"Is he single?" I asked innocently.

"Yep. He runs through the ladies. Even in college he'd never go out with a girl more than a few times. One of those confirmed bachelor types, I guess."

"I'll bet," I said as we rounded into the elevator.

"What do you mean?" Dutch asked finally catching on to my sarcastic tone.

"Nothing," I said. "That was some music he had going in there."

"Yeah, T.J.'s always had really weird taste in music. Can you believe he likes show tunes?"

"Get out!" I said, my tongue firmly in my cheek.

"I know. Weird huh?"

"And I like his sense of decor, too. Those chairs were really comfortable."

"He's always had a great eye for furniture. Did I tell you he practically decorated my whole house for me?" Dutch's house looked like it'd been decorated by a professional. Being a true guy's guy, I'd always wondered how he'd managed such style.

"It's like something out of that show *Queer Eye for the Straight Guy*," I said as we got out of the elevator.

"Yeah . . . I mean, what?"

I paused as we reached the lobby doors to the outside. "You're kidding, right?" I asked.

"About what?" he said, his face scrunching up in confusion.

"T.J.," I said, pushing backward against the door. "You do realize he's *gay*, don't you?"

"*What?*" Dutch exclaimed, completely flabbergasted as he followed me out. "He is not!"

"Is too," I sang and began to saunter ahead of him toward the car.

"There's no way!" Dutch said from behind me, his cane clicking on the sidewalk as he hurried to catch up.

I kept going but turned around to walk backward just to taunt him. "Gay as a Liza Minnelli groupie! Gay as a Barbra Streisand look-alike contest!"

"Abby," Dutch growled.

"Hello, *Dolly!*" I sang in an off-key loud voice, quite enjoying the moment and how uncomfortable my boyfriend suddenly looked. "Well hello Dolly! It's so nice to . . . *oh shit!*" I squealed an instant before a man dressed in a hooded sweatshirt and ski mask darted out from behind a building and barreled right into me, laying me out flat in the snow.

"Hey!" I heard Dutch yell a few yards away.

As I fought with the bulk of the man who lay on top of me, it took me a moment to realize he was tugging at the box I carried under one arm. My senses were momentarily dulled by the impact and he was able to snatch the box from my grasp. Just as he got up to bolt with it I heard a loud *Whack!* over my head and the thief went down on top of me again. Regaining my senses I managed to get an arm free and reached for the box, just as another *Whack!* sent echoes across the campus.

"Let go!" I shouted as I clutched at the box, as yet another *Whack!* sounded above me and my attacker groaned loudly and let go of it. I kicked at him as I pulled the box to my belly while he rolled painfully away clawing his way up to run and dart back around the building. As I got to my knees I watched him go as Dutch's cane flew in the air after him and clanked off the side of the building he'd darted behind. Still trying to catch my breath I felt myself lifted from my knees and Dutch began to poke at me checking for injuries, a rather pained look on his face. *"Son of a bitch!"* he growled, as he looked me over. "You okay?" he asked, sounding anxious.

Clutching my painful bruised side, I said, "Yeah, I think he just knocked the wind out of me. . . ."

Suddenly, from behind us we both heard a shriek and an, *"Ohmigod!!!"* The ear-piercing sounds came from the same direction and we both turned to see the source as we saw T.J. running pell-mell straight for us, waving his hand in the direction of the mugger. "I saw everything from the window!" he said when he reached us, his breath ragged from the run. "I raced down three flights of stairs! Dutch, are you all right?" he asked, his eyes panicked as he grabbed at my boyfriend to check for injuries.

"Uh . . . I'm fine, T, it was Abby who . . ."

"You could have been *killed*!" T.J. wheezed. "If it hadn't been for that cane he probably would have murdered you!"

Ah, now I knew what the whacking sound was all about.

"Really, T.J., I'm fine," Dutch said, becoming embarrassed as a few students paused to stare at the commotion. "It's Abby I'm concerned . . ."

"Oh, and to think I almost lost you!" T.J. said as he flung himself at Dutch and clutched him tightly.

Dutch caught my eye over T.J.'s shoulder and despite my own discomfort I had to flash him the full grill before mouthing, "Told you so . . ."

We made a report to the U of M campus police department, and a mere forty minutes later were on our way home again. We avoided the topic of T.J. altogether as I was sure Dutch didn't want to talk about it, but kept the conversation light for a while before Dutch finally said, "You know what's funny?"

"What?" I asked.

"Why didn't that mugger take your purse instead of going for the box?"

I looked over at him for a moment, considering that question for the very first time. I'd been so surprised by the attack that I hadn't wondered why he would fight me so hard for the box, and not my pocketbook. "Maybe because my purse was tucked securely under my arm, with the strap over my shoulder. It would have been a lot tougher to take that away from me, whereas the box was just being held in my hand."

"So why target you at all?" Dutch replied.

"What do you mean?"

"That campus is crowded with easier targets, Abby. There are women all over the place, some with purses, some with backpacks. You're just holding a box in your hand. What's the attraction?"

I puzzled over that for minute before answering, "It looks like a jewelry box. I mean, that's what I thought it was when I first looked at it."

"There's no way that guy had time to scope us out long enough to assess what type of box you were carrying before he attacked you, Edgar. Remember, we had just come out of the building."

"So what're you saying?"

"I'm saying someone knew what you had and wanted to take it from you."

"You think someone followed us to U of M?" I asked, subconsciously checking the rearview mirror.

"I'd pretty much bet on it."

"But who knew I had the . . . oh *crap*!" I exclaimed, slapping my forehead.

"Yep, that's what I'm thinking."

"But, Dutch, I just don't get that kind of vibe off of James. Really, I can't imagine he'd have anything to do with this."

"The only other person that knew about the box was Dave, and I doubt he was your attacker."

"So, do you think it was the same guy that attacked

me in my house?" I asked as a chill spread up my spine.

"Do you?" Dutch said, throwing the question back at me.

My intuition chimed in and I said, "Yeah, I do. I think it was the same guy, which doesn't necessarily point to James. Anyone could have been watching Dave and I go into that house and come out with a box."

"Who else could have known it even existed, Abby?"

My brows furrowed in frustration. I heard what Dutch was saying, but it just didn't make sense. Intuitively I knew James was a good guy, and this wasn't his doing.

That did not deter my boyfriend, however, from pulling out his cell phone and making a quick call to yet another friend of his. "Hey Milo, it's me. Listen, I need you to do a background check on James Carlier. I don't know where the guy lives, but he owns that jewelry shop in Birmingham where I bought Abby's necklace. You remember it? Good. Call me when you have something," and he disconnected.

"You took Milo with you to pick out my birthday present?" I asked.

"Have you seen Noelle's collection?" he answered, referring to Milo's wife. "Milo knows his way around a good piece of bling, let me tell you."

I smiled ruefully. Dutch was revealing lots of little secrets today.

Later that night as I lay cuddled in Dutch's arms and the sound of his steady breathing told me he'd beaten me to la-la land, the phone on the nightstand chirped and I reached for it quickly, not wanting to disturb him.

"Hello?" I whispered.

"Abby?" came a familiar voice.

"Hey, Milo, I'm sorry but Dutch is asleep. Can we call you in the morning?"

"Sorry, I know it's late," he began. "But this really can't wait. You know that guy that owns that jewelry shop Dutch wanted me to check out?"

Behind me I could feel Dutch moving groggily. He was waking up. "Yeah?" I whispered.

"His store just got robbed."

I abruptly sat up and swung one leg out of bed. "We'll meet you there," I said and clicked off.

Twenty minutes later a slightly rumpled Dutch and I pulled up to a stream of police cars lining the street in front of Opalescence. We were stopped by a patrolman who tried to wave us away, but Dutch flashed his badge, and we were allowed to park at the end of the line. As I backed into a space I spotted Milo talking with a group of police officers and off to one side I saw James with a blanket around his shoulders and a paramedic attending to a sizable welt on his forehead. "Ohmigod!" I said as I hurried to unbuckle my seat belt. "James is hurt!"

I rushed out of the car and headed in his direction, and from behind me I could hear Dutch call to me. I ignored him and beelined it for James who looked up at me and did a double take at my appearance on scene. "Abby?" he asked when I drew close. "What're you doing here?"

"I heard you'd been robbed, and I wanted to see if there was anything I could do."

"How did you hear I'd been robbed?" he asked.

Ooops. "Uh . . . it was on the news?" I tried.

"The news? It's not even eleven, and I haven't seen any reporters yet. What news station knows I've been robbed?"

"Okay, so the truth is my boyfriend is a retired cop,

and he still has his police scanner. That's him over there with the cane."

"Cane?" James said, looking at me sharply, then over to Dutch. When he looked back at me his eyes were wary. "Thank you for coming, Abby," he said, "but the police seem to have things under control, and I don't think there's anything you can do."

"Ah," I said a little taken aback. "Are you all right at least?"

"I'm fine."

"Do you know who robbed your store?"

"No." *Liar, liar . . . pants on fire . . .*

I looked at James for a long moment, the playground chant echoing clearly in my head. Why would he lie? And why was he acting so wary of me all of the sudden? "Okay, then," I said. "I'll stop by next week after you've had a chance to tend to your business and check in on my order . . ."

"Don't bother," James said with ice in his voice. "The thief took your sister's earrings along with most of my inventory. I will mail you out a refund check for your deposit tomorrow."

"Did I do something wrong?" I asked.

James let out a deep sigh and replied, "No. I'm just overwhelmed with what's happened here tonight. I'm sure you can understand."

"Of course. I'll leave you to get bandaged up and talk to the police. I'm sorry about your store, James."

"Thanks. I appreciate your coming down." *Liar, liar . . . pants on fire . . .*

Sometimes, ya just gotta throw in the towel. I nodded my good-bye to him and turned back in the direction of Dutch and Milo, who were huddled together near my car.

When I reached them Milo asked, "So what did he have to say?"

"He said he doesn't know who robbed his store."

"Baloney," Milo scoffed. "The Birmingham detective who interviewed him says he thinks the guy's a probable for insurance fraud."

"Why's that?" I asked.

"His story just doesn't add up. First of all, he says he was here late doing paperwork, but when he was asked what type of paperwork he said he couldn't remember. He claims he forgot to lock the front door, and that's when the perp just walked in, found him in his office, thumped him on the head and made him open up all the jewelry cases, leaving with about thirty grand in merchandise and all of the cash he had on hand. When the detectives asked him about the tape for his video surveillance cameras, which are all over the store, he says he never put one in the machine.

"He also couldn't give a good reason why he didn't trip any one of the six silent alarms he has planted around the shop. And he doesn't have a clear description of the suspect. All he'll tell us is that the guy was black, with an attitude."

Dutch snorted. "So that narrows it down."

"Exactly," Milo retorted frostily. "I mean, I know to white guys like him we black folk probably all look alike, but you'd think he'd be able to give us a little more to go on than black and attitude."

"Milo, I don't think James is a racist," I said, stroking his arm sympathetically. Detroit had its share of racial issues, and they often leaked north of the Eight Mile border, so I could appreciate why he was sensitive to the implication that black meant bad. "However, I do believe it's pretty obvious he's trying to throw you guys off the scent. I'm not buying into the insurance fraud theory, though."

"Then why lie about the assailant?" Milo asked.

"That I don't know."

"Still, it might be a good idea to check into his financials," Dutch said, giving Milo a measured look.

"You FBI guys have all the resources," Milo snickered. "By the way, I wanted to let you know that up until tonight, Carlier checked out okay. There's nothing in his record other than a speeding ticket two years ago and some sort of domestic dispute about five years ago involving Carlier's brother."

Buzz, buzz, buzz . . . My intuition chimed in. I cocked my head and followed the train of thought. "Milo?" I asked.

"Yeah?"

"What exactly was the dispute about?"

"Well," Milo said taking out a small notebook he had tucked away in his overcoat. "About five years ago James and Jean-Luke Carlier were living in that house you just bought over on Fern, and according to neighbors Jean-Luke was seen chasing James around the house with a knife."

"You're kidding!" I exclaimed.

"Nope, it's the truth. Turns out when the police arrived Jean-Luke had calmed down and James refused to press charges. Both men claimed there was no knife and the neighbors must have been mistaken."

"Weird," I said. My spidey-sense insisted there was a connection to what happened then and what took place tonight, so I asked, "And where is Jean-Luke these days?"

"He's in Mashburn."

"The mental hospital?" Dutch asked.

"The very one," Milo answered. "About a week after the domestic dispute Jean-Luke was declared legally incompetent and admitted by his brother who had obtained power of attorney over him."

"And he's still there?" I asked.

"There's been no release form issued, so yeah, he's still there."

I darted a look back at James who looked tired and worn down. Everyone seemed convinced he was hiding something, but intuitively I knew he wasn't about to crack. Whoever assaulted and robbed him wouldn't be revealed until James was ready to come clean.

"Come on, fella," I said tugging on Dutch's arm. "There's nothing more we can do here tonight, and I've had a long day."

Milo waved good-bye to us and took his leave, and Dutch and I headed home. During the drive I asked, "Can you really get information on James's financial records?"

"His tax returns at least."

"How long will that take?"

"Hopefully, only a day or so. I'll make a call first thing in the morning and get the ball rolling. And the next time I ask you to stop on your way out of the car, friggin' stop, would ya?"

Dutch's tone turned icy as he said that last part. His tone and the implication that he had command over me made me furious. I seethed quietly for a moment as I discreetly looked for a pothole. Finding a huge one not far up the road I aimed the Mazda toward it and just as we were about to run over it Dutch reached out and yanked the wheel back. "Hey!" he shouted at me. "What gives?"

"You're not the boss of me, you know!" I yelled, yanking the steering wheel away. Sometimes I'm *so* mature.

Dutch sighed heavily, and began in a calm voice, "Edgar . . ."

"I survived just fine on my own until you came into

the picture, you know!" I added, my anger at his verbal spanking getting the better of me.

"I'm aware of that . . ."

"No you're not! You're constantly on me about the choices I make, like I can't even go to the bathroom without your permission or something!"

"Abby . . ."

"Do you even *know* how difficult it is being your girlfriend?"

"Excuse me?" Dutch asked in a voice that was definitely taken aback.

Ooops, I'd gone a little overboard with that one. "I'm just sayin' that maybe I need a little space, you know, some room to friggin' breathe. . . ."

"You want *space?* You need to *breathe?* You got it, babe," Dutch snapped, then turned away from me and looked out the window.

I sighed and rolled my eyes. How had we offended each other so easily in such a short period of time? We'd been getting along so well lately too. A minute later I rolled into Dutch's driveway and cut the engine. Without a word he got out and walked into the house, making a point not to look back. I sat inside the Mazda for a few minutes, feeling dejected and thinking about how to make amends. Finally, I went into the house and found Dutch making up the couch. "You're sleeping down here?" I asked, failing to keep the hurt out of my voice.

"Thought I'd give you some *space,*" he snipped.

"Whatever," I answered, throwing up my hands in surrender and trudging up the stairs. I spent the night tossing and turning, while wishing that Dutch would change his mind and come up to cuddle with me, but he never did.

Chapter Nine

The next morning I hid out in Dutch's bedroom, watching television and avoiding the man downstairs. I heard him get up and shuffle around in the kitchen. Later I could just make out his voice coming from the study, but I didn't want to risk bumping into him if I went down to the kitchen. Eggy, however, finally coaxed me out of bed. Poor little guy needed to eat and water the lawn.

Quietly I crept down the stairs but came up short when I saw Dutch standing in the living room. He was easing into his coat and looking out on the street through the curtains. "Hey," I said as I stepped off the stairs.

"Hello," he answered without looking at me.

"Going somewhere?"

"Physical therapy."

" 'Kay. Let me just take a minute to give Eggy some breakfast and I'll drive you . . . ."

"There's no need," Dutch interrupted curtly. "I've called a cab. They should be here any second, and I'd rather be driven by someone who knows how to avoid a pothole."

For some reason that statement really hurt my feelings, and I bit my lip to avoid tearing up. "I see," I said after a minute, not knowing what else to say. At that moment my cell phone chirped from my purse on the coffee table. I quickly retrieved it and looked at the caller ID. It was a favorite client of mine, Candice Fusco, who was also a crack private investigator. "Hey, Candice," I said, attempting to sound breezy. "What's going on?"

"Oh, thank God I got you, Abby!" Candice said. "Your voice mail at work said you were taking January off, and I have a case that I really need your help on."

At that moment I heard a honk from outside, and without a backward glance, Dutch walked out of the house and closed the door quietly on my feelings. My eyes misted and I swallowed hard. Making an effort to conceal my emotions from Candice, I said, "Of course, I'd be happy to help. What's going on?"

"Can I come see you today?"

I blinked hard and one tear rolled down my cheek. Seeing people today was the last thing I wanted to do, but the alternative was waiting around for Dutch to get back and risk getting my heart trampled on again. "No problem. It'll take you, what? About an hour and forty-five minutes to get here?"

There was a small chuckle on the other end of the line. "Actually, I'm already halfway there. I took a chance that I'd be able to reach you. Can I meet you at your office at nine thirty?"

I wiped my eyes, trying to get a grip. "Absolutely. See you then," I said and clicked off the phone. I sat on the couch for a few minutes and did my best to collect myself. I wasn't sure who was to blame for the current state of chilly weather between Dutch and me, but I was leaning heavily toward blaming myself. The problem was I was at a loss as to how to repair it. My impulse was to gather my belongings and head on back to my place.

Whenever I'd been hurt as a kid, I'd always sought the shelter of my room, and even as an adult I tended to hermit when life got tough. Looking back, I had to admit that I'd walked away from many a relationship the moment they got hard. But I didn't want to do that here. The truth was that I was crazy in like with a certain stubborn, hardheaded, overly protective FBI agent. At times I liked that Dutch had my back. But there were also moments when the very thing that thrilled me suffocated me too.

The trick was how to communicate this to him. After all, he was already angry with me. He was pretty independent too, and if I really looked at it, I'd have to admit that it must be just as tough for him to rely on me as it was for me to rely on him. Tiredly, I ran a hand through my hair and got up off the couch. I needed the comfort of a warm shower before I met Candice. Maybe after I helped her out with her case I could talk to her about my dilemma with Dutch. Candice had a great head on her shoulders, and she always seemed to have a string of boyfriends. Maybe she could give me some advice.

An hour later I had parked my car and was just reaching for my purse when I heard a honk from behind me. I turned to see Candice's Lexus right behind me as she waved from inside. I waved back and waited by my car while she found a slot. "That was good timing!" she said as she got out and came to greet me.

"Perfect," I said, leaning in to hug her. I hadn't seen Candice in a few months, and I'd missed her. She was the most regular client I had, mostly because my service to her was rather unconventional. For all of my other clientele, the routine of looking into their futures was pretty regimented. But for Candice, my services were very rarely used to look into her personal life. Mostly, she used me as an aid to assist with the white-collar crimes she worked on. I'd helped her nail several embezzlers, cheating husbands and the like. Since our sessions together were different from the norm I always looked forward to them as a way of breaking up the monotony.

That, coupled with the fact that Candice was such a genuinely likeable person, made her appearance today far less intrusive than it could have been.

"So how ya doin', girlfriend?" she asked me as we began to walk over to my office building, located just across the street.

"I'm okay, you know, busy, but okay."

She paused to eye me critically. "Man trouble?"

I barked out a laugh and said, "It's obvious you don't need me, Candice, 'cuz there ain't nothin' wrong with *your* radar."

Candice gave me a small smile. "I can always tell. So what gives? You still dating that tall blond drink of yummy?"

I smirked at her description of Dutch. "Yeah, but we really got off on the wrong foot last night and I'm not sure how to make things right."

"What happened?" she asked as we entered my building.

"I took a cheap shot at him in a moment of anger."

"How cheap?"

"Blue light special. I may have flippantly remarked that it was really tough being his girlfriend."

We had reached the elevator by now and Candice pressed the UP button. "That doesn't sound so bad. You sure he's just not overly sensitive?"

"I suppose I should tell you that he was injured on the job recently, and I've had to play nursemaid to a guy who's been very humbled by the fact that he can't really do for himself while he's mending."

"Ah," Candice said as we stepped into the boxcar. "That's different. Well, sometimes, Abby, you just gotta suck it up and admit when you're wrong."

I nodded. "I know, but he's not in the mood to listen to me right now. When Dutch gets mad, he can pout for a couple of days. If I weren't living with him right now, I could give him some room and call him in a week and we'd kiss and make up. But the way things are going it promises to be a long couple of days before we'll be able to talk civilly to one another."

"You could always seduce him," Candice offered as we stepped off the elevator.

I smiled tiredly. "Yeah, that would be great if the doctor hadn't ordered no sex for a month."

"Sometimes a good tease goes a long way toward taking a guy's mind off the thing that he's mad about. Have you given that a shot?"

I chuckled. "Naw, mostly I've been driving over potholes." We reached my office and I moved forward to unlock the door.

From behind me I heard Candice ask, "Potholes?" but my attention was focused on the door to my office suite, which had discreetly been jimmied and stood slightly ajar.

"Shit!" I said, backing away from the door like it had bitten me.

"What's the matter?" Candice asked, putting a steadying hand on my shoulder.

"The door!" I said, pointing to it. "Someone's broken into my office!"

Candice wasted no time moving in front of me. In one graceful move she pulled out a gun hidden within her clothing and stepped close to the door, listening.

After a moment she leaned against the wall, then, with her foot, gently pushed the door open. With a quick head movement Candice scouted the interior of my front lobby, then motioned for me to stay where I was and placed a finger to her lips—I needed to be quiet. I nodded to her that I understood and she disappeared inside my office. A minute or two later she reappeared, a grim expression on her face. Reholstering her weapon and whipping out her cell phone she eyed me as she punched nine one one into the keypad. "I don't think you want to go in there, just yet."

"Why?" I asked, the blood rushing out of my face and my breath coming in quick pants.

"It's bad, Abby."

I gulped. "How bad?"

"Hurricane Andrew bad."

I groaned and moved around her, careful not to touch the door. As I stepped into my suite, my heart sank. My little lobby was a disaster. The chairs had been ripped open, their stuffing pulled out, the small table to one side was smashed and broken and the few magazines I had laid out for my clientele looked like they had exploded all over the room.

My hand flew to my mouth as I surveyed the scene, dread filling my stomach like lead and I walked on wooden legs deeper into the suite. My inner office was one huge cluster of paper, as release forms and files had been pulled from my cabinet and scattered all around the small room. My computer was smashed and broken on the floor; the fax machine was in pieces on my desk. The office chair had also been sliced open and its stuffing scattered like large clumps of snow, and my phone was unrecognizable.

I groaned and leaned against the doorjamb. Intuitively, I knew that my reading room would be the worst of all. A moment later, I discovered how regretfully right I was. As I stepped through the doorway to one of the most precious spaces in the world to me, all I could do was gasp and give in to the large wail that bubbled up inside my chest.

All the precious crystals I'd collected over the years, some of them huge forty-pound cathedrals that had cost hundreds of dollars, had been smashed to oblivion and scattered like the four winds all over the room. My two overstuffed chairs, where I'd counseled hundreds of clients, were torn and shredded, irreparable. My tape recorder had been reduced to a glob of wires and plastic and every blank cassette tape that I'd carefully arranged on my credenza had been smunched into pieces. The mosaic mirror that I'd treasured and hung with pride on my far wall lay facedown on the floor, it's center mirror splintered and cracked. The huge waterfall that had given soothing rhythm to the room for so many years lay overturned in a pool of water.

Someone had gone stark raving mad in my office suite, and the vehemence with which the intruder had taken out his angst felt like it was a physical blow to me. This wasn't just some robbery. . . . This was personal.

I mourned the death of so many treasured objects for a while, with Candice offering her shoulder to cry on. A few minutes later, Milo and a foot patrolman showed up on the scene. "Abby?" I heard him call from the lobby. "You in here? Holy cow! What the . . . ?" he said as he looked at the devastation of the room.

"Someone jimmied my lock and broke in," I said, my voice hoarse from crying.

"Did you touch anything?" he asked me, sympathy apparent in his eyes.

"No."

"Good. Where's Dutch?"

"At physical therapy. He should be done by now."

"Okay, why don't you get outta here and head home. I'll get the fingerprint crew started and meet you back at his place in an hour to get a statement. This a friend of yours?" he asked, indicating Candice.

"Yes, I'm Candice Fusco, a PI out of Kalamazoo. I can also give you a statement if you'd like."

"That'd be great. Can you get her home?"

"I'd be happy to," Candice said and took me by the hand.

I followed her through the rubble out into the hallway and down to the elevator like a lamb. I'd gone suddenly numb, the shock of being so violated far worse than when I'd encountered someone in my own home. For many reasons my office suite was even more precious to me than my house. It was the place where I connected to my spirit guides, where I'd experienced such amazing miraculous things, and I wondered if I'd ever feel safe in that space again.

As we waited for the elevator, Candice reached over to give me a gentle shoulder hug. "I know it looks bad, Abby, but with a little effort you can have it cleaned up in no time. You carry insurance, right? You can replace everything in there. Just be thankful that you weren't there when someone jimmied the lock. I'd hate to think about what could have happened to you."

"Candice?" I said as we entered the boxcar.

"Yes?"

"I really want to thank you for offering to give me a lift home, but there's something I gotta do."

"What?"

"I've gotta go see a man about a box. Want to come along?"

"Sure, but let me drive. I'm not a big fan of potholes."

Fifteen minutes later Candice parked just down the street from Opalescence. "Is that where you need to go?"

"Yep," I said and got out of the car, a determined look on my face as I marched with the puzzle box in hand toward the store.

Candice followed at a quick clip behind me, and we paused just outside as I turned to look at her. "Let me do the talking," I said, getting right to the point.

She winked at me and said, "Sure thing, I'm just here for moral support."

We opened the door and filed in, and right away spotted Maria over by one of the empty display cases, a broom and dustbin in her hand as she stooped to sweep up some broken glass. "Oh!" she said, startled. "I'm sorry, but we're closed until further notice. I must have forgotten to lock that door when I took the trash to the Dumpster," she added apologetically.

"I need to talk to James," I said without pause. "Now."

Maria looked at me for a moment, a hint of recognition in her eyes. "You were in here the other day about some earrings, right?"

"James?" I asked again, my tone and stance indicating I wasn't in the mood for small talk.

Maria hesitated for the briefest of moments, then said, "Wait right there, I'll get him."

As we waited I looked around the shop. Just as I suspected it held the same energy and trace of violence that I'd seen at my office. I was certain that the same man who had robbed James had also left his calling card at my suite, and everything led back to the box that I held in my hands. After a moment James came out with Maria, and eyed me with a rather grim expression. "Hello, Abby."

"James," I replied.

"Would you like to come back here and talk?"

"I would. Candice, will you be all right here?"

"I'm good. You go," she said easily.

I walked around a display case and followed James into his office, where he indicated the same chair I'd sat in before and took his seat. We eyed each other across the desk for a moment before he said, "So, I expect you're here for your check?"

"Cut the crap, James," I spat at him. "You know damn well who I am and why I'm here and just so we're clear, I'm not leaving until you tell me who destroyed my office."

To his benefit, James looked completely taken aback. "Abby, I can assure you, I have no idea what you're talking about. . . ." he began.

"My office was broken into, and just about every material possession that I hold near and dear was destroyed. And it was done by the same man who attacked you last night."

James didn't speak for a long moment, and I noted the mixture of emotions that flashed across his face, ranging from fear to anger to resignation. "How do you know the two events are connected?" he asked after a bit.

"Because of this," I said and placed the box on his desk. "I found this in your grandfather's house a few days ago, and ever since then someone has been hell bent on causing me grief. Now I know you're not telling me everything, James, and I'm not leaving here until you offer me a bone."

"You should have told me you were the one that purchased the house," he said.

"Why?"

"Because I could have warned you."

"About who?" I asked cocking my head.

"Him," James said tiredly.

"Your grandfather? Yeah, I got a full taste of him already, thanks."

"No, my grandfather's dead," James said, looking confused.

"Duh!" I shot back. "That's what I mean. His ghost tried to kill my handyman, thank you very much!"

"What?" James said, shocked at my statement. "His ghost? Abby, what are you talking about?"

"What are *you* talking about?"

"My brother, Luke."

"Your *brother*?" I asked, shaking my head, thoroughly confused.

"Yes, he was the one that attacked me last night. And I'm afraid he's probably set his sights on you as well."

"Wait, wait, wait," I said, holding up my hand in a stopping motion. "Isn't your brother at Mashburn?"

"He was, until he escaped two weeks ago."

A chill crept up my spine as I gaped at James. "Your own brother did all this?"

"It's not his fault," James said quickly. "He's unbalanced, and when he doesn't take his medicine he becomes unstable. He's not aware that what he's doing is wrong. . . ."

"So you sold me that haunted house knowing that your crazed brother was on the loose?"

"I don't understand what you mean by haunted."

"Oh, come on!" I nearly shouted at him. "You mean to tell me you don't know your granddaddy's one angry poltergeist?"

"Again, I don't understand what you're talking about!" James insisted. "I lived in that house for years, and I've never encountered anything unusual."

I sat back in my chair and thought about that for minute, remembering what M.J. had said about people who emitted different levels of magnetic energy. Maybe James hadn't had a ghostly encounter with his grandfather because his grandfather was neither upset by his presence nor able to show himself to his grandson. "So you don't know about the woman at the bottom of the stairs either, huh?"

The blood seemed to drain from James's face and he asked carefully, "What woman?"

My spidey-sense told me that James knew exactly what I was talking about, so I leaned in close over the desk. "The woman your grandfather murdered over this stupid bit of nothing," I said and shoved the box at him.

James recoiled like he'd been bitten and said, "I think you need to leave."

I stared him down for a long moment then I took the box back and stood up to go. "I'm going to get to the bottom of this, just so you know," I said, then walked out of his office and nodded to Candice who accompanied me out the shop's door.

"How'd it go?" she asked when we reached the sidewalk.

"Could'a gone better, actually."

"Sorry about that. Now what?" she asked as we reached her SUV.

"Let's swing by my office and pick up my car, then head back to Dutch's. I need to talk to Milo."

A short time later Candice and I walked into Dutch's living room and noted that Milo and he were already there, talking. I smiled a hello to Milo, but avoided Dutch's eyes, afraid he was still mad at me. Candice made her own introductions and she and I shrugged out of our coats, each taking a seat in one of the two wing chairs in the living room. "How ya doin'?" Milo asked me, worry in his eyes.

"Feeling like I've been sucker punched," I said to him.

"I'll bet. We finished dusting for prints in your office, and we notified the building's manager of what happened. Your landlady's worried about you and wants you to call her. She also said she could hook you up with the building's cleaning crew to help pick up the mess if you'd like."

I gave a small smile. "Yvonne is really cool. I'll give her a call later when I can stand to think about it. Right now I can't even process what's happened."

"Are you up for giving me a statement?" Milo asked as he reached for the spiral notebook tucked into his shirt pocket.

"In a minute," I said, waving a hand dismissively, "First I have to tell you that I know who broke into my office."

"You *know* who did this?" Milo asked.

"Jean-Luke Carlier."

"The guy in the mental ward?"

"Yep. He escaped about two weeks ago, so if you looked at the record you would think he was still incarcerated because no release has been issued."

"Son of a bitch," Milo said, making a note.

"*How,* exactly, do you know this, Abby?" Dutch said carefully.

Candice jumped in quickly, noting the tension in his voice, "Abby had a hunch and through my connections I was able to make a few phone calls and find out he'd escaped." *Liar, liar . . . pants on fire . . .*

I flashed a grateful smile at her. If Dutch knew I'd gone back to visit James he really would blow a gasket. "It all fits, Milo. Ever since I bought that house on Fern I've been stalked, attacked and both my house and office have been broken into. There has to be a connection, and I'm convinced Jean-Luke is it."

"What's this guy want?" Milo asked.

"This," I said, reaching over to retrieve the puzzle box I'd placed on the coffee table.

"What's that?"

"It's a box Dave and I found at the house on Fern. It was underneath some floorboards and I think that Jean-Luke had been looking for it for years."

"What's in it?" Milo asked, holding out his hand so I could hand him the box for inspection.

"Nothing at this point. But it did hold a small leather-bound journal of some kind."

"Where's the journal now?" Milo asked.

"We took it up to U of M so my buddy T.J. could take a look at it," Dutch offered.

"Your old college buddy?" Milo said.

"Yeah. He's an expert in French literature, speaks the language fluently, and since the journal was written in French, I thought he'd be able to help us figure it out."

"So what did it say?" Milo said, looking to Dutch again.

"We're not sure. We know the journal's old, and are guessing that it traveled over with Jean-Paul when he emigrated here after World War II. In it there were lots of notations about gemstones and carat weights, and a list of what appear to be names."

"Hmmm," Milo said, putting down the box and tapping the side of his head as he thought through the information. "So, the bigger question is, what does this have to do with Liza's death?"

"I don't know," I said into the silence that followed as we all thought about it for a minute. "But I know there's a connection."

"Someone's really going to have to fill me in on this," Candice said, looking at all of us a little bug-eyed.

I smiled at her and said, "It's a long story, and I don't want to bog you down with the details. I know you traveled a long way for me to take a look at your case. Could you leave me the file and I'll give you a call tomorrow?"

Candice smiled kindly to me and said, "Sure, Abby. But just so you know, my grandmother's French, and she lives in town. Remember? That's how I first found you. She gave me a gift certificate for my birthday a few years ago?"

"Oh!" I said, perking up. "Now I remember. Wow, I had forgotten about that. But I think T.J. can help out with the translation, thanks all the same."

"No problem, but you may want to consider that my grandmother also emigrated here after World War II. She's really into the French community here in Royal Oak, which is much bigger than anyone realizes, so if you need dish on anyone, I'd start with her."

My intuition buzzed in my mind. I cocked my head and listened as my guides indicated I needed to take Candice up on her offer. I grinned and thought about the coincidence of Candice needing to see me today of all days. Perhaps my guides had prompted this little visit as a way of helping me out. "You have a deal," I said. "When can I meet your grandmother?"

"Let me make a call," she replied and pulled out her cell phone, then headed into the kitchen for some privacy. Milo stood up next and nodded at Dutch and me, "I'm headed back to the station to work this Jean-Luke Carlier angle. Call me if either of you gets any more info."

I walked Milo out and leaned tiredly against the front door after shutting it. It had been an emotional day, and I was still very sad about my office. A moment later I felt strong arms around my waist as Dutch pulled me away from the door and held me in his arms. "I'm sorry about your office, Edgar."

I nodded my head as the waterworks started again, and I turned into his chest and began to weep. He stroked my hair and rocked me back and forth for a bit, periodically kissing the top of my head. After I'd had a good cry I pulled my head up and said, "I'm really sorry about that 'it's tough being your girl-friend' crack."

Dutch looked at me kindly for a long moment, then he gently kissed my lips and whispered, "So make it up to me later."

"Deal," I whispered back.

At that moment we heard an uncomfortable cough from behind us, and we both looked over at Candice as she sheepishly said, "I've talked to Nana, and she'd be more than happy to help you any way she can. She's got a bingo game tonight, but said to come by early tomorrow if you want to chat. I've left her address on the counter in the kitchen, along with that file I need you to look at."

"Thanks, Candice," I said. "I really appreciate you helping me out today."

"No sweat, Abby. Now if you'll excuse me, I've got a long drive ahead." And with that she headed out the door.

When the door closed I looked up at Dutch and asked, "What now?"

He smiled, gave me a peck on my forehead and said, "Since you're convinced this Jean-Luke Carlier character is the one that attacked you, let's take a road trip to the mental hospital and see if we can find out anything."

I smiled back at him and nodded. I got my purse, my coat and we headed out the door too.

Dutch navigated as I drove and we kept the conversation short, neither one wanting to disturb the newly found peace treaty between us. The ride took about twenty minutes, and led us to a town about three cities north of Royal Oak, to Pontiac. We passed the now deserted Pontiac Stadium, which the Detroit Lions once called home, and kept going for another five minutes before Dutch said, "Turn here."

I pulled onto a side street and followed the winding road until he pointed right and we headed north again for a little ways until I saw a sign ahead that read MASHBURN HOSPITAL. I turned where the sign indicated and pulled into a large parking lot surrounding a one-story brick building that stretched out and back a good way.

I found a spot near the door and Dutch and I got out and headed toward the front entrance. We walked into a lobby with shiny parquet floors and the smell of antiseptic. A reception desk greeted us and we moved forward to the middle-aged man behind it.

"Good afternoon," Dutch said good-naturedly as he pulled out his badge and flipped it open for the man. "I'm Agent Rivers, this is my associate Abigail Cooper and we're here investigating the disappearance of one of your patients."

The man behind the counter moved closer to inspect the badge, and I couldn't help but notice that he also sat up straighter in his chair. "You must be here about Jean-Luke Carlier," he said to Dutch, reaching for a phone on the desk.

"That's the one," Dutch said tucking his badge away.

"Why don't you take a seat in the lobby and I'll page Doctor Michaels for you."

I sat down while Dutch stood nearby, leaning heavily on his cane. "Another tough session today?" I asked, noting his stance.

Dutch gave me the barest of nods and said, "No pain no gain, right?"

"How much more do you have to go through before you get the all clear?"

"You mean before I can make a dishonest woman of you?" he asked, bouncing his eyebrows.

I rolled my eyes and smiled, "We'll need to do something soon, sugar. It's getting harder and harder to sleep next to you, you know."

"About the harder part? Yeah, I know," he said with a chuckle.

I giggled. "You're bad, Dutch."

"No, sweethot . . . I'm actually really, *really* good," he replied with a knowing wink that made me want to jump him right there.

Just then a door opened off the lobby and a very pretty blond-haired woman about my age dressed in a white lab coat walked out. "Hello," she said when she spotted us. "I'm Doctor Michaels. I understand you're here about Jean-Luke?"

Dutch walked forward pulling out his badge and handing it to the doctor. "Yes, I'm Agent Rivers of the Troy field office of the Federal Bureau of Investigation, and this is my associate, Abigail Cooper. Is there someplace we can talk?"

She inspected Dutch's badge briefly and took note of his cane. "This way," she said and walked us back through the door she'd first entered from.

We followed her down a long corridor with offices and hallways jutting off to either side, before we reached a wooden door with a nameplate that read, DR. MICHAELS.

The doctor unlocked the door and held it open for Dutch and me. We entered into a moderately spacious room and I took in the surroundings.

Dr. Michaels had nice taste. Her office was a soft

rose color, wth sheer curtains cutting out most of the glaring sun that was streaming in through the window behind her desk. Against one wall was an overstuffed couch, off-white in color, and laden with several silk pillows in a variety of styles and patterns. A matching chair was angled to the side of the couch and it too held a few pillows. In front of the couch was a low table, an Indian statue centered prominently in the middle and a Kleenex box off to one side.

Against the opposite wall were several gilded frames that housed medical degrees and certificates. To the right of those was a large bookshelf filled to capacity. Dr. Michaels's cherry red desk was neat and organized, but loaded on the right side with a large stack of files.

When we were all inside, she waved her hand toward the couch and chair, indicating we should take our seats, and walked around to her desk where she sat and leaned her elbows on the surface, her hands folded over each other.

Once Dutch and I were settled she asked, "How can I help you Agent Rivers?"

I leaned back on the cushion, keeping my lips shut. I had a feeling we were on pretty dicey ground here, as this was hardly an official investigation, so I was content to let Dutch do all the talking. This would also give me a chance to snoop into Dr. Michaels's energy while she talked with him.

"What can you tell me about Jean-Luke Carlier?" Dutch asked, taking out a spiral notebook and flipping it open.

"What would you specifically like to know?"

"We understand that Jean-Luke was committed here approximately five years ago by his brother, James. I know you may not be able to give us much due to patient-client privilege, but anything you can offer us might help."

Dr. Michaels looked at Dutch and me for a long moment, probably wondering what this was all about. "Exactly what has Jean-Luke done that warrants an investigation by the FBI?" Dr. Michaels asked.

"For starters, he attacked an aid to the FBI and re-sisted arrest," Dutch said, as I hid a grin thinking he must be referring to me as the aid to the FBI, and his smashing Jean-Luke with his cane as resisting arrest.

Dr. Michaels's face blanched. "We've made a point to inform the local authorities to Jean-Luke's violent tendencies and are working diligently to find him."

"I know, and we appreciate it," Dutch said kindly. "Again, without putting you in a tight spot with that doctor-patient privilege, anything you can tell us might be useful."

Dr. Michaels gave a small wave of her hand and said, "Based on his current medical diagnosis, and the fact that he has escaped, privilege is waived."

I breathed a silent sigh of relief. If this were true, then we might be able to get some real answers here.

"He's a threat to himself or others," Dutch said, understanding why privilege would be waived.

"Yes."

"Can you tell us what his current medical condition is?" Dutch asked.

"Jean-Luke was originally committed to the hospital by his brother on the grounds that he was suicidal. He was kept for observation until we were able to make a determination as to his mental state. Shortly thereaf-ter he was found to have a textbook case of borderline personality disorder with dissociative tendencies."

"Can I have that in English, Doc?" Dutch asked, smiling.

"For all intents and purposes, Jean-Luke is a predator without conscience," Dr. Michaels began. "He would look to gain the trust of unsuspecting and vulnerable individuals, then take great care in planning their downfall. He is dispassionate about suffering. In fact, it is an emotion he cannot clearly understand, yet works very hard to evoke from anyone unfortunate enough to come into contact with him."

"Yikes," I said from the couch, a chill running up my spine.

"Yikes is right," Dr. Michaels said, her face composed but her eyes revealing a deep worry. "In recent years Jean-Luke has become increasingly violent. He had attacked several patients and an intern before he was taken out of the general population."

"So how would you treat someone like that?" Dutch asked.

"Typically we medicate with an assortment of mood-altering drugs and sedatives. In Jean-Luke's case, however, this method was ineffectual because he proved deeply resistant to most of the medications we had him on, both through his ingenuity at avoiding taking them and the fact that his own body chemistry was reluctant to absorb them to their fullest effects."

"He was able to avoid taking the drugs? How could he get away with that in a place like this?"

Dr. Michaels gave Dutch another long look and said, "You are obviously underestimating Jean-Luke's intelligence. This is an individual who tested at a 168 IQ. That qualifies him for membership into Mensa."

Dutch whistled. "168?"

"Eight points higher than genius," Dr. Michaels said. "Which makes him infinitely more dangerous."

"That changes things," Dutch said, looking pointedly at me. "Dr. Michaels, do you have a photo of Jean-Luke?"

"Yes, one moment," she said and stepped to a filing cabinet. After a moment she pulled a file, opened it and extracted a photo. She handed it to Dutch, who studied it for a moment then handed it to me.

I looked at the photo and winched. Jean-Luke stared back at me disheveled and very angry. He had wild dark hair that stood up on end in several places and appeared matted and tangled. His beard was overgrown, obsuring much of his facial features, and his eyes were like daggers staring into the camera. He was wearing a blue jumpsuit and it too looked rumpled. I looked for the resemblance to his soft-spoken, well-dressed brother, but other than being roughly the same build, these two men were worlds apart.

"Can you tell us how he managed to escape?" Dutch asked. "I mean, I would think you took some extra precautions given the level of danger with this guy."

"I can assure you, Agent Rivers, we took every imaginable precaution."

"So what happened?"

"As I said, Jean-Luke's intelligence and patience levels far exceeded our expectations. We weren't able to imagine the way he got out, and to be honest with you we're still puzzled. We found one of the nurse's aides, unconscious and heavily drugged, by a door that Jean-Luke should never have had access to. The nurse's aide doesn't remember a thing and I'm perplexed as to how Jean-Luke pulled it off. However, that's beside the point—the real problem now is that he's out there among an unsuspecting public and has more than likely already selected a victim."

"So who would he target?" Dutch asked.

"Someone who could most effectively meet his needs."

"Like what?"

Dr. Michaels sighed. "Well, he'll need money, food and shelter in the short run, and in the longer run transportation and an identity. He will probably look for a victim that he can manipulate into helping him with obtaining all of these things."

"Do you think he would go to his brother for help?" I asked, my spidey-sense tingling.

Dr. Michaels focused on me and said, "James Carlier is a good man, who deeply cares for his brother despite his brother's inability to return that feeling. In the beginning James came to visit Jean-Luke just about every week. Then something happened and James stopped coming, so although I've alerted James, no, I don't think Jean-Luke would go to him."

"Do you know what happened?" Dutch asked.

"No. I just noticed that James abruptly stopped his visits. But he did come to see Jean-Luke about three days before the escape, which was the first time he'd been here in several months."

"Three days?" I asked.

"Yes."

"What was the date?"

"Well." Dr. Michaels paused, pulling her calendar close. "Let's see. . . . I remember it was a Tuesday, because I had rounds in the morning, so it must have been on December twenty-ninth."

"Your birthday," Dutch said softly, winking at me.

"And the day we made an offer on the house," I said, another chill traveling up my spine.

Dr. Michaels looked confused, "Excuse me?"

"Nothing," Dutch said quickly. "Listen, I think we have everything here we need. Thank you for your time, Doctor," Dutch said, standing up stiffly.

"You're welcome," Dr. Michaels said, also getting up to walk us out.

I stayed seated for a moment and looked quizzically

at the doctor, something really bothering me about
her energy. She and Dutch walked to the door, then
turned toward me when I didn't follow. "You coming?" Dutch asked.

"It's not your fault," I said, directing my statement
to Dr. Michaels.

She gave me a half smile and answered, "It's hard
not to feel responsible when someone like Jean-Luke
is on the prowl."

"Not about that," I said, a message swirling with
great intensity inside my head. "You tried to save her,
but she wasn't someone who could be saved."

Dr. Michaels's face turned very pale and she stepped
backward as if I'd just hit her. "What did you say?"
she asked me, her eyes wide.

"Your patient. The one who committed suicide. It
wasn't your fault. The wounds were just too deep,
and there was nothing you could do. You didn't fail
her. . . . Life did."

"How . . . ?" Dr. Michaels asked me, her eyes
misting.

"Something I forgot to mention," Dutch said quietly, his voice lowered with the heaviness that had
filled the room. "Abby is a professional psychic."

Dr. Michaels snapped her head at Dutch, then back
to me, her eyes still wide.

"It wasn't your fault," I said again, the intensity of
the message beating like a deafening drumbeat in my
brain. "That's really, really important for you to know,
Doctor."

Dr. Michaels swallowed hard, and fought back the
tears that were leaking down her cheeks. "Her name
was Olivia," she said after a moment. "She was a
lovely girl who'd been kidnapped and raped repeat-
edly by a Detroit gang when she was fourteen. She
never moved beyond the event, despite my best ef-

forts. She was a patient here over the summer, and we all thought she was well enough to go home, but yesterday I heard from her father that she had committed suicide last weekend."

I shook my head sadly. "It wasn't your fault," I repeated. "You've got to believe that, I can't tell you how important it is. There's an opportunity in your energy for you to throw in the towel, and your guides are insisting that you reconsider this. There are so many patients that you have helped, and so many people left to help that if you quit now you really will be doing all of them a disservice."

Dr. Michaels's jaw dropped, and it took her a moment to speak. "Abby, is it?"

I nodded.

"I had been thinking of quitting. With Jean-Luke's escape and Olivia's death . . . well, let's just say it's been a difficult month."

I nodded again, the message about it not being her fault finally subsiding in my head. Good, she'd heard and listened. The rest was up to her, but at least I'd done my part.

"We should go," Dutch said discreetly, looking at me proudly.

I shot him a shy smile and got up from the couch, and we walked back through the corridors in silence, Dr. Michaels leading the way.

We paused in the lobby to shake her hand and as I pumped her palm she leaned in and said, "Thank you for what you said, Abby. I needed to hear it."

I winked at her and grabbed Dutch's arm and we left the hospital.

On the drive home Dutch said, "Nice job."

"She needed to hear it."

"I know, that's why I'm tellin' you, *nice job.*"

I gave him the full grill and kept driving.

"That, however, does not mean I'm going to let you out of my sight now that I know Jean-Luke's got you as his next target."

My left side felt heavy as he said that and I turned again to look at him. "Whaddya mean?"

"It's obvious after you've been attacked twice that Jean-Luke's got you in his sights."

Again my left side felt thick and heavy. I shook my head from side to side and replied, "No . . . it's not me he's after."

Dutch looked askance at me and said, "You could have fooled me."

"I know what it looks like, but that's not syncing up with my radar. Jean-Luke's got someone in mind, but it's not me. And there's a connection to the box that we found, but for the life of me I can't figure out what he'd want with it."

"He must have been after the notebook inside."

Again my left side felt thick and heavy. Again I shook my head and said, "Nope—wrong again."

Dutch sighed, exasperated, and asked, "Well, then what's your spidey-sense telling you he's after?"

"Not sure . . ." I said as a picture began to form in my mind. I followed the image and watched as a familiar swallow circled the puzzle box and landed on top. The swallow then began to tap on the crest etched into the wood. I blinked as I focused on the road for a minute, finding it hard to concentrate on my driving because of the intensity of the image swirling in my mind. "Hold on," I said and pulled into a fast-food restaurant.

"Awesome," Dutch said as we rounded into Burger King. "I'm starved."

I smiled as I pulled forward into a space. He didn't know about the image in my head. "Why don't you go in and get us something to eat," I said. "I need to make a few notes about something."

"Radar buzzin'?" he asked.

"Yep."

"Here," he said, handing me his notebook and pen, "use this if you want. I'll be back in a few," and with that he got gingerly out of the car.

"Don't eat the fries before you get back!" I called as he shut the door. My boyfriend's idea of "sharing" a meal involved wolfing down his own french fries before making it back home, then resorting to pinching half of mine.

Dutch smiled and saluted, then limped into Burger King. After he walked away I closed my eyes and focused again on the image playing inside my head. Again I saw the swallow flying in a circle above the puzzle box, and coming to a rest on the lid. The bird tapped three times on the crest, stopped, then tapped three more times.

Weird . . . I thought and jotted down the image. I vaguely remembered the crest on the top of the box. It had something to do with an eagle holding a rose with a shield in the background. I wondered suddenly who the crest belonged to. There was a feeling of royalty associated with it, and again I shut my eyes. I focused my radar and saw the image of Julie Andrews in her famous scene walking the hills and singing her heart out. I opened my eyes and scratched my head. The crest had to do with Julie Andrews?

Left side, heavy feeling . . .

I scowled. Again I closed my eyes and focused, and again I saw Julie Andrews in the hills singing. My eye kept going to the hills surrounding the image, the grass seemed greener and richer than I remembered from the movie, and then I had it. It wasn't about Julie Andrews; this was about the land itself. The crest was connected to Austria.

Right side, light and airy feeling . . .

"Jackpot," I said just as the passenger side door opened.

"I swear I didn't eat any fries yet," Dutch said as he got in. *Liar, liar . . . pants on fire . . .*

I smirked as I took the bag away from him, "Right . . ." I said and chuckled.

"What's jackpot?" he asked as he got settled, scooting his rubber doughnut underneath his bum, and his breath coated with the smell of hot potato.

"The crest on the top of the puzzle box. It's Austrian."

Dutch screwed up his face in a, "Huh?"

"You know," I said. "The crest on the top of the puzzle box? It has something to do with this whole mystery. And there's a connection to Austria."

"How do you know?"

"Julie Andrews."

Dutch scratched his head, opened his mouth to ask a question, then shut it just as quickly. Finally he said, "Okay, Edgar, whatever you say. Let's get home and look at the crest."

We got home a little later, the fries half gone but our burgers still intact. After getting indoors we parked ourselves on the couch and unloaded our meals. Dutch unpacked an extra burger, plain without condiments. "What's that for?" I asked as I saw him open the lid and remove the bun.

"Here, Eggy," he called to my pooch drooling by my knee.

I smiled broadly at him as the gesture took me by surprise and touched me. Dutch was always taking care of me in small ways that added up to a larger sense of comfort. As Eggy wolfed down the patty, I leaned over and gave Dutch a big slurpy kiss.

"What's that for?" Dutch asked, a grin on his face.

"That? Oh, that wasn't from me," I said. "That was from Eggy."

"Well then," Dutch replied, "remind me to get him the whole Happy Meal next time."

I chuckled and went to the kitchen and retrieved the puzzle box. Bringing it over to the couch I sat down and ran my fingers over the crest, tracing the shape of the eagle, the rose, the nest and the shield. "What do you think it means?" I asked, picking up my own burger and taking a bite.

"Not sure. Why don't we take a digital of it and e-mail it over to T.J. He's into all this European history stuff."

I nodded at him while I chewed. That felt right. "Has T.J. been able to get anything for us yet?" I asked, reaching for my Coke.

"Nope, he's been busy with his classes. He says that the beginning of the term is always the roughest, but he'll have time to look into the notebook later in the week."

"Cool." We ate in silence for a minute when my intuition buzzed in. "Check your voice mail," I said to Dutch.

"Huh?" he asked through a bite of burger.

"Your voice mail, you have a message," I said matter of factly and reached for Dutch's business phone, which he'd brought in earlier from the study and left on the coffee table. I handed it to him and returned to eating my burger.

Dutch shook his head at me and clicked the ON button of the phone. Sure enough there was an interrupted dial tone that even I could hear. "Told you so," I said, smirking in spite of myself.

"Someday you're going to have to teach me how you do that."

I shrugged my shoulders and munched on a fry while he hit the speed dial to his voice mail. After a moment he got up and went to his coat where he'd left his notebook and pen. Bringing these back to the couch he sat down and began to write quickly. When he was done he pressed a button on the phone and clicked it off.

"Who was it?" I asked.

"My buddy Peter."

"The one from Interpol?"

"Yep. He's got something for us on our guy Jean-Paul."

"Well call him!" I said excitely.

"Can I eat my burger first?" Dutch whined.

"You can have the rest of my fries if you call him right now," I said. I was too impatient to wait.

"Gee, all three of them?" Dutch asked sarcastically, looking at my cardboard container.

"Please?" I asked, fluttering my eyelashes and giving him a Bo Peep smile.

Dutch rolled his eyes, took a rebellious, huge bite out of his burger and dialed the number he'd written on the pad of paper. When the other end picked up he set the phone down and pressed the button for speaker so that I could join in on the conversation.

"Hey Pete!" Dutch called, his mouth still full of burger.

"Dutch?" came the reply.

"Yeah, sorry to put you on speaker but Abby's here and I know she'd like to hear what you've found out about our man Jean-Paul."

"Nice to meet you, Abby," Peter said.

I smiled, because it was obvious Dutch had talked

about me to his friend. "Hey, Peter. Nice to meet you too. So what can you tell us?" I said.

"You don't waste time do you?" Peter said good-naturedly.

Dutch chuckled. "She's a little anxious to put this one to bed."

"No sweat. Okay, here's the scoop. Jean-Paul Carlier was born in Lyon, France in 1905. His father Jean Carlier owned a small café there until he died in World War I, and Jean-Paul and his mother took over the café. Jean-Paul married Avril Loisclair in 1935 and they had one child, a boy named Paul.

"When France fell to Germany in 1940, Jean-Paul became part of the French Resistance, and played an integral role in obtaining identities for fleeing enemies of the Reich. Mostly these were people of power and influence who were resistant to Hitler's regime, and as German occupation swept across Western Europe, many of these families relocated to Lyon and were given a chance to fly under the Gestapo radar, mostly due to Jean-Paul's underground resistance efforts. After the war he was awarded several medals and commendations from the French government for his role in the Resistance, and was well known throughout Lyon as a hero. Then shortly thereafter in 1945, Jean-Paul moved to the United States to set up a jewelry shop where he worked until his death in 1990."

I listened to Peter with furrowed brows. This man was a hero? My radar wasn't buying it. Something was wrong with this picture, but I couldn't put my finger on what it was.

"So that's it?" Dutch asked after Peter had finished. "There's nothing else on this guy? No smoking gun or skeleton in the closet?"

"Not that I could find, but then, we're talking records that are sixty-plus years old, pal. At best, they're sketchy."

I shrugged my shoulders and looked at Dutch in an "I give up" way. There was nothing here that was going to help us with our case.

Dutch nodded and said into the phone, "Thanks for your help, Peter, I appreciate it."

"No sweat. Hey, I'll be stateside in a couple of months, want to grab a beer?"

"You buyin'?" Dutch chuckled.

"Don't I always?"

"That's because the Euro is so strong against the dollar. It costs you less," Dutch joked and Peter laughed. "Sure, pal, come on in and you, me and Abby will all go out for a night on the town."

I smiled, happy that he had included me and nudged Dutch's knee playfully.

"Talk to ya," Dutch said and clicked off the phone.

"That wasn't much help," I said gloomily.

"Just because the guy did a few good deeds doesn't mean he wasn't capable of some pretty bad ones," he reasoned.

I nodded and yawned, feeling the effects of a very long day.

"Come on, Edgar, let's get you to bed," Dutch said, standing and gathering up all the wrappers and bags. I watched him clean up with a smirk on my face.

"You take good care of me," I said after he'd thrown out the trash and come back into the living room.

"Someone's got to," he said seriously.

"Then I'm glad it's you," I said, taking his hand and following him up the stairs.

Chapter Ten

The next morning I was up early, and headed downstairs without waking Dutch. I had woken with a start this morning when I remembered Candice's folder and that I had promised to tune in on it. I wanted to get to it while I was sure I wouldn't be disturbed.

I found the folder on the kitchen table, and after heating up a cup of tea I sat down and pulled the file close. Inside was a large envelope that I opened first and from which I pulled out three large pictures. The first was a photo of a woman, in her early to midthirties. She had shoulder-length wavy brown hair, perfectly styled in a way that complimented her beautiful features. She had soft brown eyes, a narrow nose and highly arched brows. Her energy, however, held no beauty whatsoever.

The more I looked at her photo, the more I knew this woman was up to no good. Abruptly, I grabbed a sheet of paper from Dutch's notebook in the living room then returned to the kitchen table. I sat down, closed my eyes and focused.

Almost instantly an image came into my mind's eye; it was of the woman in the photograph and as I watched she put a mask over her face. The mask was white and somewhat faceless. After a moment the mask was removed and a new face was revealed, one I recognized. The face was Liza's. My eyes snapped opened and I stared again at the woman's photograph. What was the vision trying to tell me? Had this woman been murdered too? I looked at the woman's photo again. There was no flat, plastic appearance to the image, which told me the woman was still alive and well. Intuitively, however, I felt a connection of some kind between the woman and Liza, but I wasn't sure what. I wrote down on the piece of paper everything I had seen and moved on to the next photograph.

This was a picture of a man who appeared to also be in his early to midthirties. He was handsome in a rugged way, with a bold square jaw, broad shoulders, thick wavy brown hair and nice eyes. His energy wasn't nearly as distasteful as the woman's, but there was a hint of something underhanded. I closed my eyes and followed my intuition as I focused on his energy, and right away I got the image of a triangle. I looked at the triangle and noticed one corner held a wedding ring. Ahhh. He was married and having an affair with the brunette. Men could be so stupid sometimes.

I opened my eyes and jotted down a few more notes about the cheater, then picked up the last picture. This held the photo of an older man, roughly fifty to sixty, dressed in an expensive-looking suit and sharp tie. He looked very well groomed, and immaculately put together. Right away I knew he was a man of power and influence. I closed my eyes again and focused on him. Immediately I saw a marble bust of Julius Caesar. Nothing else came to mind, so I opened my eyes and thought about the image for a minute, tapping my fingers on the tabletop. It suddenly dawned on me that Caesar had been betrayed, stabbed by his own friends.

I picked up the photo of the younger man again and looked at it, the name *Brutus* swirling in my head. Curious.

I came back to the woman and tried to connect the dots. What did the mask mean? After a moment of trying to think it through I gave up and pulled the file close to me to read through some of Candice's notes. I always put off reading about the case until after I'd tuned in on the energies of the people involved so that I could avoid any preconceptions. When I flipped to the first page everything clicked together and I was able to decipher what my guides were hinting at.

Nancy Bradshaw was the name of the woman in the photo. She worked at a large insurance firm in Kalamazoo, and had recently brought a ten million dollar lawsuit against the CEO of the company, Jackson McBride, who was the older man in photo number three. Her witness was one of the company's adjusters, Mark Calloway, photo number two, who claimed to see Jackson making inappropriate advances toward Miss Bradshaw.

The insurance company was seriously considering firing their CEO and settling with Bradshaw, and Candice had been hired independently by McBride to clear his name. McBride claimed he never made any kind of advance toward Nancy, inappropriate or otherwise. After focusing in on McBride's energy, I was inclined to believe him.

As I scanned the rest of the file, something popped out at me toward the end of Candice's notes. Nancy Bradshaw's credit history revealed only two accounts: a Visa and a car loan, both only two months old. Prior to that, Nancy Bradshaw had never existed on paper.

Now I knew what the mask was all about, and I also had a very large clue into Liza's mystery. Quickly, I got up and retrieved the phone from the coffee table. Trotting back to the kitchen I dialed Candice's number and winced when the line was picked up by a groggy voice.

"Hello?" she said, obviously still half asleep.

"Oh, God, Candice, I'm sorry!" I said, noting the clock on the wall read seven thirty.

"Abby?"

"Yeah, I didn't realize it was so early."

"Is something wrong?" Candice asked, alarm in her voice.

"No, nothing's wrong, I just tuned in on your file and got excited about what I hit on."

"Shoot," Candice said, shaking the sleep from her voice.

"Well, your girl Nancy Bradshaw isn't really Nancy Bradshaw."

"I'm not following you."

"Identity fraud. Nancy Bradshaw is an alias."

"Whoa. Are you sure?"

"My radar says absolutely."

"Abby, if you're right, then this is awesome!" Candice said excitedly. "What else did you get a bead on?"

"The younger guy, Mark Calloway, he's lying his ass off."

"Yeah, that was obvious to me too. What I can't figure out is, why?"

"He and Nancy are gettin' busy, if you catch my drift."

"Really?" Candice asked, surprised. "This guy's married with three kids and according to his coworkers, one hell of a devoted husband and father. I mean, it's not like I haven't seen this kind of thing a thousand times before, but the word around the office was that he and Nancy loathe each other, and that's why it was such a shock to everyone when he stepped forward to back up her story. The shareholders figured that if her biggest enemy was backing her up, then the allegations must be true."

"Appearing to loathe someone is a good cover for an affair, wouldn't you say?"

"I'm with you," Candice said. "So did you get anything on McBride?"

"He's innocent. Completely set up."

"Good to know, Abby. Listen, this helps a ton. Thank you so much!"

"No sweat. I'm going to call your grandmother later on this morning to see if I can stop over. When is a good time to call?"

"Anytime, she's an early riser. Probably been up for hours already."

"Still, I think I'll wait till nine or so."

"Cool. I'll catch you later, girl. Tell Nana I said hi."

"Will do," I said and disconnected. Just then Dutch came into the kitchen and gave my neck a nibble as he reached around my waist and pulled me back into him.

"Hey there, cute stuff. Who ya talkin' to so early in the morning?"

"Candice. I came down early to focus on her file, and I wanted to tell her about the results."

"Good news?" he mumbled into my neck.

"Yes, in fact. Turns out I was able to give her a direction that should really help her client. And while I was at it I discovered something interesting about our friend Liza."

"Oh?"

"That wasn't her real name."

"It wasn't?"

"No. She hid her identity from Jean-Paul."

"Come again?" Dutch asked, swiveling me around to face him.

"Liza hid her identity from Jean-Paul. I don't know why, but I do know that she was pretending to be someone she wasn't."

"And when he found out about it, he killed her?"

I thought on that for a moment and played it against my radar. My intuition said that there was truth to that statement, and yet it wasn't the complete story. "Maybe," I said after a bit.

"So we're still in the dark about how everything fits together?"

"Yes, but hopefully not for long. How about I make us some omelets, then call Candice's grandmother? Maybe she'll have some answers for us."

Dutch's stomach growled. "I'm in," he said, giving my rear a friendly pat.

I made us breakfast and we were in the middle of eating when the phone rang. Dutch picked it up off the table, scanned the caller ID and handed it to me. "It's your sister," he said by way of explanation.

I grabbed the phone and depressed the ON button. "Hey, Cat," I said happily. It had been a few days since I'd heard from her.

"I'm at the airport," she announced.

I nearly choked on the bite of hash browns I'd just eaten. "Excuse me?"

"I'm coming to Michigan."

"*What?*" I squealed into the phone. "But *why*?"

"*Because I just can't take it anymore!*" Cat shouted. "Abby, our parents are *crazy*!"

"Thanks for the news flash, Cat. But that still doesn't explain why you're coming here. What's happened?"

"They've locked me out of the house."

"Who?"

"Claire and Donna."

"Your housekeeper?"

"Yes! I did everything I could to prepare that stupid guesthouse for Claire and Sam, and they refuse to move there! Instead, they've taken over my house and don't seem to want to leave, and when Tommy forced me to go over there to kick them out, Donna slammed the door in my face!"

"But *she* works for *you*!" I said, aghast that Cat was taking this abuse.

"I know, and I realize I should call the police and have them all physically removed from my home, but I just can't, Abby. I have to get away for a few days and get some distance from all this. I just called Tommy and told him that I have to fly to Michigan to check on the progress of our investment property, and he's going to stay with the boys at the Four Seasons until I get back."

"Cat, do not come here," I said sternly. The last thing I needed was for my sister to insert herself into the mess of the house on Fern and make herself a target for Jean-Luke.

"They're calling my flight. I've got to go. We'll talk when I get there." With that the line went dead.

I depressed the OFF button and bonked myself in the head with the phone.

"Trouble?" Dutch asked, working hard to hide a smirk.

"Yes, and her name is Cat," I said, setting the phone down with a sigh.

"She can't stay here," Dutch said, looking pointedly at me. He and Cat got along swimmingly just as long as they spent no more than fifteen minutes together in the same room.

"Relax, Cowboy," I said, leveling a cool look at

him. "If I know Cat, she's already booked the penthouse at the Hilton."

Dutch looked relieved and said, "Why's she coming into town anyway?"

"Apparently, the state of Massachusetts isn't big enough for my parents and my sister."

Dutch gave me a blank look and then changed the subject. "So what time are we going to see Candice's grandmother?"

"You're coming?" I asked.

"Edgar, until this lunatic is caught, I'm not letting you out of my sight."

"But what about your physical therapy?"

"I can do a lot of the exercises at home."

I cocked an eyebrow of doubt in his direction.

"Really," he insisted. "It's basic stuff."

I rolled my eyes and reached for the phone. "I'll call her now and see what time she can talk to us."

Ten minutes later I'd hung up the phone after having a very lively conversation with Madame Brijitte Dubois, who was quite bubbly about the prospect of assisting in a thirty-year-old murder mystery. I put the phone on the charger and turned to Dutch, "We're due at Madame Dubois's in an hour. I'll shower first."

Dutch grunted from his seat at the kitchen table, absorbed in his newspaper, so I headed up the stairs and into the bathroom. I turned on the faucet allowing for the water to heat, then headed into the bedroom where I rooted through my suitcase to find a pair of clean jeans and a sweater.

The weatherman had predicted a warm front moving in from the south, and this meant unseasonable temps for the week in the upper forties—a true rarity for these parts in mid-January.

I carried my clothes and makeup case into the bathroom, shutting the door and sealing in the steam; then

I pulled back the shower curtain and jumped as a gasp escaped me.

"Come on in," said my *very* naked boyfriend. "The water's just right." And with that he scooped me into the shower, pajamas and all.

"*What* do you think you're doing?" I asked as my tank top became soaked.

"Saving time," Dutch replied as he began to undress me, "and water."

"Dutch," I said, stifling a moan as his soapy fingers went to work, and his lips connected to my neck. "Hey, the doctor said no hanky-panky for another week."

"Mmmmm . . ." he replied and wound his fingers through my hair. Bending my head back he kissed my mouth and I suddenly found myself kicking off my pajama bottoms. Months of suppressed passion seemed to erupt between us as the shower rained warm and inviting water down on us. My fingers found their way along his slippery skin, curling over his muscular arms, his developed pecs and his deliciously narrow hips. Within seconds I found myself completely absorbed in the passion of the moment. I wanted him *bad* and I suddenly didn't give a rat's ass about doctor's orders.

But just as Dutch and I were entering uncharted territories there was a horrible crash from downstairs, and an instant later Eggy's frantic barking reverberated throughout the house.

With speed and reaction time I hadn't imagined he possessed, Dutch let go of me, flew out of the shower and out the bathroom door. I stood a little dazed for a half second against the wall of the shower, then shook myself and quickly turned off the spray. Launching myself out of the tub I grabbed a towel and followed the trail of wet footprints down the stairs, through the living room and was about to step into the kitchen when I heard a sharp, *"Stop!"* from Dutch.

I looked questioningly at him and he pointed to the floor, which was covered in glass. Among the shards I noticed small specks of blood and I looked back at Dutch who was holding one foot tenderly off the floor, and a squirming Eggy in his arms. "Are you okay?" I asked anxiously.

"I'm fine. Just got a foot full when I came into the kitchen. Can you go get me a towel?"

It dawned on me that he was still naked, and a little embarrassed. I nodded, then rushed upstairs where I retrieved a towel for him, a pair of boxer briefs and a T-shirt from his bureau and his slippers. Before heading back downstairs I stepped back into the bathroom and grabbed a bottle of peroxide, some cotton swabs and Band-Aids, then rushed back to Dutch.

I found him in the kitchen, with Eggy sitting on one of the kitchen chairs watching Dutch intently as he was doing his best to sweep the glass into a pile. The poor guy was shivering slightly as a cold breeze blew in from the broken window over the sink. A brick lay on the counter, and I noticed with a bit of shock that there was a piece of paper attached by a black string poking out from under it.

"Here," I said extending the towel, clothes and the peroxide. "Do you need help with the glass in your foot?"

"Naw, it was just one big sliver, and I got it out okay. Thanks," he added, setting the broom down and coming over to me to retrieve my bundle. He avoided stepping into the living room, because his foot was still bleeding. He quickly mopped himself off with the towel and then donned the boxers and the T-shirt. I snuck a few extra peeks before the boxer briefs covered the important parts, inwardly groaning that we'd come so close and I was just destined to be wound with sexual tension for eternity.

After getting dressed, Dutch hobbled over to a chair to tend to his foot while I raced back upstairs and got dressed as quickly as possible, then ran back to take over sweeping duties in the kitchen. I had a neat pile within a minute or two and looked around for a paper bag to deposit the broken glass in. Dutch read my thoughts and pointed to a corner by the fridge. I got the bag and said, "Someone sure wants to get our attention."

Dutch got up and walked over to me. Putting a hand on my shoulder, he asked, "You okay?"

I looked up at him, the question catching me by surprise. "If you're asking if I'm rattled, yeah, a little, but I'll get over it."

Dutch looked into my eyes and after a moment he kissed me on the forehead, then walked over to the brick on the counter. Using a pair of tongs from the utensil drawer he picked the brick up and turned it over, then extracted the note from the string and, using a pencil and the tongs, he unfolded it.

"What's it say?" I asked as I dropped the last of the glass into the bag.

"Give it back," Dutch read, "or else."

"The box?" I asked, and as I said this, my left side felt thick and heavy.

"I guess," Dutch said, running a hand through his wet hair.

I watched the move and noticed that there were goose bumps along his arm. He was cold and the open window wasn't helping. "Hey," I said to him, "you get upstairs and get some clothes on. I'll call Dave and have him come over to fix the window."

Dutch nodded and left the kitchen. I called Dave and told him what happened, leaving out the shower scene.

"If all this guy wants is that stupid box, then I say put it out on your front doorstep and be done with it, Abby," Dave said after I'd filled him in.

"If I thought that would make him go away, I'd take you up on that, but my spidey-sense is telling me he's after something more."

"Like what?"

There was a buzz in my head as Dave asked that question and I tuned in to the message for a moment. In my mind's eye I saw the swallow again, landing on the puzzle box and pecking at the crest on the lid. There was something about that crest that was significant. What exactly, I wasn't sure, but I obviously had some homework to do. "I'm trying to figure that out. In the meantime, do you think you could come over and fix the window?"

"I'll be there in ten," Dave said and clicked off.

Dutch joined me in the kitchen and asked, "Did you get a hold of Dave?"

"He's on his way. Listen, can you take a picture of the crest on the box and e-mail that to T.J.?"

Dutch looked at me quizzically for a moment. "You in a hurry about it?"

I looked pointedly at the window, then back at him. "There's a connection. I don't think Jean-Luke is after the box itself, and I doubt he's after the notebook. There's something else he wants and that crest is the key."

Dutch nodded. "I'll get the camera."

While Dutch was off taking care of the box, I called Madame Dubois back to reschedule.

"But of course," she said with her thick French accent when I asked if we could postpone to later in the day. "I will be here for ze afternoon, come when you can."

I thanked her and hung up, heading off to find Dutch in his study. When I entered I announced, "Madame Dubois can see us anytime this afternoon."

"Good," Dutch said as he made several keystrokes on his computer. I noticed that both the camera and the box were on his desk. "We have an errand to run first, anyway."

"What errand?" I asked as I took a seat in one of the leather chairs in his study.

"We're going to get some answers out of your friend James Carlier."

I sat up straighter in the chair. "We're going to talk to him?"

"Yep. When's Dave getting here?"

Just then the doorbell rang. "My spidey sense tells me any minute!" I joked.

"Ha, ha," Dutch said, coming around the desk and messing my hair on his way to the door.

I followed him out to the living room and waited while he opened the door for Dave. "Morning," I said when he walked in.

"What's up with your sister?" Dave asked me in an accusing tone.

I blinked several times and asked, "What?"

"Your sister. Cat. She just called my cell phone from a plane now circling Metro Airport and demanded a status on the house on Fern."

"Uh-oh," I said.

"When I told her I wasn't going back into that house until it'd been leveled, she got all huffy on me and hung up!"

I groaned, "You actually *said* that to her?"

"Well, yeah. I thought you told her we weren't

touching that house until someone performed an exorcism."

"Nope," I said setting my shoulders. This wasn't good. Cat was far easier to deal with when she was eight hundred miles away versus up close and personal. Now that the cat was out of the bag, so to speak, about our investment property, there was no telling what she'd do with the information. If Dave had only kept his yap shut I could have stalled for a few more days or even weeks.

"Did I goof?" Dave asked me, noting the expression on my face.

"No, but I did by not handling Cat this morning when she threatened to come into town," I said with an exasperated sigh.

"Sorry," Dave said sheepishly.

I shook off the tension setting in my shoulders and said, "Don't sweat it. Listen, Dutch and I are headed out. Will you be okay here by yourself?"

"Sure. I've got the wood in my truck. I'll board up the window same as I did at your place, take the measurements and order you a new window from the Depot. It should only take a week or two to come in."

"Thanks, buddy," Dutch said as he handed my coat to me. "We'll be available by cell if you need us."

We left the house and headed to my car. I noticed that Dutch had left his cane inside and I said, "You leaving the third leg behind?"

"Yeah," he said, rounding to his side of my car. "It's time I started walking on my own."

I smiled encouragingly at him. After all, the sooner he was back to normal the quicker we could get on with getting acquainted, and given my current level of horniness I figured that was definitely a good thing.

I got in my side, and when Dutch was seated I

started the car and pointed it in the direction of Opalescence. Noting the direction I was headed, Dutch chimed in with, "We're not going to the shop, Abby."

"We're not?"

"Nope. He doesn't open for business until eleven a.m. It's only nine thirty. We can surprise him at home."

"How do you know what his hours are?"

"I remember from when I went shopping for your necklace."

"Ah," I said, nodding my head. Dutch had a fantastic memory for these sorts of small details, which definitely came in handy in his line of work. "So where are we going?"

"Fourteen and Lahser, he's got a house in a sub over there."

"Just let me know where to turn," I said.

We arrived a little while later in front of a good-size Colonial nestled among similar looking houses in a fairly affluent part of Bloomfield Township, a neighbor to the west of Royal Oak. The houses in this neighborhood had a little land between them, and each home hosted a spacious front yard. James's house was beige with black shutters and had an attached garage.

I parked my SUV in the driveway and as we got out I noticed movement among the front curtains as they were pulled slightly apart, then, when I darted a look, pulled firmly closed again.

I followed Dutch as he limped up the walkway careful not to put too much weight on his injured foot. I consciously slowed my pace so he wouldn't feel rushed. Poor guy, we'd had our share of injuries lately and I wondered when things would ease up for us.

We got to the front door and Dutch pushed the doorbell. From inside we heard the "Bing-Bong!" announce our arrival. While we waited at the door I took in the surroundings, and noticed that James still had his Christmas lights up. I figured with all the commotion at his shop lately, he probably hadn't gotten around to taking them down yet.

Dutch and I waited probably sixty seconds before he hit the doorbell again. "I know he's home," he said.

"I'm right there with you," I replied. "I saw the front curtains peel aside when we first pulled up." As we waited again, I noted something that wouldn't normally have caught my attention, but for some reason made me cock my head and listen. "Hit the doorbell again," I said to Dutch after a minute. He did and I listened again. It was what I didn't hear that bothered me, but before I had a chance to say anything to Dutch, the front door opened a fragment and two dark brown eyes peeked out through the crack.

"Go away!" hissed James.

"Good morning, Mr. Carlier. I'm Agent Rivers with the FBI, and you remember Abby?" Dutch said, flashing his badge for effect.

"I said go away!" James repeated.

"Not until you talk to us," Dutch said calmly.

"I can't talk now," James insisted. "I have to get ready for work."

"Where's your dog?" I said, asking about what had bothered me since Dutch pressed the doorbell. All dogs bark at doorbells, and I'd noted the silence that followed our arrival on James's front steps.

"I had to give her away," James said, his eyes flickering to me.

"Why?" I asked, trying to keep him talking.

"She was too much . . ." James tried to explain. "She was too much trouble." *Liar, liar . . . pants on fire . . .*

"But I thought you said she was a great dog," I

insisted. Something really bothered me about James giving his dog away. He was lying through his teeth about it and I couldn't figure out why.

"Well, I was wrong. Now if you'll excuse me," he said and began to shut the door.

Dutch put his hand on the door, not forcing it open, but definitely preventing it from shutting. "James, we need to know about your brother, Jean-Luke. Is he here?"

There was a gasp from James, who said, "I can't talk about him!"

"Listen, if you're hiding him here there could be severe consequences for you," Dutch said, his hand still firmly on the door. "He needs to go back to Mashburn where he can be monitored and treated."

From the other side of the door came a hollow laugh as James said, "Luke won't go anywhere he doesn't want to, Agent Rivers."

"It sounds like you're afraid of him?" Dutch said again. "We can help you, James. We can protect you."

Again James laughed. "He's smarter than you think. If he wants to inflict pain, he'll find a way."

"So tell us what he wants with the puzzle box," I said, my voice calm and low.

"He wants his treasure back," James replied cryptically. "His bloody, dirty, treasure!" And with that he slammed the door in our faces.

"What the hell was that?" I asked Dutch as we heard the dead bolt slide home from the other side of the door.

"You got me, sweethot," he answered, scratching his head. "Come on, he's not going to play nice today. Let's go see Candice's grandmother."

We backtracked across town and headed northeast until we got to Pleasant Ridge, a town that buffers Royal Oak and Ferndale. Pleasant Ridge is a small community, but known to have real estate tags higher than Royal Oak. We made our way along the quaint streets dotted with typical midwestern suburban homes until we arrived at the address on the piece of paper Candice had given me.

Again I parked in the driveway and got out, waiting for Dutch to take the lead. We used the knocker this time and the door was promptly opened by a beautiful old woman with shiny silver hair, perfect makeup and nearly flawless skin. I smiled as she greeted us and extended my hand. "Madame Dubois?" I asked.

"Ah, you must be Abby Cooper, no?" she asked me, her English exotically laced with a French accent.

"Oui," I said, remembering the only word I'd retained from four years of high school French.

"Bonjour!" she said happily as she waved us indoors. "Come in, come in from ze cold."

We walked into the stifling heat of her front hall, Dutch taking off the light jacket that he'd worn on the unusually mild day. I quickly followed suit as the thermostat had to be set in the mideighties. Madame Dubois took our coats and set them on the banister leading to the upstairs. "Come, come," she said and fluttered into the living room. "Would you like some tea to warm your bones?" she called over her shoulder. "I've just put on a fresh pot."

I smiled gamely at Dutch who was tugging at his shirt and eyeing me with a "She's kidding, right?" look.

"We'd love some, thank you," I called and elbowed Dutch in the side as I mouthed, "Behave!"

As Madame Dubois set off to fix our tea, Dutch and I headed into the living room and both of us came up short as we caught sight of the décor. The room was an explosion of pink, pillows and lace.

I gaped at the surroundings as I took in walls that

were papered, a pattern of pink and white stripes, the carpet a dusty pink pastel. The couch was soft rose, with half a dozen assorted pink and lace-trimmed pillows. Facing the couch sat two blush-colored wing chairs draped with their own chenille pink afghans. The room was like an eruption of Pepto-Bismol.

Dutch gaped with me, his features reflecting something between horror and disbelief. After a minute he looked at me as if to say, "Where do I sit?" and I rolled my eyes and pointed to one of the wing chairs. He sat carefully on the edge of the chair, afraid some of the color might rub off on his clothes. I took the other chair and tried to get the thought of indigestion out of my head.

Just then Madame Dubois swept back into the room carrying a white tray with a pink teapot and several matching cups and saucers and cookie plates. Dutch got up to help her with the tray, and she shooed him away with a smile. She set the tray down and arranged each plate on the coffee table in front of us, then poured each of us a cup of tea and set those out as well. Without pause she shuffled back into the kitchen and came out with another, larger plate, stacked high with cookies in the shape of hearts with pink frosting.

Dutch smiled and took a cookie, but his face said he'd lost his appetite. As Madame Dubois came around the table and took her seat she drew a deep breath and waved a hand at the room. "You like?" she asked us. "I decorated eet myself."

"Very nice," Dutch said. *Liar, liar . . . pants on fire . . .*

"Lovely," I added as my lie detector went off again in my head.

"So, you want to know about zis man, Jean-Paul Carlier?"

I took a tiny sip of tea, more for show than for thirst and said, "Yes. Did you happen to know him?"

"But of course," Madame Dubois said as she poured her tea. "Everyone knew Jean-Paul."

I caught Dutch's eye and winked at him, then turned back to Madame Dubois. "What can you tell us about him?"

"Well," she began, settling back on the couch and raising a finger to her chin as she collected her thoughts. "For starters, he was, how you say . . . a rat bastard."

Dutch sputtered his tea, and followed that with a heavy cough, and Madame Dubois and I both turned to look at him. "Sorry," he said as his face flushed red. "Wrong pipe."

I rolled my eyes at him and turned back to our hostess. "You were saying?"

Madame gave Dutch one more curious look while he pounded his chest with his fist. She continued, "He was a real shit."

"I see," I said, stifling a laugh. "Because . . . ?"

"Well, for one sing he was a thief."

"Thief?"

"Yes. It was well known among ze French community here zat eef you needed your diamond jewelry cleaned, you avoided Jean-Paul's. My dear friend Anna-Marie took heem her two-carat diamond broach, and returned with a one-point-six carat broach. Jean-Paul would switch ze diamonds and tink noting of eet."

"Why didn't she get the police involved?" I asked.

"Oh, mais oui, but she deed. However, she could not prove zat ze diamond had been switched, because she had no pictures, and no sales receipt. Ze broach had been in her family for generations, and Jean-Paul got avay with eet."

"So, other than larceny, was there anything else that Jean-Paul was underhanded about?" Dutch asked.

"But of course," Madame said, taking another sip

of tea, and then biting off a bit of cookie before continuing. "He broke hearts everywhere he went."

"He was a ladies' man," I summarized.

"Why, yes. After hees wife's death he had a string of girlfriends. But zen he settled with one woman for nearly twenty years, until he died."

"Until, *he* died?" I asked.

"Why, yes. But, of course, he broke her heart too."

"What do you mean?"

"Jean-Paul cheated on her with a much younger woman."

My radar began buzzing and I set my teacup down, then leaned in toward Madame Dubois. "Do you know who this much younger woman was?"

"Mais non," she said with a sigh. "I saw her a few times, but we were never introduced."

Dutch had also leaned forward in his chair. "What did she look like?"

"She was pretty, blond and petite. She was like a little doll and no one could understand what she saw in Jean-Paul."

It was Liza, I thought excitedly. Madame Dubois was talking about Liza! "What happened to her?" I asked.

Madame Dubois said, "Je ne sais pas. One day Jean-Paul was back weeth Simone."

"Simone?"

"Oui, ze woman I told you about who cared for heem until Jean-Paul died."

"Is Simone still alive?"

"Oui, yes."

"Where can I find her?" I asked, reaching into my purse to pull out a pen and piece of paper.

"Why, she is living with her sister, two streets over. I will get you ze address if you'd like."

"Yes, please!" I said excitedly.

Madame Dubois got up from her pink couch and shuffled into the kitchen. As she exited I looked at Dutch and mouthed, "Jackpot!"

He nodded and whispered, "Let's get the address and get the freak outta here."

I stifled a chuckle as Madame came back into the living room, toting a pink lace-covered address book. "Here eet ees," she said as she paused on a page. "Simone lives at 126 Arlmont. If you take a left at ze stop sign and go two streets over you weel find her street right away. Hers ees ze tird on ze right."

"Merci!" I said, jumping up after I'd written down the address. "Madame Dubois, thank you so much for your time. We've kept you too long and really must be on our way, but thank you again for your lovely hospitality, and valuable information."

"My pleasure," she said sweetly, beaming at Dutch and me as we hurried over to our coats. Just as I was wriggling into mine, Dutch's cell phone chirped, and he nodded to Madame Dubois and ducked out the door. I smiled, shook the sweet woman's hand, and followed behind my boyfriend, relishing the cooler air outside the moment it hit my face.

Dutch was waiting for me on the front lawn, his hand on his forehead and his mouth a small "oh" as he listened intently. "She's driving a *what*?" he asked, looking at me with wide eyes and shaking his head in disbelief, then he added, "And she drove it over *what*?"

I walked to him, wondering what the commotion was about, just as Dutch began laughing. Someone must have said something incredibly funny on the other end of the line because he suddenly doubled over and began clutching at his sides.

His laugh was contagious, and I found myself chuckling with him, as I waited for him to tell me what was so funny. Finally, he said, "Okay, Milo, we'll be there in a few minutes. Try not to make her madder." He clicked off the phone.

"What was that about?" I asked as my boyfriend continued to laugh so hard his sides shook and tears leaked out of his eyes.

"I think I'm gonna have to show you this one, Edgar. Come on." And with that he walked to my car and waited for me to unlock the doors. Curious, I followed after him—my spidey-sense giving me the feeling that whatever Dutch wanted to show me, I wasn't going to like it.

Chapter Eleven

Dutch said only one thing to me between chuckles as I started the car: "Make your way over to Fern Street, Abby."

I groaned as I pulled out of Madame Dubois's driveway. "What's happened?" I asked, but this made Dutch only laugh more.

Ten minutes and lots of really annoying laughter later, I was thoroughly irritated. "Will you *please* tell me what the hell is going on?"

"Can't really put it into words, sweethot," Dutch said, torturing me.

When we pulled onto Fern Street I understood completely what he meant. On the front lawn of my investment property, perched in the cab of a bulldozer and waving her arms as she yelled at the police surrounding her, was my sister, Catherine. "Ohmigod! She's gone over the edge!"

Dutch ducked his head and began shaking with laughter again. I stepped on the gas and sped toward the scene, hitting him with my free arm and yelling, "It's not funny!"

I screeched to a halt and tore out of the car, running to Milo who was holding a bullhorn to his lips, ready to yell through it at my sister.

"Milo!" I shouted.

He swiveled his head toward me and lowered the bullhorn. *"Thank God* you're here!" he said as I neared.

"What the hell's going on?" I asked.

"Your sister's a lunatic!" Milo bellowed. His eyes large and angry, his fingers clenched around the handle of the horn as he raised it and shouted, *"Lunatic!"* at Cat, who turned in the cab to glare at him and give him the finger.

"Where did she . . . ? What has she . . . ? How . . . ?" I stammered as I looked at the havoc my sister had apparently caused. The fence that had once lined the property lay in a crumpled heap where it had been squashed by the dozer that was inching toward our investment property, while a group of police officers stood bravely in front of it and tried to get my sister to stop.

"She ran over my car!" Milo shouted through the bullhorn as he pointed it at me, the sound so loud it rang through my head like a gong.

I gasped as I turned back to him, "No! Not the beemer?"

"Yes!" Milo shouted again through the bullhorn but directed it this time at my sister.

"But *why?"*

"Because she's a *lunatic!"* Milo yelled again, swiveling the bullhorn back in my direction as I ducked and plugged my ears.

I backed away from the horn and looked around. Over by the neighbor's fence I saw a crumpled heap of black metal that was once a shiny sedan. Dutch was standing next to it doubled over, his guffaws audible from way over here. Milo followed my gaze, caught Dutch laughing and shouted at him through the bullhorn, *"It's not funny!"*

That was enough. I yanked the bullhorn away from Milo and marched directly toward the bulldozer. When I got up alongside it I raised the horn and shouted, "Catherine Cooper-Masters! Get out of that thing right now!"

Cat worked the levers in the cab of the dozer as though she hadn't heard me and continued her slow march toward the house, a determined and half-crazed look on her face. I ran in front of the dozer and planted my feet, the officers giving me room. Cat pushed it to within a foot of me before she let up off the gas, and we had ourselves a little staredown.

"Get out of the cab," I said through the horn.

"No!" she yelled back, working the gears threateningly.

"Get out of the cab so we can talk about this, Cat!"

"No!"

"Oh for the love of God, Catherine!" I yelled, completely fed up with her. "Get out of the friggin' cab or I will call Mother and tell her what you've done!"

That did it. I saw Cat blanch, then succumb to a hail of tears. I threw the bullhorn aside and scrambled up onto the dozer, making my way along the oblong wheels and tapped on the side of the cab. After a minute Cat unlocked the door and I held it open as she blubbered her way out onto the dozer's giant tread wheel and grabbed me in a desperate hug. I gently moved her along the side of the dozer over to the edge, careful to watch our footing, noting that Cat was dressed in a typical three-thousand-dollar designer suit with matching Manolo Blahniks. As I moved her to the edge of the wheel, I saw one of the officers move in, reaching behind him for a pair of cuffs.

Protectively, I pulled her back along the edge. "Milo!" I shouted. "Call off the dogs, and let's talk about this!" There was no way I would let them cart Cat off to jail without a fight, and if that meant that I had to go along, well then, so be it.

Milo glared at me and kept his mouth shut, but thankfully Dutch came up to him and said something in his ear. I saw Milo protest, then throw up his hands and wave the officers away. With great care I lowered my sister, who was still clinging frantically to me, to the ground and I jumped down after her. I walked her to the car and noticed half a dozen onlookers from the neighborhood ogling us. I put the burbling Cat in the passenger seat of my Mazda, whispered, "Let me go take care of things, okay?" and handed her a tissue from the glove box. Then I trotted over to Dutch and Milo and said, "So tell me what happened."

"Your sister's a . . ."

"I know that already," I said, cutting him off. "Milo, focus here! Tell me exactly what happened."

Milo was as mad as I'd ever seen him, but to his credit he made a great effort to neutralize his facial expression and speak in slow measured tones. "We got a call from the station that some psycho woman was driving a bulldozer erratically down Woodward Avenue. I didn't think much of it until someone else called in that she had turned off Woodward, and was heading in the direction of your house on Fern. Since all the stuff that's been happening to you seems to revolve around this house, I took the call and headed over here. When I arrived I found your sister, locked in the cab of the bulldozer, heading straight for the home. She'd already run over the fence when I pulled my car in front of her to stop her forward progress. I got out and was trying to *reason* with her when she flipped me off and *ran over my car!*"

"Okay," I winced as he shouted that last bit. "Listen, if it helps any, my sister is loaded, and I'm sure that after she calms down she'll be more than willing to replace your Beemer."

"I *loved* that car!" Milo said, a small tear forming in the corner of his eye.

Dutch had to turn away, his shoulders shaking again with laughter. I ignored him and continued, "Can we avoid an arrest?"

"*Are you crazy?*" he asked me, a look of astonishment on his face. "No way! Do you *know* how many laws she's broken, Abby?" he asked me, then he began to list them, ticking each one off on his fingers as he went. "Assault with a deadly weapon, malicious destruction of property, hazardous driving, driving without a valid license . . ."

I gave an exasperated sigh. "Come *on*, Milo," I pleaded. "Be reasonable. Listen, she's had a really tough week, and I think all she wanted to do was vent a little, and this is Cat's way of venting."

"*Bulldozing an innocent BMW?*" Milo shrieked.

I winced again and said, "No, not that. I think she just wanted to take it out on that house and your car simply got in the way."

"She doesn't have a permit to do that, Abby!"

"Yes, I know. But, again, she's had a tough week."

"Most people just go to the gym, you know," he said through gritted teeth.

"Milo, haven't I always helped you when you asked? And wasn't it because I provided you with the winning lottery numbers that you were able to afford that car in the first place?" I added.

Milo glowered at me, then lowered his head and kicked at a rock on the ground. After a long moment he said, "She gets on a plane tonight, and I don't want to see her again for a *very* long time."

"Deal," I said, and was about to leave.

"But first," he said stopping me, "she needs to buy me a new car."

Two hours later we were ready to leave the BMW dealership, Milo in his shiny brand-new black sedan and Cat writing a notation for seventy thousand dollars in her personal checkbook.

"I'm going to take Cat to the airport. Why don't you head back with Milo and I'll meet you back home later on tonight?" I said to Dutch.

Dutch gave me a torn look, which I understood all too well. His best friend just got a brand new toy, with a few extra upgrades, but he was worried about leaving me to my own devices once I dropped Cat off. "I don't know . . ." he said, thinking it through.

"Oh, for Christ's sake, Dutch. I'll be fine. I'll come home right from the airport. Honest Abe."

"Is your cell phone charged?"

"Check!" I saluted.

"Is it turned on?" he probed.

"Check, check!"

"Fine, but no detours. Okay, Edgar?"

"Check, check, check!"

"Smart-ass . . ." he said as he winked at me, ruffled my hair and walked away toward Milo.

I didn't wait for him to change his mind but hurried over to my car and climbed in. Cat and I had a long talk ahead of us. "I booked a flight for seven," she said, sounding tired.

"Good, that'll give us some time to talk."

Cat played with the belt of her designer coat for a minute, before saying, "Thank you for getting me out of that."

I shook my head, marveling at the audacity of my

sister. "So . . . where'd you learn to drive a bull-dozer?"

"I paid the guy I rented it from two grand for a quick lesson, and his promise to look the other way when I drove it off the construction site."

"Construction site?"

"Mmm-hmm. They're putting up an office building two blocks over. I figured I could level the house and have it back to the site in an hour or two, with no one really the wiser."

"Good plan," I said sarcastically.

"It seemed like a good one at the time."

"So, what brought all this on?" I asked.

Cat played some more with her belt before answering me, "I don't know. . . . I guess it's about how Claire makes me feel every time she's near me. I mean, I'm a big cheese, Abby. I run a multimillion-dollar company that I built with my bare hands. I tell thousands of people what to do, but when my mother's in town I'm five years old again, and I can't even get the respect of my own housekeeper."

"Ah," I said. "Well, then, I guess you have no choice."

"No choice about what?"

"No choice but to get your power back."

"What do you mean?"

"Well, today, you defied the law, the police and common sense, Cat. That took balls. Big brass ones at that," I added with a chuckle.

"Go on," she said, smirking herself.

"See? There's no reason someone like that, someone with *cajones* that big, can't kick a couple of unwanted houseguests out of her home, and fire her disloyal housekeeper."

"I know it sounds easy, Abby, but the moment I see Claire's face . . ."

"Cat," I said slowly, "today you ran over a seventy-thousand-dollar automobile and didn't think twice about it. You then proceeded to stare down five cops and come very close to bulldozing a house! What's telling Claire to pack her bags and get the frig out of your house compared to that?"

Cat chuckled. "I see your point."

"You can do this, honey. Take back your power! You're not five and powerless—you're thirty-five and invincible!"

"I can do this?"

"Abso-friggin-lutely!" I said triumphantly as I mentally crossed my fingers.

"I can do this!" Cat said and sat up straighter in her seat.

"That's the ticket!" I said and beamed her the full grill.

"I need a drink before I do this!" Cat said, a note of panic in her voice.

Ah, crap. So close . . .

I looked at the digital clock on the dash. Well, we had time for a shot or two before we needed to be at the airport. I got off the highway at the next exit and made a detour into a little bar and grill that Dutch and I were fond of. I parked and Cat and I got out and went inside. We found two seats at the bar, and Cat ordered a double vodka martini, and I ordered a Coke. Cat downed her drink in about two swigs, and I ordered some food, hoping to soak up a little of the alcohol before she became too obnoxious.

As I was trying to catch the waiter's attention my spidey-sense went off. I had the feeling I needed to turn around, and I swiveled in my seat and stared across the restaurant. There, hidden by the darkness of a booth was James Carlier, watching me with a menacing stare.

As he watched me I got the smallest shiver up my spine. It made me angry to think that it was too much of a coincidence we might be here at the same time. I got up from my seat and whispered to Cat, "I'll be right back," and took a step in James's direction.

As soon as I did that though, he got up, threw some money on the table and headed out the door. I stopped midway to the lobby, knowing that I'd already lost him.

Shrugging my shoulders, I headed back to Cat, and watched as she swigged another glass of vodka. I rolled my eyes and made a slicing motion across my neck to the bartender, cutting her off. Our food arrived and I managed to shovel some into Cat, although it wasn't easy because she was definitely tipsy. I glanced at my watch, and decided to quit while I was ahead. I paid the bill and poured my sister out of the restaurant and into the back of my car and headed for the airport.

An hour later Cat had sobered up a little, and I left her teetering slightly at the security entrance. "I can do this," she said as she hugged me, her words a little slurred.

"I know you can," I answered, and mentally told my inboard lie detector to shut the hell up.

I made it home by seven and walked in the door feeling exhausted. Dutch was sprawled out on the couch reading a book. "Hey, there," he said when I walked in. "Did she get off okay?"

"Yeah, and it only cost me a couple of martinis."

Dutch smiled and grabbed my hand, pulling me down on top of him. "I had a good time with you this morning," he said playfully as he nibbled on my ear.

I smiled, enjoying the delicious feeling. "You mean at breakfast?"

"After breakfast."

"With Madame Dubois?" I giggled as he moved to my neck.

"Before that," he whispered, his hands finding their way underneath my clothes.

"At James's?" I said, only now remembering the encounter at the restaurant.

"Earlier . . ." he said, nibbling on my neck. "Remember? It was warm, wet and soapy."

"Hmmmm," I purred. "I remember something about a shower, but do you think you can refresh my memory?" I pulled my face up to hover my lips alluringly over his.

"I thought you'd never ask," he said and kissed me.

I moaned and curled my fingers into his hair. No one kissed like Dutch. He had the perfect blend of full lips combined with soft touch and skillful tongue. I swooned on top of him as parts of me went moist and parts of him went hard. And then . . . the phone rang.

"Son of a bitch," he swore as he pulled away and reached for the receiver. Looking at the caller ID he groaned and hit the ON button. "Rivers," he barked.

There was a pause, and then he sat up, moving me to the side and grabbing a pad of paper and a pen from the coffee table. "Yes, sir," he said, jotting down a few notes, "Yep. . . . Okay, I got it."

There was another pause. "I'd appreciate it, thank you, sir." He disconnected.

I looked quizzically at him as he stood up and squirmed in his jeans, while giving me a sly look. "Seems the universe is against us consummating our relationship, sweethot."

"Why? Who was that?" I asked.

"My boss. If I come off workman's comp one week early and do a little work from home, they've agreed to give me back my vacation time."

"But you haven't taken a vacation," I said, getting up with him.

"True, however, before workman's comp kicks in, the Bureau soaks up a week of vacation pay. I'd rather take you someplace warm and sunny than spend my vacation hours having you play Nurse Nelly."

"So you have to work?" I asked, looking at my watch and noting the late hour.

"Yeah, there's a file I've gotta run through tonight and give a synopsis to my boss before morning. I'm afraid I'm not going to be any fun for you tonight."

"I can't keep doing this, you know!" I groaned.

"What's that?"

"This!" I insisted pointing to the couch. "I mean, I have *urges,* you know."

Dutch chuckled in spite of himself and came over to cup my chin in his palm. "Listen to me," he began. "I promise you that just as soon as I get the okay to drive I'm gonna whisk you off someplace and satisfy *every single solitary* urge you have. Deal?"

"Whatever," I said, feeling disappointed as I tried to turn away. It always seemed to be something with us.

"Hey," he said holding on to me. "I'm doin' the best I can, you know."

"Yeah, yeah," I said, refusing to let him off the hook, even though I knew it wasn't his fault. "Go to work, cowboy. I'm headed upstairs with Eggy for a little telly."

Dutch gave me a long, deep, parting kiss, then walked into his study. Sexually frustrated, I watched his perfect derriere as he walked away, then sighed, picked up Eggy and trotted up the stairs.

The next morning I was up early again. Dutch had come to bed around three in the morning, and fallen immediately to sleep. I, on the other hand had tossed and turned all night long. When all you can think about is how much you really want a little nooky, there's nothing worse than having to sleep next to someone who could put a little "ooo" in your "ooo-la-la" if only he wasn't snoring.

Sleep deprived and tense, I trotted downstairs, Eggy in tow, and peered into the fridge. Not much stared back.

"Time to go shopping," I said to Eggy, who answered me by wagging his tail. I walked over to a window and peeled back a curtain. The first wisps of sunlight were beginning to streak across the lawn. I looked back at Eggy, who put the tail wagging into overdrive, adding a little snap of his jaws as if to say, "Well get to it!"

"Fine," I said and pulled my coat out of the closet. "I'll go." Eggy hopped up on his back legs and did his version of a Snoopy happy dance. "Yeah, yeah," I said as I opened the door and ran to my car, shivering in the frigid temperature. The market was only a few blocks over and I navigated the streets easily on the way there. I found a parking space in front and headed inside.

Grocery shopping is right up there on my list of least favorite things to do. For a multitude of reasons I can't stand to do it. In part it's because I'm inherently impatient, and buying food that I have to lug home, unpack, put away, only to get it back out again and cook just seems like far too much work.

It's also that I can't stand the long lines. Almost without fail I will get stuck behind some mother of three who has eight thousand coupons ready to be scanned, processed and notarized until the bill for her overflowing grocery cart is less than my gallon of milk. The whole thing drives me bazonkers.

This morning, however, the store was relatively empty and it was clear there'd be no line for me to wait in, which made the shopping a little less of a pain in the tookus. I zoomed through the aisles, pulling down anything that looked good. Mostly ready-to-serve stuff, but here and there I added a few things that required actual work to make . . . like cookie dough, and brownie mix.

A short time later I headed to checkout. As I was unloading my cart my antennae buzzed. I looked around sharply. There, across the store near the exit was James Carlier. "Son of a bitch!" I hissed. What was with this guy? I glared at him as he stared back at me, his face blank. "What?" I mouthed as I challenged him. He held my gaze for a long moment then turned abruptly and left the store.

The whole thing really gave me the creeps because it was obvious he was following my every move, and I had no idea why. What did he want with me that he was unwilling to confront me about? As I set the rest of the items on the counter I made up my mind to find out.

After paying the bill, and groaning at the charge, I wheeled my bags to the car and looked around the lot. There was no sign of James, but I kept a lookout just in case.

I shoved my cart into the buggy post, and headed back to Dutch's, keeping one eye firmly on the rearview mirror. I was almost disappointed that no one seemed to be following me.

Dutch was waiting for me when I came in the door, my arms loaded to the gills. "Where have you been?" he demanded, his brows low and dangerous.

"No, that's okay," I said, struggling to bring in the bags. "I got it . . . don't bother yourself."

Dutch rolled his eyes and grabbed a few of the bags. "I was worried," he said gruffly. "You could'a left me a note, you know."

"You were sleeping."

"Writing me a note would not have woken me up."

"What's the big deal?" I said as I got the bags to the kitchen counter. "I went *shopping*."

"Abby," Dutch began, putting his set on the counter as well, "you know damn well what the big deal is. I told you yesterday that it's not safe for you with that lunatic running around, and the first chance you get you're out the door without an escort."

"Cut me a break, Dutch," I said, annoyed, as I began to feel smothered. "I can take care of myself."

"Really?" Dutch snapped, his voice rising. "And did you come to that conclusion before or after we had to take you to the hospital the other day?"

I turned my back on him. My scare at the grocery store, being cooped up with my demanding boyfriend and all the other events that had recently turned my life topsy-turvey made my frustration bubble up to the surface. Fuming with anger, I began shoving the groceries into any available cabinet, mindless of where they actually belonged, and slamming doors and cabinets as I went about it.

"Or are you talking about when you were tackled at U of M?" he continued.

I shoved the eggs in with the glassware and continued to ignore him.

"Or how about when you narrowly missed getting the stuffing beaten out of you at your office?"

I put the brownie mix and potato chips into the fridge and slammed the door. "I don't need a babysitter, Dutch!" I said as I stomped away into the living room.

"I'm taking your car keys!" he yelled at my back.

That stopped me. I pivoted on my heel and came

back into the kitchen, fury coiling along my limbs. "Don't you *dare!*" I shouted, but it was too late, he'd already plucked them off the counter.

"It's for your own damn good, Edgar. If you won't behave, then I'm just going to have to limit your mobility." And with that he snatched my purse off the counter and rooted around inside.

"Hey!" I yelled and reached for my purse, "Give me that!"

Dutch held it away from me and found what he was looking for, my spare set of keys.

"You are a *son of a bitch!*" I yelled and stormed out of the room, absolutely livid.

"It's for your own good!" he called to me. "I'm only doing it because *I care!*"

"Bite me!" I snapped as I stomped up the stairs, tears stinging my eyes. I hate being treated like a child, and I hated it even more that Dutch was the one treating me like one.

A half hour later I heard Dutch come up the stairs. He walked into the bedroom and sat down on the bed where I was watching television. "Can we talk about this?" he said in a low measured tone.

I reached for the remote and turned the volume up. I'm such a grown-up.

"Abby . . ." he tried.

I turned the volume up higher.

"Fine," he said, then set something on the nightstand and left the room.

After he'd gone I looked over at what he'd placed on the nightstand. A perfect Spanish omelet complete with hash browns and toast sat there looking warm and inviting, and in spite of my angst, my stomach rumbled. Glowering at the food, I leaned over and picked up the plate. "Jerk," I grumbled through a mouthful of food.

After I'd polished off the breakfast I gathered up the plate and utensils and walked them downstairs. I heard music coming from Dutch's study. Good. I tiptoed into the kitchen, and placed my plate and fork on the counter being careful not to make any noise. Then I picked up my coat, which I'd tossed on a chair, and carefully opened up the back door.

One of my worst habits is locking my keys in the car when I stop to pump gas. After calling AAA several times, I'd finally gotten wise and invested in a magnetized Hide-A-Key, which I'd stashed inside one of the wheel wells. Dutch may have thought he was a clever boy for thinking to grab my spare set, but I still had a thing or two left to teach him.

Ducking low along the side of the house, I shuffled over to the passenger side of my car and ran my hand up inside the rear wheel well. My hand connected with a small metal case, and I smiled wickedly. I pulled the Hide-A-Key loose and slid the top open. "Bingo!" I whispered. One car key, and one house key. I didn't waste any more time congratulating myself. I needed some space between me and lover boy, and I needed it pronto.

As I hopped in the Mazda and peeled out of the driveway, I couldn't help but laugh as I imagined the look on Dutch's face when he discovered I'd outsmarted him. "Take that, Cowboy!" I exclaimed and punched the button for the CD player. U2 jammed the interior and I smirked all the way to my house.

I parked my car one block over, because I didn't put it past Dutch to have it towed if he discovered it in my driveway, and trotted back to my front door. When I got inside I shivered. I'd set the thermostat low while I was away. I headed into the kitchen and got a Coke out of the fridge. I stood in the kitchen while I popped the top, trying to think of what to do next.

I really needed to buy some more furniture for my

sparse digs, and I also needed to get to the office and clean up the mess there. My heart sank when I thought of my office and I decided I couldn't face that particular task quite yet. I looked at my watch, and seeing that it was a little after nine a.m., decided to head over to the furniture store.

As soon as I walked into Englander's, I was immediately surrounded by salespeople, all vying for my attention. Within the throng I noticed the guy who'd sold me my couch and I pointed to him. "John, right?"

"Yes! I remember you," he said, shooing the other clerks away. "Did you come back for the puzzle box?"

I smiled and said, "No, thanks. I think I'm still gonna pass on that. What I do need to buy though is the rest of my living and dining-room. What can you show me in the way of an entertainment cabinet?"

John pulled me over to a section of the store and walked me through the purchase of an entertainment cabinet, coffee table, dining room table and chairs and a desk for my study. The process took a while, mostly because my brain was elsewhere and it was hard for me to focus. The truth was that I was beginning to regret my tiff with Dutch this morning. That didn't mean I thought he was right to treat me like a child; however, now that my initial anger had passed I was able to see that he was trying to look out for me.

Still, I needed to establish the ground rule that Dutch could not dictate when I came and went. Outsmarting him by taking off was just good for our relationship—I reasoned. It set the precedence that he couldn't order me around. Then again, I didn't really need to overdo, so I could probably head back to his place after I'd finished with my shopping . . . having made my point and all.

Around ten thirty I was done with my furniture shopping and ready to leave. Just as I was tucking the sales receipt away my intuition buzzed and the hair on my arms stood up on end. I jerked up my head and turned to my right. There, just inside the door was James Carlier . . . again.

Anger welled up inside me and I began to march in his direction. I'd taken only a few steps when I heard my name called from across the store, "Miss Cooper! Miss Cooper!"

I stopped short, and spun around. The voice belonged to the cashier who had just rung me up, and she hurried over to me waving my credit card. "You almost forgot this!" she said as she huffed to a halt in front of me.

With effort I smoothed my features and accepted the card. "Thanks," I said, casting a glance over my shoulder—James was gone. "I must have forgotten it on the counter."

"You don't want to leave that lying around," she said. "Not with all this identity theft going around."

As she said that my intuition went haywire, and I blinked and took a step back.

"You okay?" she asked, putting a concerned hand on my arm.

"Uh . . . yeah . . . fine. Listen, I've gotta go. Thanks for getting this back to me," I said and tucked the card back into my wallet.

"You look a little pale," she insisted.

"Low blood sugar," I offered, and smiled at her.

"Oh, we have doughnuts here if you want one."

"No, thanks. I've got a protein bar in the car. And I gotta fly." Not waiting for her to respond I turned and left the store. I trotted to my car and got in, my mind set on one purpose. I turned the engine over and pointed the car in the direction of *Opalescence*. It was time to have a little tête-à-tête with James Carlier.

Chapter Twelve

The drive to James's shop took a lot longer than expected. The moment I hit the road I noticed cops on what seemed like every street corner. I had little doubt that Dutch had called in a few favors and was even now having the streets scoured for any sign of me. Trying to avoid detection forced me into taking back streets and side alleys.

The problem is that I have a vanity plate that makes it really easy to spot me. When I'd purchased the Mazda, I'd indulged in a plate that noted my profession: LTWRKR.

For those not in the know, lightworker is one of those hip and trendy metaphysical terms that means someone who works with the Light. As I know of no better way to describe what it feels like when I'm in psychic mode and giving a reading, I'd always had an affection for the term. Now, as I navigated the bumpy back alley of a hardware store, anxious to get to Opalescence, I was beginning to regret my impulsiveness at the DMV.

At around eleven thirty I finally arrived at the jewelry store. After parking in a garage two blocks over and out of sight, making sure to back into the parking space, I double stepped it over to James's shop, keeping a lookout for police cars or foot patrolmen. I made it to the store without incident, and just as I reached for the handle the door swung open unexpectedly.

"Whoa!" I said, jumping back as a woman carrying a box nearly crashed into me.

"Excuse me," she said with a sniffle.

After taking another look at her, I realized this was the salesgirl who'd gone to lunch when I'd first met James. "Oh! Hello," I said as I held the door open while she struggled with her box. "Maria, isn't it?"

Maria nodded and pulled her head down low in an attempt to hide her face, which I only now noticed was tear streaked. "If you'll excuse me," she said as she pushed past me.

"Hey," I called as I let go of the door and moved to walk next to her. "What's the matter?"

Maria kept walking, her head low and tears dribbling down her cheeks. "I'm fine," she said and hitched up the box.

"You don't look fine," I said, refusing to go away. "Come on, what's the matter?"

Abruptly, Maria stopped and dissolved into a fit of shoulder-shaking tears. I took the box from her, which was about to slip through her hands anyway, and laid it on the ground, only now noticing that it was full of small personal effects—an umbrella, an empty Tupperware container, a small radio and a box of Kleenex. I took one of the tissues and handed it to her. "Hey, there," I said gently, putting a consoling hand on her shoulder. "It's okay, really. Whatever this is about can't be all that bad."

"He fired us!" she wailed.

"What?" I asked. "Who?"

"Mr. Carlier. He just walked in this morning and told Josh and me to pack up our things and clear out. No explanation, no severance pay, just handed us our final paychecks and buh-bye!"

"Oh, Maria," I said, rubbing her shoulder. "I'm so sorry!"

"I've worked there for three years! I *loved* that job!" she blubbered between sobs.

My heart went out to her and I offered comfort the only way I truly knew how. "Do you know what I do for a living, Maria?"

She shook her head and waved the tissue at me like she couldn't care less.

"I'm a professional psychic, and what I see for you right now is you'll have about two weeks where you're feeling a little lost, unsure of what to do, but then there will be a terrific job opportunity for you, doing pretty much the same thing you did here."

Maria's sobbing subsided a bit. "Really?"

I scanned her energy to be sure, "Yes. You're definitely going to be working with jewelry again. You're good at it. And I see a little more money too. There's something about a raise, or a promotion, so I would say that whoever is lucky enough to hire you will give you more responsibility, and even a little more money than you were making here."

Maria looked at me. "And I only have to wait two weeks?"

"Don't hold me to that," I warned. "I'm not the greatest with time, but there's definitely the number two in my head and a feeling of immediacy, which typically means within two weeks. It could be just a tad bit longer though, so let's say three just to be safe."

"I can wait that long," Maria said. "Still, I'm really going to miss this place. And Mr. Carlier too. I really liked him, and that's what makes his firing me so hard. He was such a great boss—until recently, that is."

"He's been different lately?" I asked, my intuition buzzing.

"Yeah, about a week ago he started acting all weird."

"Like what?"

"Well, for one thing he was always checking the back door, to make sure it was locked. And he would jump when the phone rang. Then he got robbed and things got extra weird."

"I can imagine that getting robbed would make anyone act a little off."

"Yeah, I mean, we expected him to be even more paranoid, but instead he just didn't seem to care about business anymore. He'd show up late, leave about ten minutes after he got here and couldn't care less what we sold for the day. Mr. Carlier used to be a real stickler for details and the books, and all of the sudden he just doesn't want anything to do with it. Then, yesterday, I heard him on the phone with Mr. Breger and he was yelling at him really loud . . ."

"Who's Mr. Breger?" I interrupted.

"Willy Breger," she explained. "He's our accountant. From what I hear he's been the store's accountant forever. He even did the books for Mr. Carlier's grandfather when he owned the store. Anyway, I heard them arguing, and at the end James says, 'If you don't like it then I'll go find another accountant!' and slammed down the phone. I guess I shoulda known then, huh?"

I had been listening intently to Maria, and her question took me off guard. "Should have known what, Maria?"

"That Josh and I were next to get the ax. Josh was

so mad he didn't even stick around to pack his box. He just grabbed his tools, flipped off Mr. Carlier, and walked out the door. I really liked Josh. Damn, I'm gonna miss him!" And with that Maria dissolved into another round of tears.

I rubbed her shoulder some more and looked around self-consciously. People were beginning to stare. "Hey, now," I said. "Come on, Maria. It'll be okay. My feeling is that you'll see Josh again, and you'll love this new job too."

Another gulp and Maria nodded her head, then bent down to retrieve her box. "Thanks," she said. "Sorry to lay this all on you. You've been really nice, but I just want to go home, okay?"

"Sure," I said with a smile. "Good luck to you."

Maria gave me a sad smile and walked away. As I watched her go, I felt an even more powerful wave of anger wash through me. Who did this Carlier guy think he was, anyway? Maria was a good, loyal employee; her energy said as much. Why would he fire someone like her?

I pivoted then on my heel and walked back to the store, stopping abruptly in front of a sign posted there that read CLOSED UNTIL FURTHER NOTICE.

I tried the door but it was locked so I cupped my hands around my eyes and peered through the pane. The interior was dark and no movement was evident from inside. "That was fast," I said out loud as I moved away from the door. In the time that I'd walked halfway down the block with Maria, and talked with her, Carlier had closed up shop and vacated the premises.

I scowled as I backed away from the door, pissed that I'd wasted so much of my afternoon chasing after some nutcase. Wasting no more of my time, I pivoted around and headed back to the parking garage. When I came out of the stairwell my day got a whole lot worse.

Parked in front of my Mazda was a shiny, brand-new BMW 750i sedan with two occupants I knew very well. Milo sat in the driver's seat and smirked as I came closer to the car. Dutch sat next to him and wore a look that could freeze a polar bear's ass.

"Shit," I said under my breath, as I looked around nervously, wondering if I should bolt or cop an attitude. "What?" I demanded as I got up to the car, opting for the latter.

Dutch got out, his look darkening to a level that made me shiver involuntarily. "Get in the car, Abby," he growled.

I thought about giving him a smarty-pants reply and running for it, but didn't have it in me. With a shrug I got in the backseat of Milo's car and pouted with my arms crossed.

"Hey, Abby," Milo said, eyeing me in the rear-view mirror.

"Milo," I answered as Dutch got in next to me.

"This is how it's gonna go down," Dutch said, pivoting to eye me critically. "You're going to hop into your car, and drive back to my house like a good girl. When we get there, you and I are gonna have a serious little chat."

"Bite me," I said, lowering my own eyebrows. I don't cotton to being talked to like a child—just ask my mother.

"Abby," Dutch said in a tone that meant business.

"Who do you think you are to tell me what to do anyway?" I said, my voice rising as my temper flared.

"I *think* I'm the guy who's trying to keep you from being another *murder statistic,* that's who!" Dutch yelled.

"Oh, for crying out loud!" I shouted. "I can bloody

well take care of myself!" And with that I began to get out of Milo's car.

"Hey!" Milo shouted at both of us. "Abby, hold on, and Dutch, shut up and sit there!"

I paused with my hand on the door and one foot out of the car, waiting Milo out. "What?" I asked finally.

"Abby, let's go back to Dutch's and the three of us can talk about it, okay?"

"He took my keys!" I yelled, refusing to give in.

"Obviously, you found another set," Milo said, indicating those I held in my other hand.

"He can't treat me like a child, Milo," I insisted as I got the rest of the way out and slammed the door. I walked over to my car without looking back at either of them. I hated that Dutch was being such a jerk, and debated with myself about the wisdom of going back to his house to work things out, even with Milo playing referee.

I got in my car and started the engine, and waited grudgingly while Milo backed up the Beemer and allowed me to pull out. I drove for a few minutes, trying to let the rational side of my brain talk some sense into the angry five-year-old side and eventually it worked because I ended up back at Dutch's, noting with only slight irritation that Milo pulled in right behind me and cut off my exit.

We filed into Dutch's house and I took a seat on the chair next to the couch, pulling a pillow protectively over my lap and screwing my face up into half pout and half snarl.

Dutch and Milo sat on opposite ends of the couch, and after getting settled Milo said, "Abby, I know you think that Dutch is being overprotective, but you've got to give the guy a break. I mean, the entire time he's known you, you've had one crazy psycho after another coming after you."

I gave that statement some thought, and had to admit that in the last couple of months I'd seen my share of nutcases. Even now, there seemed to be another one lurking around every street corner, grocery store and furniture gallery. "It's not like I go looking for this stuff, ya know," I said defiantly. "Stuff just happens to me."

Dutch rolled his eyes and shook his head at his partner as if to say, "See what I have to put up with?"

For obvious reasons, this really hurt my feelings, and as tears stung my eyes I snapped at him, "If you don't like it, Cowboy, then all you have to do is wash your hands of me and walk away."

"Oh, come on, Abby! Cut me a break, would ya?" he snapped back.

"Seriously, if you're sick of babysitting me, then maybe we should just go our separate ways and be done with it." The words were flowing out of my mouth of their own accord, and even though I didn't mean them, I was saying them anyway.

"Is that what you want?" Dutch asked, glowering at me.

"Hey, guys," Milo said, his hands in a time-out gesture.

"Maybe," I sneered.

"You know where the door is," Dutch said and turned his head away from me.

"Whoa!" Milo said and stood up, his hands going to his hips as he chastised us. "You two are just about the most pigheaded, stubborn malcontents I've ever laid eyes on." Turning to me he said, "Abby, do you know that all Dutch ever talks about these days is *you*? The guy's crazy about you. Head over heels. Gaga . . ."

"Milo," Dutch warned, shooting daggers at him.

"And, Dutch, Abby is so nuts about you that she was willing to put her life on hold for a full month to nurse your sorry bullet-riddled butt back to health, a job trained nurses wouldn't take if you paid them."

I squirmed uncomfortably in my chair, as it dawned on me what this entire argument was about. I was used to my independence and freedom, not to mention a certain amount of alone time. Ever since I'd moved in with Dutch, I'd felt confined, and cagey. When he'd taken my keys away, he'd also taken my only ticket to freedom, and that's what I was really upset about.

"Now that we've established that you two really, really like each other, what say we call a truce and agree to talk about what steps we need to take to protect you," Milo said, pointing to me, "without making you feel smothered and what you," he said, pivoting now to Dutch, "can do to give her a little space until we catch this guy."

"It's not safe for her out there," Dutch replied.

"Agreed, but you can't watch her every second, buddy. She's a grown woman."

There was a long pause among us as we all pondered that. After a minute I looked at Dutch and said, "I keep my keys, but agree to an escort for a while. And by escort I don't always mean you."

"Like who?" Dutch wanted to know.

"Like Dave, or Milo or Mary-friggin-Poppins if she's available," I said moodily.

Milo gave Dutch a look that said, "I'd take that deal if I were you."

"Fine," Dutch said and got up to walk into the kitchen, where he returned a moment later with two sets of keys. "Here," he said, dropping them into my outstretched palm. They jingled when they hit my hand and a moment later Dutch closed his hand over mine and said, "I'm only trying to look after you because I am a little nuts about you, Edgar."

"Good to know," I said with a small smile.

"Thank God that's over," Milo said, sitting down on the couch again and lifting the remote. "I should get paid for this stuff," he added as he tuned the TV to ESPN.

Just then Dutch's office phone rang and he headed to the study to answer it. I sat in the chair for a long moment, fingering the keys that he'd given back to me and thinking about the two of us, wondering how couples managed to wade through all the shit that complicates a relationship. Sighing I got up and headed into the kitchen to put my keys and purse away. My intuition buzzed just then and I had the feeling I needed to look on the counter. There, my eye fell on the phone book and the name Willy Breger floated into my mind.

Curiously, I opened it and toured the B's. Sure enough I found a listing for W. Breger in the town next to Birmingham called Bloomfield Hills. I wrote the address and phone number down and decided to tell Dutch and Milo about my conversation with Maria. Maybe we could call him and get some dirt on James.

As I came back into the living room, Dutch was walking back in from the study, carrying a small stack of papers.

"What'cha got there?" I asked.

"Carlier's tax returns for the last three years."

"His tax returns?" I asked, peering over his shoulder to take a better look.

"Yeah. My buddy at the Bureau just e-mailed them to me."

"Anything interesting?" Milo asked, hitting the MUTE button on the TV.

"Only one thing I've noticed so far," Dutch said, thumbing through the returns.

"We're waiting," I said when he paused to turn back to a page he'd already viewed.

"Do you know if Carlier's Jewish?" he asked me.

I looked at him oddly for a moment, then I remembered the small crucifix I'd seen in James's office. "No, I don't think so. I believe he's Catholic, why?"

"He makes a sizable donation to the Holocaust Survivors' Fund every year."

"How sizable?" Milo asked.

"Fifty thousand last year alone."

My jaw dropped. "Did you say *fifty* thousand?"

Dutch nodded his head. "Another forty-six the year before, and thirty the year before that."

Milo whistled. "That's some profit he must be turning to be able to afford that kind of a donation."

"That's just it," Dutch said, looking the papers over once again. "His profit for all three years was only two times that. By this account he donates half his profits to this one charity."

I remembered my conversation with Maria just then and chimed in, "I may know of someone who could help us find out a little more about that particular line item."

"Who?" Dutch asked, finally looking up from the papers.

"Carlier's accountant. I talked with one of his ex-employees today, and she suggested that James had it out with his tax man, and they went their separate ways. I've got the guy's name and number right here if you'd like it."

Dutch grinned at me, his features so much softer than a mere twenty minutes before. "Good job, Edgar. Milo, you up for a road trip?"

"As long as I get to drive," Milo said, standing up.

He got no argument from Dutch and me as we followed him out the door.

Fifteen minutes later we arrived at a small office building on the southern end of Bloomfield Hills. Milo parked his Beemer in the very last parking slot at the back of the building, miles from any other car. "Don't want anyone to scratch my new toy," he said when Dutch and I gave him a look.

"No sweat, buddy," Dutch said in a flat tone. "I mean, I'm only recovering from a bullet hole in the thigh. The remote possibility that this baby could be scratched is worth any extra discomfort."

Milo gave him a look. "Well, ain't that a pain in the ass," he deadpanned, and got a glower from Dutch as I smiled at the pair. We all got out then and headed into the building, pausing once we got inside to check the wallboard and look up the suite number for Breger. Milo spotted his name first. "He's on the second floor, suite 207."

Dutch groaned as we headed toward the stairs, because even though he was getting around now without his cane, stairs were still tough for him. We made our way slowly up and down the hallway, pausing in front of Breger's suite. Dutch knocked on the door and a moment later we heard a gruff voice say, "Come in!"

We stepped inside a small, single-room office with a desk at the far end, stacks of folders piled everywhere on the floor and no one in sight behind a huge barrier of paper lining the edge of the desk, like the Great Wall of China. We all came up short at the scene, and after a beat or two up rose Breger. He was taller than I expected, almost as tall as Dutch, with an additional fifty pounds of girth. He had a broad brow, eyebrows that looked like furry caterpillars and jowls so pronounced that they pulled the corners of his mouth down.

"Yeah?" he asked while we stared at him.

"Mr. William Breger?" Milo asked.

"Mr. Breger was my old man, you can call me

Willy," he corrected, cocking his head to the side like a big bulldog.

"Nice to meet you. I'm Milo Johnson of the Royal Oak Police Department," Milo said, flipping his badge open for Willy's inspection. "This is Agent Rivers of the FBI and our associate, Abigail Cooper. We're here to talk to you about one of your clients."

"Got a warrant?" Willy asked, quick on the draw.

Milo smiled turning on the charm and answered, "We don't need one in this case, Mr. Breger. We're really just here to ask some character questions about a James Carlier."

"You mean the son of a bitch that owes me ten grand and won't pay up? Ask any question you want, Detective, I'll be happy to answer off the record until you get a warrant." Willy said in a change of demeanor that took us all off guard.

"He owes you how much?" Dutch asked, taking out his notebook to jot down some notes.

"Ten stinking grand. I do his books all year for him, and get his taxes ready early on account of he's been my client for so long. Hell, his grandpappy was my client for nearly twenty years. And all a sudden, he decides he wants to do his own taxes and tells me to go to hell. Son of a bitch. Ooops. Sorry, hon," he said, noticing me.

"It's okay," I said. "I've been known to use that term myself."

Dutch coughed pointedly and I elbowed him while Milo asked, "When did he tell you he didn't want you to do his books anymore?"

"The other day," Willy said, leaning against the desk and threatening to topple over one of the great stacks with his bulk. "I call him to review his deductions and go over his donations and when I get to that part he goes ballistic. He tells me that I'm fired, and not to file anything or he'll sue me. Forty stinking years of hard work down the toilet like that," Willy lamented, snapping his fingers.

My intuition buzzed and I asked, "You mentioned something about donations—we know that Mr. Carlier had been giving generously to the Holocaust Survivors' Fund. Can you tell us a little bit about his motivation for doing that?"

Willy scratched his head. "Wish I could, 'cuz it's been a big fat mystery to me for as long as I've done his books. His grandpappy sure never donated to no charity. Hell, that miser'd steal from his own mother. But James was different. The moment he inherited the store he got rid of all the inventory, mostly at a loss, and started selling only opals. Then every year he'd scrape together the profits, cut them in half and donate that to the Holocaust fund."

"Is he Jewish?" Dutch asked.

"No, and that's why it was so odd. I mean, not that you have to be Jewish to donate to the Holocaust fund, but as far as I knew he didn't have a direct connection to the organization, the Holocaust or any of the victims. He would never tell me why he did it, he just insisted I write the check and send it. Like, this year, he told me two weeks ago that he wanted to donate the entire proceeds of a house he'd sold, plus fifty percent of last year's profits, then two days ago he yells at me for making out the checks. The guy's gone wacko if you ask me."

Something else was tickling my mind and I asked, "You mentioned that James got rid of all his inventory when his grandfather passed away. Why the change from traditional jewelry to opals?"

"Beats the hell outta me. Jean-Paul . . . uh, that's

his grandpappy, he used to do pretty good, let me tell you. He was also obsessively meticulous about his records. Do you know I still have every record of every sales transaction that guy ever made?"

Dutch looked around the cramped room. "Here?" he asked.

"Naw. I got a storage place in Pontiac."

"Why would you keep all those old records?" Milo asked.

"Well," Willy thought, rubbing his scruffy chin, "Most of it's just 'cuz I'm lazy, and the other part is 'cuz when Jean-Paul was alive, he insisted on keeping track of his inventory, even after he'd sold it. Now that I've been fired, I guess it's high time I got rid of that old junk, huh?"

I smiled at Willy. Despite his gruff exterior, I liked the guy. Just then my intuition buzzed again, and I said, "Willy, could we take a look at some of those sales receipts before you toss them?"

"Sure, I guess. I'll have to get them out of storage, though. How about you folks come back around here tomorrow around six and I'll let you cart away as many boxes as you'd like."

"How many boxes are there?"

"Oh, I'd say around ten or so."

"Are they big?"

"Banker's Boxes, you can manage them," Willy said, giving me a wink. "Jean-Paul didn't move a ton of merchandise, mostly 'cuz his prices were so high, but what he moved he made a tidy profit on."

"It's not too much trouble?" I asked, looking at Willy's energy and noting an area of caution around him.

"Nope. I need to clean out the old bin anyway."

"Just don't overexert yourself," I said, troubled by

the yellow light I saw blinking in my head. "If you want our help with the boxes, we can meet you at the storage place."

Willy waved me off. "Naw, it's fine. Listen, you guys get outta here while I get back to work and make some time for myself to go to the storage place tomorrow, okay?"

"We appreciate the help Willy, thanks," Milo said, taking his leave.

"See you tomorrow at six," I said as I nudged Dutch, who jotted something down before following us out the door.

We headed back to the car and piled in. Milo started the engine but didn't take the Beemer out of park. Instead he turned in his seat to me and Dutch and asked, "So, what do you make of it?"

"Not sure," Dutch said, looking through his notes.

"It's like one giant puzzle, with all these layers of interconnected pieces," I said, shaking my head. "And the truly screwy part is that I know they all fit together, but I don't know how."

"There's one lead we haven't tracked down yet," Dutch offered.

"What's that?" I asked.

"Simone Renard."

"Madame Dubois's friend?"

"And Jean-Paul's ex-girlfriend."

"What're we waiting for?" Milo asked, pulling out of the space. "Just tell me where to go," he said, and we headed back toward Royal Oak.

We arrived at Simone's house a little while later, and I noticed a light on in the living room. "Good," I said when we pulled up. "It looks like they're home."

We piled out of the car and headed up the front walk. Before we even got to the door it opened and a small woman with large eyes and a hawkish nose peered out the storm door at us. "Yes?" she asked meekly.

"Simone Renard?" Dutch asked, heading up the steps and extending his hand in a warm gesture.

"Yes?" she asked warily.

"How do you do?" Dutch asked, trying not to scare her. "I am Agent Rivers with the FBI, and this is my associate, Detective Johnson, and our associate Miss Abigail Cooper. May we come in and chat with you for a few minutes about an old friend of yours, Jean-Paul Carlier?"

Simone's face wavered between fear and curiosity before curiosity won out. "Come in," she said after a moment.

We walked into the house and were struck by the smell of Ben Gay, which hung cloyingly in the air. The house was furnished almost completely with antiques and vintage collectibles. Simone led us into the living room and indicated two weathered couches, arranged in an L, for us to sit down on. Dutch and I took one side, Milo took the other and Simone remained standing. "My sister is sleeping in the bedroom, so I'd appreciate it if you'd keep your voices low," she said.

Dutch nodded and took out his notebook again. Flipping it open he began, "As I said, we're here to talk to you about Jean-Paul Carlier. We understand the two of you were quite close at some point?"

Simone fiddled with the necklace at her neck. "Yes, we knew each other quite well for many years. We used to go together."

"Can you tell us a little bit about him?" Dutch asked.

Simone's face seemed to soften ever so slightly. "I met Jean-Paul at a local dance in 1969. My parents were French immigrants, you see, and even though my sister and I were born here, our parents insisted that we immerse ourselves in the local French community. The community put on dances several times a year and I'd been attending them since I was in high school. I stopped going after I was married, but started again after my husband was killed in the Korean War.

"I met Jean-Paul at one of these functions and he was a looker. He was so handsome back then, and full of himself too, let me tell you," she said with a chuckle. "He thought every girl wanted to be with him because he was rich, and handsome, but I liked him because he was smart."

"So you were with him for all those years until he died in 1990?" I asked. Something was tugging at me and I was anxious to follow the lead.

Simone turned to me with one eyebrow raised, almost in challenge. "Yes, we were together for nearly thirty-one years."

"Was he a faithful man?" I asked boldly.

"As much as he could be," she answered, her guard going up. "Besides, in the end he always came home to me. It was me he wanted at the end of the day, me who nursed him through his illness until he died in my arms. There was no one else of consequence in all the time we were together," she sniffed.

"And, what about Liza?" I asked, digging in.

A look of surprise flashed across her face, she'd been caught off guard. "I'm sorry, who?"

"We know Jean-Paul had another girlfriend for a period of time. A young woman who lived with him until she disappeared. You must remember her."

"I don't know who you're talking about," Simone said sharply as my lie detector went haywire. "As I said, there was only me. Jean-Paul may have stepped out a few times with the women that were constantly throwing themselves at his feet, but I was his true love. In the end it was me he came crawling back to every time."

There was such a tone of bitterness in that last sentence that I almost backed off. But I remembered suddenly the beautiful woman at the bottom of the stairwell, and pushed Simone a little more. "What do you think happened to her, Mrs. Renard?"

"Happened to whom?"

"Liza," I said, irritated that this crotchety old woman was protecting a dead man. "You must know he killed her—after all, I'm sure he told you everything."

Simone's hand flew to her mouth to hide the gasp that nearly escaped her. "I think you should leave now," she said when she'd recovered herself.

"You did know, didn't you?" I said as I scanned her energy.

"My sister will be up soon, and I cannot have the three of you disturb her," Simone said, her voice shaking.

"And you know even more beyond that," I said, watching and assessing her carefully. "You're hiding the rest of his secrets, aren't you?"

"I don't have any idea what you're talking about," Simone snapped. "And I've asked you to leave!"

Dutch and Milo got up together and nudged me to back off and follow them. I was mad for reasons I couldn't really identify, so as I got up I couldn't resist saying to her, "We're going to figure it out, Simone. We are going to find out exactly who she was and why he killed her, and if you had anything to do with it, we'll make sure you get exactly what you have coming to you."

That did it. Simone reacted as if I'd struck her, and she recoiled backward slightly, her hand fluttering to her heart as she said, "I don't know what happened to her!"

Dutch and Milo paused on their way out of the living room, giving her their full attention, and I sat back down on the couch.

"But you know something," I prodded, waiting her out.

She looked at me like a scared rabbit, her eyes large and her lips quivering. "You have to understand," she began, "she was much younger than Jean-Paul, and she was pretty. He was lured by her advances, duped by her schemes. . . ."

"What schemes?" Dutch said, returning to the couch.

Simone shook her head back and forth, fighting with herself about whether to talk or stay quiet. While she fought her internal battle she began fiddling with the necklace at her throat again. It was only then that I realized how stunning the diamond necklace was.

"That was a gift from Jean-Paul, wasn't it?" I asked, intuitively knowing that it was flashy enough to assuage a guilty conscience.

Simone's hand dropped to her waist. "She betrayed him," she said by way of answer.

"How so?" Milo asked as he hovered in the doorway of the living room.

Simone sighed, and her shoulders slumped, and she started from the beginning. "Liza came here in the early seventies. She showed up one night at the dance hall at the Community House on Main Street. I remember the night she made her first appearance. She was younger than most of the rest of us, and she was very petite and pretty. She spotted Jean-Paul right away, and before I knew it the two were off by the punch bowl, or dancing right in front of me. It was a slap in the face, and I demanded that Jean-Paul stop flirting with her.

"He waved me away and told me to go home, he'd be along later. But he never came over. After that night he also stopped calling and before I knew it the two of them were quite the item. It was outrageous!" Simone said, bitterness heavy in her tone. "She was less than half his age, and we all knew she was up to no good, but Jean-Paul was blind to her treachery. Then, one day, Liza disappeared, and Jean-Paul came crawling back to me, begging me to take him back. He said that Liza had stolen his most precious gems and fled the country, and he never spoke of her again."

"But you knew differently," I said, noting the shift in her energy. She was still hiding something.

Simone gave me a cold, hard look. "He used to talk in his sleep," she said.

"What did he say?" Dutch asked.

"It wasn't anything specific," Simone insisted. "Just that there were times when he would ramble, and he would say things like, 'Give them back or I'll kill you!'"

"Give what back?" Dutch again.

"I don't know," Simone said, shaking her head back and forth. "But there was one night where he had a particularly vivid dream, and he almost killed me."

We all kept silent and waited for her to continue. After a moment she said, "He was calling her name, like he was trying to find her, and then he just grabbed me by the neck and started to choke me. He kept calling me Liza, and screamed that I had betrayed him. Luckily, I managed to wake him up before he strangled me, and I never slept in the same room with him again."

"What else can you tell us about her?" Dutch said.

Simone looked thoughtful for a moment, then offered, "I knew she wasn't French, even though she claimed to come from the same region as Jean-Paul."

"How did you know?"

"It was her accent," she said. "She spoke perfect

French, but it was almost too perfect. And there were times when she would slip, and there was a hint of something . . . maybe a German influence that we noticed. But Jean-Paul refused to acknowledge it. He was blinded by her beauty and interest in him."

"Do you know her last name?" I asked.

"Proditio," Simone answered.

"That doesn't sound French," Milo said.

"It's Latin," Dutch said. "It means betrayed."

As I cocked an impressed eyebrow at my boyfriend, Simone swallowed nervously, perhaps feeling like she'd revealed too much. "If there are no more questions, I would like it if you would leave now."

Her request was more demand, and I nodded as we all stood up to leave. Partway to the door, however, Dutch turned back to her as something occurred to him and he asked, "How did you get along with Jean-Paul's grandsons, James and Jean-Luke?"

Simone scowled. "Those two," she said with a wave of her hand, "horrible boys."

"Really?" he prodded.

"At least Jean-Luke was. Always up to something. After his grandfather died he insisted I move out of the house. I'd been living with Jean-Paul and taking care of him throughout his illness, not that either of them ever lifted a finger. They forced me to move in with my sister without even so much as a thank you. Ungrateful scamps."

"Thanks again for the information," Dutch said, and took out one of his business cards, which he set on an end table near the doorway. "If you think of anything else, please call us."

Simone gave him a cold stare. She'd call just as soon as the forecast in hell projected a winter storm warning.

We left Simone's house and I involuntarily shivered. "You cold?" Dutch asked me, taking note.

"Naw," I answered with a smile. "Just that the energy in that house is pretty awful. By the way," I said as we headed toward the car, "you have a message on your voice mail that you need to pick up."

Dutch grinned as we all got in the car, and as Milo started the engine he reached for his cell phone and checked all his mailboxes. Sure enough there was a message on his office phone from T.J. "He's got something on that crest I sent him," Dutch explained while he listened. "Let's grab dinner first, then head back and call him."

We called in a carryout to Prontos! Deli and Milo double-parked while I dashed in to pick it up. We were home a few minutes later, and Milo distributed the food, while I grabbed the beer and Dutch called T.J. "He's not answering," Dutch said as he tried another number.

"What time did he leave the message?" I asked, wondering by how long we'd missed him.

"About two minutes before you told me to pick up the voice mail," Dutch said with a grin as he listened to T.J.'s recorded voice through the phone line. Dutch left messages on all T.J.'s lines and we dug into our dinners.

While we ate we talked about all of the pieces we'd discovered and the possible ways they interconnected, but there were still some pieces missing, and I kept reiterating that I felt the box and the notebook were the keys. If we could only unravel why they were so important to Jean-Luke, and what their connection was to Liza, maybe we could uncover the truth behind her murder, and Jean-Luke's obsession.

As I was cleaning up from dinner the phone rang. Dutch answered it, and I heard snatches of the short conversation, "Uh-huh. Yep. Sounds great. See you then." And he hung up.

I came into the living room as he set the phone down and he explained. "That was T.J. He didn't want to discuss it on the phone, and he's asked us to take another road trip to Ann Arbor tomorrow."

"I'm in," I said.

"I'm not," Milo said, disappointment on his face. "I've got a meeting downtown with the mayor and the city council for most of the day."

"Hmmm, aren't *you* the up-and-comer?" I teased Milo.

"It's not like that," he said, waving me off.

I honed in on him for a moment, noticing something new in his energy. "Yes it is. Why didn't you tell us you were interested in a political career?"

Dutch looked sharply at Milo, surprise on his features, as Milo scowled at me. "Does anything get past you?" he asked.

"Not much," I said with a grin. "You should go for it, by the way. You'd make a great addition to the council. That's what you're thinking of running for, right?"

Milo rolled his eyes at me and sighed. "Damn it, Abby. A man needs to keep certain things to himself, you know."

"You're going to win . . ." I teased.

This news brightened Milo's mood considerably, "Really? 'Cuz there's only one slot open in the next election, and even now there are a lot of interested candidates."

"I'm not saying you won't have some competition. But if you play your cards right and campaign hard, you'll win the election all right."

Milo grinned, even while Dutch looked at him skeptically. "Politics?" he asked his friend.

"What?" Milo said. "I'm supposed to stay a detective my whole life?"

Dutch shrugged his shoulders and said, "Okay, okay . . . whatever you want, buddy."

At that moment Milo's cell phone chirped, and he looked at the readout with a frown. "Uh-oh."

"What?" I asked.

"Noelle," he said, indicating his wife. "She's probably wondering where I am, and I promised to be home in time for dinner."

I smiled wryly and said, "Hope you left room, 'cuz something tells me she's not going to like the fact that you already ate."

"Good point," Milo said and flipped open the phone. "Hey, honey. I was just about to call you . . ."

Liar, liar . . . pants on fire . . .

After Milo left to eat his second dinner for the evening, Dutch and I sat on the couch near enough to be companionable, but not close enough to touch. Finally he looked at me and asked, "You still mad at me?"

"A little. You still mad at me?"

"A little," he said with a grin, then swept his arm around my waist and pulled me close. "I don't like fighting with you," he said when he'd settled me in the crook of his arm.

"Then don't."

"Sometimes, it's so hard to resist . . ."

"I know what you mean."

"I have some work to do. Is it okay if I wake you when I come to bed?"

"Yeah," I said, getting up to head upstairs. "Just don't make it too late, okay Cowboy?"

Dutch stood up as well. "You got it, pardner." And he bent low to kiss me and give a little taste of my wake-up call for later.

The next morning I woke up to an empty bed. I sat up and looked around the bedroom, remembering that Dutch was supposed to sweep me off my feet and carry me to some blissful place that I had yet to visit. "Jerk," I said into the empty room.

I threw off the covers, grabbed my robe and headed downstairs, following the sound of sawing logs into Dutch's study. He was sitting reclined in his office chair with his mouth open and a terrific sound filling the room. I rolled my eyes and headed into the kitchen where I put on the coffee and began to scramble Eggy's breakfast.

After I'd fed Eggy and Virgil, I padded back into the study with a steaming cup of black coffee and wafted it under Dutch's nose. He snarfed and grunted a few times, then woke with a start. "Wha . . . ?" he asked, coming around and rubbing his bloodshot eyes.

"Hey there, Romeo," I sang with a smile.

"What time is it?" he mumbled, taking the coffee and giving me a wink.

"Seven thirty."

"Oh, shit!" he said looking at me guiltily. "Why didn't you come down and get me?"

"Like *you,* I was sleeping," I deadpanned.

"Sorry, sweethot. I'll make it up to you, I promise."

I nodded with a smirk. "I'm counting on it."

"We're supposed to meet T.J. at nine thirty before his first class. Why don't you head up and get ready first."

"Will I be showering alone?" I asked playfully.

"Uh . . . ." Dutch hemmed. "The thing is I still have a little work to do. But I . . ."

"Promise to make it up to me later, yeah, yeah," I said with a flip of my hand as I walked away.

"I will, you know!"

"Promises, promises," I called back from the hallway.

Two hours later we were in T.J.'s office sitting in his plush leather chairs while he finished up the phone call he'd been on when he waved us in from the hallway. "Sorry about that," he said as he replaced the receiver.

"No problem," Dutch said with a smile. "We're just really glad you could help us out on this, T.J."

I wasn't sure what Dutch had said to T.J. in the days following our last visit about T.J.'s obvious affection for him, but the two seemed to have come to an understanding and had gotten past any uncomfortable feelings toward one another. And I had to admit, the fact that Dutch was a pretty open-minded guy made me feel that much more affection for him. "So whata'ya got for us?"

T.J. clapped his hands together excitedly as he said, "I haven't had a chance to analyze the notebook any further, but I have come across something quite interesting about that crest you e-mailed me."

Dutch nodded and leaned forward with interest. "I'm all ears."

"The crest is from a noble family with a long history out of Vienna, Austria."

Dutch's mouth opened and he turned to me. "Julie Andrews . . ." he said.

"The hills *are* alive." I winked back.

"I'm not following," T.J. said, looking back and forth at us.

"Not important, you were saying?" I said to him.

T.J. shrugged and continued. "Anyway, the crest is of the von Halpstadt family, a prominent and extremely wealthy clan with ties to Austrian nobility way back when."

"Way back when as in no longer?" Dutch asked.

"That's the interesting part that I'm just getting to," T.J. explained. "You see, the family had a bit of good fortune in the sixteenth century when raiding Turks invaded Austria and gained significant ground until they reached the von Halpstadt stronghold. Under the guidance of Helmut IV, the Turks were soundly defeated and sent packing. As a reward for defending the territory against the invading marauders, the Austrian adjunct to Pope Gregory XIII awarded Helmut significant landholdings and other various treasures."

"So, what happened to the family?" I asked, with a sinking feeling in the pit of my stomach. Intuitively, I knew this was Liza's heritage we were discussing.

T.J. sighed and said, "Sadly, like so many other noble families of the time and in the area, they appear to have fallen victim to the perils of the Third Reich.

"You see, even after Austrian nobility went the way of more modern forms of government, the von Halpstadts appear to have remained quite powerful. The last prominent male heir I can trace was Helmut IX, who was the only son of Pieter VII. He came into prominence just after World War I and appears to have been rather outspoken—speaking out against Austrian unification with Germany in the years leading up to 1940.

"I have traced his whereabouts to a posting at the University of Salzburg, from 1932 to 1939, and then on a hunch, I checked out a few listings at the Universities of Bern, Lausanne, and Geneva, and hit paydirt on Lausanne from 1939 to 1941."

"He fled to Switzerland," Dutch said, and I found myself grateful that he knew more about geography than I did.

"Yes, which was quite common at that time given the Reich's iron fist when it came to outspoken men of learning. It was a sign of the times that many men of noble birth often took postings at university if they didn't take an active role in politics. Helmut, it appears, followed these lines until 1941 when he and his family simply disappeared."

"How many were in the family?" I asked.

"From the records I've found, there appeared to be four in total: Helmut, his wife, Frieda, their son, Pieter, and a daughter, Eliza."

The hair on the back of my neck stood up on end. "Eliza?"

"Yes."

"It's her, isn't it, Abby?" Dutch asked as he watched me carefully. "It's Liza."

My right side immediately felt light and airy. I nodded to him with a sad smile.

"Liza is this woman you say was murdered?" T.J. asked.

I nodded again at him and asked, "So what could have happened to them?"

"That's what I'd like to know," T.J. said. "The war made record-keeping a nightmare. The Germans kept meticulous records of things they wanted to document, and meticulously didn't keep records of things they didn't want to document, and while they never invaded Switzerland, there was much collusion between the two countries. Switzerland was in a rather precarious position, and if they hadn't fully cooperated with the Germans, they might have felt the same stinging backlash as other countries like Poland and Hungary.

"If Helmut was as outspoken as some of his published papers displayed prior to 1939 and 1940, he would have posed a significant threat to the Nazis. Back then, they had ways of making you disappear."

"You think the Swiss turned the family over?"

"It's possible," T.J. said, scratching his head. "In fact, it's even probable. Right now I'm working on a different angle for you."

"What's that?" I asked.

"Frieda's side of the family. Her lineage is also of noble lines, the von Stiessen family. If I can trace that lineage to someone alive today, I might be able to get in touch with a relative who can tell you what happened to the family."

Dutch looked at me, his face telling me he was missing something. "So how does this tie in with Jean-Paul?"

"Who?" T.J. asked.

"Jean-Paul Carlier. He was a French café owner in Lyon who was heavy into the French Resistance during the war."

T.J. looked sharply at Dutch. "In Lyon, you say?"

"Yeah." Dutch nodded.

"Well, *why* didn't you say so?" T.J. chastised.

"Why? Is that significant?" I asked.

"Yes, of course, because if Helmut feared he was about to be turned over to the Nazis by the Swiss, his only choice would have been to get to Lyon. It would have been dicey, but it's highly likely that he would have tried it. In fact, there is a central railway leading right from Lausanne to Lyon. This may be where the family headed, then changed their identity to avoid detection from the Nazis."

"But I thought France fell to Germany in 1940," I said, recalling my high school history.

"Yes, that's true," T.J. said, nodding at me. "The Germans invaded France in the spring of 1940 and divided the country in two. There was the Occupied Zone in the north, and the Free Zone in the south. The southern zone was run from Vichy, a small spa town in the center of the country, but the most important city—economically, politically and socially—was Lyon. Before the war, the population of the city proper was about five hundred thousand. But in the few years before and after France declared war on the Reich there was a massive influx of refugees into the south of France. Jews, Spanish republicans, Belgians and, of course, anyone unlucky enough to have made themselves unpopular with the Reich in the early years of the administration."

"So, if you got to Lyon, you were home free?" I asked.

"No, not necessarily," T.J. cautioned. "You see, even though Lyon was allowed a measure of freedom so to speak, and a 'free' French government was set up, it was merely a puppet of the Gestapo who ruled with tight control. Lyon had citizens of power, influence and money, and the Gestapo sucked it dry."

"That's got to be it," I said looking at Dutch. "That's got to be how Liza came into contact with Jean-Paul."

"So what's the missing link?" he asked me. "Why would she show up here thirty years later and steal from him?"

My intuition buzzed and I looked at T.J. "It's the notebook," I said. "That's the missing link. There's something in there, boys, that ties this whole mystery together. T.J, could you try and decipher it?"

"I can try," T.J. said. "I should have some free time this weekend. Will that be soon enough for you?"

"It'll have to be," Dutch said, looking at his watch and standing. "Thanks, buddy, we really appreciate all the help."

"Absolutely," T.J. said. "You know I love this stuff."

"We'll let you get back to your classes," I said as I shook his hand and Dutch and I left.

On the drive home we were quiet, both of us lost

in thought about what T.J. had told us and how it fit in with what we already knew. Suddenly, I looked at Dutch, my intuition on high. "There was something else in the box!" I said.

"What?" he asked me.

"In the box! The one with Liza's crest! It's not the notebook that was kept hidden. There was something else in there before the notebook."

"Like what?"

In my mind's eye I saw a large diamond in the shape of an egg. "Gems," I said, following the line of intuitive information dancing in my head. "Treasure . . . like the kind the adjunct of a pope would give you for saving the country from Turkish invaders."

Chapter Thirteen

When we got home, Dutch called T.J. and left a message to get back to him about what specific kind of treasure the von Halpstadt family had received for its dutiful service against the Turks. Then, while Dutch worked on his FBI brief, I puttered around the house until about five thirty when Milo arrived and we all headed back over to Willy's office. Knowing Dutch's injury was bothering him, I insisted on driving so that we could get a decent parking slot close to the building.

Milo didn't put up much of a fight about it, and it was then that I noticed he looked like he'd had a long day. "Politics not the bag of fun you thought it would be?" Dutch goaded when were all nestled in the car.

"Let's just say there's a lot of room for improvement," Milo quipped from the backseat.

When we got to Willy's we headed inside and waited for Dutch to catch up as Milo and I reached the second floor well ahead of Gimpy. We chatted as we walked down the hallway and noticed Willy's door slightly ajar.

Milo pushed through first and came up short at the scene in front of him. The office was in ruin. The large stack of papers that yesterday had been piled neatly along the edge of Willy's desk now lay scattered about the room like enormous bits of confetti. The desk chair had been overturned, a filing cabinet had been knocked over and now leaned against the desk, the files spilled out onto the ground and one of the windows held the impression of something large and heavy that had smashed into it. The signs of a struggle were all over the room, and to make matters worse as I gawked at the floor and the mess my eyes fell on a family photo of Willy, his wife and their three kids.

Looking flat and plastic from out of the frame was a smiling accountant, and my heart sank as I realized he was dead. "No!" I said as I went to reach for the photo.

"Whoa!" Milo said grabbing my arm. "Abby, hang on there! You can't touch anything here."

"No!" I wailed again, my eyes misting at the thought that Willy's family had just suffered such a tragic loss.

"Abby?" Dutch said, alarm in his voice as I continued to struggle against Milo, wanting to reach the picture, to be sure that I wasn't mistaken. "Abby, what's wrong?"

"He's dead," I said, my voice now a whisper.

"What?" Milo asked, looking to where I was now pointing.

"The picture," Dutch said as he looked at his former partner. "She can tell when someone's dead by their photograph."

Milo looked around at the room. "Wait here," he said as he shoved me out the door. "Do not move," he warned and disappeared inside the room, grumbling about contaminating a crime scene, then he came back out into the hallway holding the picture with the edge of his coat. "Look closely," he offered. "Are you sure?"

I was leaning against the wall in the hallway feeling like the air had been let out of me. I looked at the photo closely, but the image did not change. Willy was flat and plastic looking, one-dimensional. The rest of his family smiled up at me, vibrant with life. I nodded and turned away, as a tear slipped down my cheek. "Poor Willy," I said to no one in particular.

Immediately, Milo pulled out his cell phone and dialed 911. "This is Detective Milo Johnson of the Royal Oak P.D. I'm at 2670 Long Lake Road, suite 207. Reporting a possible homicide and requesting police and CSI immediately!"

An hour later the police had come, taken our statements and were now processing Willy's office. Milo had indicated that I was especially gifted at knowing when someone had fallen victim to foul play, and the fact that he backed me up in the face of two very skeptical Bloomfield Hills detectives was testament to his faith in me. After talking with them for almost a half hour, Milo came back to Dutch, who was holding me close and watching the crime techs take their pictures and dust for prints.

"They're looking through the building for a body," he said as he got to us.

"It's not here," I said.

"How do you know?" Milo asked.

I tapped my temple and squeezed my eyes closed, wanting to shut out the scene. Intuitively, I knew there was a connection to our investigation, and the fact that Willy had paid the ultimate price for merely trying to help us was weighing heavily on my conscience. Just then, my intuition buzzed and I said, "Milo, there's something in his car."

"Whose car?" he asked.

"Willy's," I said. "There's something important in his car. A clue of some kind."

"Where's the car?" he asked me.

"Here," I said. "In the parking lot. Look for a light blue sedan."

Milo pulled out his cell phone and hit a number on speed dial. "Hey, Tina. Detective Johnson here. Can you get me the make, model and license number for a car registered to a William Breger of Bloomfield Hills?" Milo fished out his notebook, waited a minute or two then jotted down the information when Tina gave it to him. "Got it, thanks," he said and flipped his phone closed.

Turning to me he said, "You're on the ball today, Abby. Light blue Oldsmobile. Let's head downstairs and find it."

We found Willy's car parked in the back of the building, and as Milo peered inside the windows, careful not to touch the glass, he said, "No body, but there are a couple of Banker's Boxes on the seats."

"There's a clue in those boxes," I said.

Milo nodded. "I'll head up to the detectives upstairs."

I stepped in front of him, my intuition buzzing. "They won't let you have them."

"Well, it is their crime scene," Milo reasoned.

"We don't need all of them," I said, hating that I was even thinking about this.

"What are you saying?" Milo asked warily.

"Just one should do it . . . that one," I said and pointed to the one in the front passenger seat. "We could just take that one and no one would be the wiser. Hell, they probably won't even think about his car for another couple of hours yet."

"You want to get me *fired*?" Milo asked, his voice rising at the audacity of the suggestion.

"How about this," Dutch said as he gave me a pointed look. "How about you go get us a soda across the street, buddy, and we'll meet you back at Abby's car, in say, oh . . . ten minutes?"

"Dutch!" Milo exclaimed, "Are you *crazy*? Do you know what kind of trouble you could get in if anyone found out you contaminated a crime scene and stole evidence?"

"I'd like a Coke. Abby? What's your poison?"

"I'll take one of those as well," I said, beaming up at him.

Milo sputtered at the two of us for another few seconds before stomping away in the direction of the drugstore across the street, while muttering things like, "You're gonna get us thrown in *jail*!"

When he was far enough away Dutch said, "Can you go next door to that dry cleaners and get me a wire hanger?"

I smiled at him as I looked in the direction he pointed to. "Man! You notice everything, don't you?"

"I'm a detail kinda guy, sweethot," Dutch said and bounced his eyebrows a few times.

I rolled my eyes and trotted to the dry cleaners, returning to Willy's car a few minutes later with a coat hanger in tow. Dutch took the hanger from me, then placing me in front of him he said, "Block the view, would ya?"

I nodded and turned my attention to the parking lot, playing lookout. Dutch had the car open within seconds and with a grunt hauled out the Banker's Box. He used his good foot to close the door and nodded at me as we traversed the parking lot and I beeped my car doors open for him so he could put the box in the backseat. We then hopped in and waited for Milo, who was taking forever.

Finally, Milo appeared from the drugstore carrying three Cokes in his hands and walking toward our car doing his best to look casual. He got in and I put the pedal to the metal, peeling out of the parking lot with my heart racing.

We cruised home sipping on our Cokes as Milo pouted in the backseat. When we got to Dutch's, Milo got out the second I turned off the engine and walked over to his car without a backward glance.

"Aren't you coming in?" I called to him as he reached his car door.

"I want no part of *that*!" Milo said as he pointed to the box Dutch was carrying to the house.

"I was gonna make chicken Marsala for dinner," Dutch called over his shoulder with a grin. Milo's favorite meal was Dutch's chicken Marsala.

Growling, Milo yanked open his car door and popped inside, leaving us with a final, *"No part!"*

Dutch and I laughed as we headed inside. Dutch deposited the box on the coffee table while I took off my coat. "Are you really making us dinner?" I asked hopefully. Between the two of us, he was far more domesticated. My idea of cooking usually involved a bowl, some ramen noodles and the microwave.

"Yep. Why don't you look through Willy's box while I get dinner started. Shout if you find anything interesting."

I nodded and headed to the couch where I lifted the lid off and peered inside. The container held folders all neatly arranged and labeled by month. Within each folder were small stacks of handwritten sales receipts dated some forty years earlier. I sorted through the folders, at first just randomly pulling out files and taking a cursory look, then filing them back away. When I went to the oldest folder from March of 1965, I noticed something peculiar. There was a name at the top of the slip, a small notation really, in the corner next to the date. The name was German and I cocked my head as I read it. "Itzak Kleinburg," I said aloud.

"What's that?" Dutch called from the kitchen.

"Itzak Kleinburg," I repeated louder.

"It's a—who?" he said, appearing in the doorway, a bowl in one hand and a whisk in the other.

"Here," I said, showing him the slip. "Look at this."

Dutch read the slip while he whisked and said, "That the guy he sold the diamond to?"

I turned the slip back to me and read down the paper to the notation about the one-point-seven carat diamond set in yellow gold. "No," I said, pointing to the lines above that notation. "Here, see? This is who he sold it to, Christopher Fletcher of 206 Roxberry Court."

"Weird," Dutch said as he tapped the whisk on the side of the bowl.

"Very," I said, turning back to the slip. My intuition continued to buzz, so I set the slip aside and dug through a few more files. After just a short search, I came across similar slips, some had the same "Itzak Kleinburg" notation at the top, and others had different names, like "Jakob Weinstein," and "Samuel Katzberg," and "Elijah Goldschtadt."

There was something familiar about the names, and after a moment with the sales slips all spread out on the table, I closed my eyes and let my radar take me where it would. In my mind's eye I saw the same swallow that had appeared in so many of my visions of late, and I followed it as it fluttered about a room and landed on the puzzle box. This time, however, when the bird pecked at the crest on top of the box, the box opened and the little fellow pulled out the notebook hovering in the air with it in its beak.

"Ohmigod!" I said as my eyes flew open.

"What?" Dutch said, coming into the room. "What's happened?"

"These names!" I said excitedly. "They're the same names as in the notebook!"

Dutch looked at the sales slips scattered on the table, picking them up one by one and sorting through them. "They're Jewish names," he noted. Then he snapped his head up and said, "Hang on," as he headed into his study. A few minutes later he came back out carrying a book and flipping through the pages. "I was a history buff once upon a time," he said as I took note of the book in his hand titled, *Trail of Death: The Jewish Diamond Trade 1938–1940.*

"You're a World War II buff?" I asked, looking at him quizzically.

"History was my minor in college. I'm not as up on it as T.J., but I remember doing a paper on the European diamond trade pre– and post–World War II. This book was a really good read and I ended up keeping it. Here it is," he said as he found what he was looking for. Reading from the book he said, " 'The diamond trade pre–World War II was primarily populated by Jewish merchants, dealers and craftsmen who lined the route between the Netherlands where diamonds were imported almost exclusively at the time, down through Europe reaching all industrialized sectors. As Hitler's power within Germany grew, and hatred for Jews reached fever pitch, many prominent Jewish families who had dealt in diamonds and precious gemstones for generations found themselves in a rather precarious and dangerous situation. Some bought their way out of occupied zones, some were captured and their inventory seized as they were summarily sent off to death camps. Others hid their most precious gemstones within the lining of their clothing, waiting for the day they could escape or be released from the Third Reich's iron fist.' "

"These were diamond merchants," I said as I pawed through the receipts, another piece of the puzzle slipping into place.

"T.J. said that there was quite a population of Jews making their way to Lyon."

Dutch nodded agreeably. "Now we know how he got his inventory and how a café owner from France became a jeweler in the U.S."

"So, he traded their freedom for gems."

"Wouldn't surprise me."

Just then the phone rang and Dutch picked it up to inspect the caller ID. Noting the number he placed the phone back on the coffee table and hit a button. "Hey, T.J. I've got you on speaker so Abby can listen."

"Hi guys," T.J. sang through the phone. "Listen, I got your message and I canceled my last class because I found something that you two may really be interested in. You know how you asked me about what kind of treasure the adjunct to the pope might bestow on an Austrian nobleman? Well, as it turns out, a pretty significant one. Pope Gregory VIII bestowed a small collection of priceless gemstones upon Helmut von Halpstadt in 1584. His gift was a collection of three brilliant perfect white diamonds of nearly thirty carats each!"

"Whoa," Dutch said as my eyes widened.

"The diamonds, known as the Schwalbe Eier Diamanten or Swallow's Eggs Diamonds were named for their odd shape, size and color. Even back then they were worth a fortune."

I caught my breath as T.J. spoke. Even I was surprised by the coincidence of the swallow in all of my recent visions.

"In fact, the crest of the von Halpstadts changed after this priceless gift to reflect the pope's generosity. Before, the eagle in the crest held only the rose. The nest and the three eggs representing the family's great fortune were added shortly after the pope showed them favor."

"Where are the diamonds today?" I asked, the hairs on my arm standing up.

"No one knows. They were last documented on an insurance form filed by Helmut IX in 1926 when he'd had them set into a necklace and gave them to his new bride, Frieda, on their wedding day. The diamonds' whereabouts remain one of Europe's great mysteries."

"T.J.," I said into the phone, "do you have the notebook there with you?"

"Yes, it's here."

"I need you to check it for something," I said, mounting excitement coursing through my veins.

"What?"

"Look through the book for the name Itzak Kleinberg and see if there's a notation there."

"Okay, hold on," T.J. said as Dutch and I listened to paper rustling. After a few minutes T.J. said, "Yes, here it is. Itzak Kleinberg, and there's a long list of diamonds and other gemstones of various carat weights here."

I grabbed up all seven of the sales receipts with Itzak's name on them. "Can you read a few of them off for me?" I asked as I arranged them in a row on the table.

As T.J. went down the list I picked up the corresponding sales receipt to the gemstone he called off. When he was done, I'd checked off twenty diamonds, rubies, emeralds and sapphires listed both in the note-book and on the receipts.

"That confirms it," Dutch said as he took the receipts from me. "Jean-Paul got his inventory from fleeing Jews during the war."

"And may be why he left in such a hurry after the war . . ." I added.

"Uh, hang on a second," we heard through the speakerphone.

"What's up?" Dutch asked, turning his attention back to T.J.

"There's a name in here that I recognize."

"You're kidding," I said. What were the odds?

"Ira Jacobson . . ." T.J. said softly. "I wonder . . ." he added and we heard more shuffling. "Hold on a minute, guys," he said and we listened as he put the phone down and seemed to walk away.

I looked at Dutch, and he looked at me and we both shrugged our shoulders. While we waited for T.J., Dutch got up to check on dinner, and my stomach growled as the house filled with the smell of delicious food. Dutch came back after a minute and said, "We can eat as soon as T.J.'s done."

I gave him the thumbs up just as T.J. came back to the phone. "Sorry about that," he said, "but I had to look for the book written by a man of the same name. Ira Jacobson was a Dutch Jew who fled with his family to Lyon, France in 1939. His father, whose name was also Ira, was a wealthy diamond merchant who had arranged for safekeeping through a local Frenchman. One night, when Ira's father went to meet the Frenchman, he disappeared, along with most of the family's precious inventory.

"Ira's mother learned later that her husband had been turned over to the Gestapo, and was executed as an enemy of the state within hours of his disappearance. The rest of the family barely escaped with their lives as Ira's mother was luckily quick enough on her feet to use what little money she had left and move the family deeper into the south of France. Later, when Ira grew up, he became a pretty famous professor at the University of Toulouse, where I studied for a year. I never had him as a professor, but I heard about him and bought his book."

"You think the Frenchman mentioned in Ira's book was Jean-Paul?" Dutch asked T.J.

"Yes," I answered before anyone else could, feeling my right side take on a light and airy feeling. "And that's what happened to Liza's family too," I added definitively. "Hey T.J.?"

"Yes, Abby?"

"Can you go back to the notebook and see if there's a notation for the von Halpstadts?"

"I'm looking," T.J. said as we heard pages flipping. Then, finally he said, "Nope, there's no mention of the von Halpstadts. And no other notation to indicate the Schwalbe Eier diamonds either."

"Doesn't matter," I said into the silence that followed.

"Hey, hold on a minute," T.J. said as we heard pages turning.

"What?" Dutch and I asked together.

"There's a page missing from the back of the book. I can see a little bit of it in the seam here."

"That must be the page Jean-Paul recorded the Swallow's Eggs diamonds on," I said my right side feeling very light. "He took them, and he turned the family over to the Germans. I just know it."

"There may be a way to find out for sure," T.J. said.

"How so?" Dutch asked, sounding a little surprised.

"Remember I told you that I was digging into Frieda's family tree? I got a hit on a connection. Turns out Frieda's sister went with the family to Lausanne when they fled Austria. The sister met and married a Swiss man about a year later and they had a daughter in 1945 who as it happens moved to Canada."

"Where in Canada?" I asked, my spidey-sense buzzing.

"Windsor," T.J. said triumphantly.

"Damn!" Dutch exclaimed. "That's right next door!"

"Thought you'd like that one. I'll e-mail you her name and address so you can look her up."

"T.J., I owe you big-time for this. Thanks for all your help," Dutch said.

"Happy to do it, my friend," T.J. said.

Dutch clicked off the phone and got up from the couch while I sat and pondered things a while. He came back a little later with two plates of chicken, artichoke hearts and pasta, setting one down in front of me and the other down in front of himself. "So, what'cha thinking?"

I reached for the fork and knife and said, "That's what Jean-Luke is after."

"What do you mean?"

"The diamonds. He thinks we have the diamonds."

"So, if we don't have them, and assuming Jean-Paul never sold them, where are they?" Dutch asked me.

"That's the sixty-five-million-dollar question, my friend," I said as my intuition buzzed. In my mind's eye I saw the swallow again, and I now understood the bird's connection to the treasure once held by the puzzle box.

"You think Jean-Luke killed Willy?" he asked, interrupting my thoughts.

"Yes," I said, my shoulders slumping. I'd almost forgotten about the poor old accountant.

"Abby," Dutch said soothingly, "it's not your fault."

"I should have seen it coming," I said, swirling my noodles as my appetite disappeared.

"Oh, now you're omnipotent?"

I scowled at him. "No, but I should be able to pick up the kind of violence that took place in that office."

"How much time did you spend pointing your radar at the guy yesterday?"

I shrugged my shoulders. "I don't know, a few seconds or so."

"Ah, well, I'm amazed you didn't pick it up then," Dutch said sarcastically. "Listen, he's not your client, you weren't sitting down together in your regular space doing your regular thing. You weren't looking for it because you had no reason to and that's why you missed it. Does that make sense?"

"A little," I agreed, trying to follow his logic.

"The point is, it's okay to be human," Dutch said. "Now eat your food before I get a complex."

I smiled at him and took a few bites. "So, are we going to Windsor tomorrow?"

Dutch nodded, chewing his food a bit before answering me. "Yep. But this time I get to drive."

"The doctor gave you the okay?" I asked.

"Just as soon as I have my last therapy session tomorrow. Do you mind taking me?"

"What time's your appointment?"

"Nine thirty."

"Doable."

"And, while we're in Canada, why don't we take a little detour and head straight up to Toronto while we're at it?" Dutch asked, his eyebrows bouncing.

"You mean tomorrow?" I asked.

"Yeah. It's Friday, and we can make a long weekend out of it. It'd be good to get out of Dodge for a few days, especially since that maniac's running loose. What do you say?"

"I'm in," I grinned and nudged him with my knee. "I'll have to take Eggy to the vet in the morning to board him."

"Great. Why don't you get packing and I'll do the dishes," Dutch offered.

I smiled at him and my heart softened a bit. I really had landed a good guy after all. "Don't have to ask me twice," I said as I bounded up the stairs.

I packed my suitcase with just about everything I'd brought with me to Dutch's, which was enough for a significantly longer stay than just two days. It's hard to pack for such an impromptu event as the spontaneous romantic weekend. What does one bring? Lots of clothes or just a few? I opted for the lots, making sure to pack my Victoria's Secret teddy right on top— ready to grab at a moment's notice.

Dutch came up much later after working to wrap up his Bureau file and tiredly he pulled out his duffle bag, throwing in two pairs of jeans, two sweaters and a couple of changes of underwear. I scowled at how simple he kept it.

He crawled into bed next to me and pulled me close. "You feel nice," he said nibbling at my neck.

I giggled and said, "Save your strength for the weekend, Cowboy. You're gonna need it."

Dutch made some sort of sound, half purr, half growl and a few minutes later I felt the soft, gentle breeze of his even breathing on the back of my neck. Wrapped in his arms with that for a lullaby was a really nice way to fall asleep.

Chapter Fourteen

The next morning Dutch and I were up early doing last minute chores and tidying up the house before our long weekend. I packed a bag for Eggy, who seemed to know we were leaving and thus moped in the corner of the kitchen giving me a pathetic look every chance he got. Dutch hurried to lay out extra food for Virgil, who seemed to have the decidedly opposite feeling of Eggy, and was happily purring a figure eight through Dutch's legs, encouraging him to leave town faster.

At eight twenty we piled into the car and stopped off at the vet, where I delivered a sulky dog to a friendly receptionist, my heart dropping a little as I waved good-bye. I got back in the car and we took off toward the PT's office.

"Is she gonna make you go back in the pool today?"

"Yeah," Dutch groaned. "It might be kind of a long wait. Will you be okay in the lobby until I'm through?"

"I have to wait there? I thought I'd run a few errands and meet you after you're done."

"Tell me you're kidding," Dutch said seriously.

"What?" I asked, looking at him like he'd just grown another head.

"Did you learn *nothing* at Willy's office?" he asked me stiffly. "Abby, there's a maniac on the loose looking for priceless diamonds he thinks we have. Don't you think that's enough of a reason for you to stick close until he's captured?"

I pondered that for a moment, then shrugged my shoulders. "Fine."

"You'll wait in the lobby then?" Dutch said, more statement than question.

"Yes, I'll wait in the lobby," I answered, my voice only slightly sneering.

"You're gonna drive me to drink, you know that?" Dutch said, letting out an exasperated sigh.

"I do what I can," I said with a grin.

We arrived at the PT's office a short time later, and I waved to Dutch as he headed through a door on his way to the pool. Looking around the lobby I found a quiet spot in the corner, and sat down wondering how I was going to fill an hour and a half. I reclined in the seat and closed my eyes, thinking maybe I could catch a catnap. As I got comfortable, my intuition began to buzz, and reflexively I tuned in to the message coming into my head.

In my mind's eye I saw the same swallow that had been fluttering through my visions since the start of this whole ordeal, and I smiled as I watched it fly about, thinking about how interesting it was that this same little bird had led me all along to discovering the clues to Liza's mystery. I focused with rapt attention as the swallow fluttered about a blank room, then came to rest on a little nest. Inside the nest were three eggs that sparkled and caught the light.

Schwalbe Eier, I said in my head, and the little bird

nodded. An instant later my eyes flew open and I jumped out of the seat. "Ohmigod!" I said. "I know where they are!"

"Are you okay?" an elder gentleman asked me.

"Uh . . ." I stammered, looking around at the other people in the lobby who were all staring at me. "I'm fine, thanks," I said, grabbing my coat and walking quickly to the receptionist.

The woman behind the counter eyed me quizzically and asked, "Can I help you?"

"Yeah," I said, anxious to check out my theory before Jean-Luke beat me to it. "If Agent Rivers gets done with his therapy before I get back, please tell him to wait right here, and I'll call him as soon as I'm done." And with that I ran out the door.

I dashed to my car with my heart racing. Why hadn't I put the clues together before now? It was so obvious where Liza had hidden the jewels, and such a simple solution to hide them in plain sight. Before I called in the cavalry, though, I had to be sure. After all, I didn't want to make a fool out of myself.

I got to the house on Fern about ten minutes later, and I knew I was right on the money the moment I parked my car. I had a good view into the backyard from the driveway, and there it was, just what I was looking for.

I sat still for a beat, my intuition on hyperdrive, and a small smile playing across my face as I dug out my cell phone from my purse.

"Yello!" came a familiar voice.

"Hey, Dave, it's me, Abby."

"Hey there girl, what's happenin'?"

"I need a ladder."

"I got one I can spare."

"I need you to bring it to me as fast as you can."

"Sure. You at Dutch's?"

"No. I'm at Fern Street."

"Oh, *come on,* Abby! You know I hate that place! And I just threw out the holy water!"

"This is nonnegotiable, David," I said sternly, the grip on my cell phone becoming tighter.

" 'David'?" he mimed. "Sounds serious."

"Just get your ass over here!" I yelled and hung up the phone. True, I was being overly harsh but I needed a ladder and I didn't have time to deal with Dave's squeamishness.

I sat in the car for about twenty minutes, my eye constantly going to the dashboard clock until finally I growled under my breath and reached for my phone again. I must have been a little too over the top for Dave so I dialed his number intent on sweet-talking an apology, but his line went directly into voice mail indicating he'd most likely turned off his cell. As I scowled down the street it was pretty clear he wasn't coming. "Damn!" I swore as I tossed the phone on the passenger seat and got out to stand next to the car. I stood there for a beat or two thinking about what to do next.

Spotting the garage at the end of the long driveway I walked the cracked pavement to it, pausing before the big rusty aluminum door when my eye fell on what appeared to be a shiny brand-new padlock. "Hmmm," I mused as I lifted up the lock. *Why would James padlock the garage?*

Looking back toward the road I sighed again as I watched for cars coming down the road. Still no sign of Dave. I shrugged my shoulders and went around to the side of the garage and, spotting a window, peered in. Sure enough, hooked onto the far side of the wall was a ladder. "Paydirt!" I said aloud as I tried the window. The thing wouldn't budge. I pushed and pulled and shimmied on the pane for a few minutes until I finally gave up and looked around on the ground. Finding a brick in one of the flowerbeds I picked it up and hurled it through the window. Hey, it was my house; if I wanted to break a window that was my prerogative.

Taking off my coat and wrapping it around my hand I knocked out a little more of the glass and reached up to unlock the window. With my hand still wrapped in my coat I pushed up on the pane and it opened. "Yay!" I said as I shook the glass from my coat, and put it back on. Carefully, I hoisted myself up and swung a leg over the ledge, putting it through the window, and shimmied the rest of me through the opening, dropping to the floor of the garage a moment later. It was darker than I'd thought inside and as I turned to head toward the ladder I tripped over something large and went down like a sack of potatoes.

"Crap!" I said as I landed hard on the floor of the garage. Turning to see what I'd tripped over I nearly fainted from fright as the large unseeing eyes of Willy Breger stared back at me. *"Ohmigod!"* I screamed and scuttled backward, away from the body, my own eyes large and horrified.

"The diamonds aren't in there," called a voice from the window.

Startled yet again I looked away from Willy to the owner of the voice, and was shocked to see James Carlier standing at the window, a .44 Magnum trained at my head.

"Wha . . . ?" I said stupidly, my brain not quite computing everything I was seeing.

"The diamonds. I tore this garage apart years ago, and they're not in there."

"I know," I said before I could stop myself.

James looked startled at my statement, then amused. "You know where they are, don't you?"

Watching the Magnum, I nodded my head slowly. "If you put the gun down, I'll tell you where they are," I said, my breathing a little ragged.

"Or," James offered, "I keep it and you get them for me."

I thought about that for a minute, until James took the safety off the gun. "Okay!" I said. "Okay! I'll get them!"

"Good girl," James said. "Now hurry up."

"I need the ladder," I said getting to my feet, my legs feeling like rubber.

"It's right behind you."

Slowly, I turned to the wall and got the ladder down off the hooks it was on. Awkwardly I began to walk it forward toward the window, wondering how I would manage to get it through the hole.

"Hang on," James said. "I'll open the door." He disappeared and a moment later I heard him at the lock on the garage door. I quickly set the ladder down and began to move to the window, but faster than I would have expected I heard the padlock drop to the ground and the door begin to open. There was no way I'd make it if I tried to run.

With pounding heart I waited while the door creaked open and sunlight burst through the garage. James stood in the light of the open door and as he noticed the ladder cast aside and my position a few steps closer to the window he grinned as he trained the gun on me again. "Thought you could run away?"

Something about his smile made me catch my breath, and for an instant I was lost in the memory of the first time I'd visited him at his shop. Then, I realized what troubled me so much about James's smile and my hand flew to my mouth as I figured out another giant piece of the jigsaw puzzle.

"What?" he asked me as I ogled him.

"You have crooked teeth," I said as I lowered my hand and pointed a finger at him.

James snapped his mouth shut, his eyebrows lowering to dangerous levels. "So what?"

"You're not James," I said after a moment. "James had braces. You're Jean-Luke!"

"Very good," he said after a moment, his grin widening again. "You figured it all out. Now, come on out of there and show me where the diamonds are . . . *now!*"

On wobbly legs I walked back to the ladder and picked it up. I needed to stall in order to think of a way out of this mess, because I had no doubt that Jean-Luke was just crazy enough to kill me just like he'd murdered Willy. "So why'd you kill him?" I said, pausing with the ladder by Willy's body.

Jean-Luke looked down at Willy with a snarl. "That old geezer wouldn't give me my tax returns. In fact, he actually took a swing at me!"

"So you killed him over tax returns?" I asked, horrified.

"No, and I didn't kill him. He tried to hit me and I shoved him, and we sort of wrestled around his office, and then all of a sudden he's grabbing his chest and turning purple. I'd known the guy since I was little and I had a moment of weakness, so I loaded him into my car and headed in the direction of the hospital, but he died on the way. I couldn't very well drop off a dead man . . . too many questions. So I brought him here."

"What about his family?" I asked horrified. "Didn't you ever think what they must be going through, not knowing where he is, or what's happened to him?"

"I don't know his family, and I don't care about them. Make no mistake," Jean-Luke warned me, "if you don't cooperate, I will kill you. It runs in my family, after all." And with that he let out an evil laugh.

"Where's James?" I asked, still stalling.

"Tucked away," Jean-Luke answered with a wicked smile. "Now get a move on."

I trudged awkwardly with the ladder out of the garage over to the center of the backyard, where I put the ladder against the pole at the base of a birdhouse. I looked at Jean-Luke and said, "It's only a guess that they're in there, you know."

Jean-Luke regarded me with a hard look. "For your sake, let's just hope you've guessed right."

I gulped and began to climb the ladder. I got to the top and clutched the birdhouse—I'm not overly fond of heights—and began to inspect the little structure.

It was a wooden octagon, with holes for eight nests and little perches pegged underneath each hole. It was a birdie condo. Grass, twigs and feathers overflowed from every hole, save one. That one had been plugged with a small piece of cork. Luckily, the cork was weathered and aged, and it crumbled as I dug at it until I could get a few fingers into the hole. A moment later I felt something small and leathery underneath my fingertips. I carefully wedged another finger into the birdhouse and scraped the object closer. When I had it up against the opening, I pulled my hand out and repositioned my fingers forming a hook and, after a moment, I was able to lift a small leather pouch out of the hole.

I paused up on the ladder for a moment, knowing that Liza and her family had been killed for the contents in this bag, and feeling very sad that such a small thing could wreak such karmic havoc.

"Bring it down," Jean-Luke insisted.

I scowled at him and came down the ladder, holding the pouch in a tight grip. When I reached the bottom

I stood by the ladder defiantly and didn't offer up the pouch.

"Give it to me," Jean-Luke said, waving the gun in one hand while he extended the other.

I looked at the bag in my hand, resigned to giving him what he wanted, when my intuition buzzed in with an idea and I said, "No."

"You seem to forget, Cooper, I'm the guy with the gun."

"Finders, keepers," I taunted.

"Give it to me!" Jean-Luke screamed.

"No problem," I said and tipped the ladder off the pole with a hard pull from my free hand.

I watched in slow motion as Jean-Luke's expression turned from absolute hatred to one of complete shock as the ladder made a slow arc toward him.

I didn't pause long enough to see it hit him, because the moment his eyes left me I bolted across the lawn. I headed straight for my car and heard Jean-Luke swear as the ladder made a connection with what I hoped was his head. A moment later I heard another sound that made me jump and duck low. A gunshot rang across the yard and spurred me to even greater speed.

Even as I heard the sound I felt something hot and fast whiz by me, landing in the dirt just to my left. "Shit!" I swore and began to swerve in a zigzag, hoping Jean-Luke's aim was as off as his mental state. Ten feet from my car I heard another gunshot, this time the shot kicked up dirt right next to me. I veered sharply out of the driveway toward the house, looking for any kind of cover, and barreled right into my handyman as he came around the front corner.

We both went down with a loud thud, the ladder he'd been carrying toppling off his shoulder to the ground. Even as Dave and I tumbled over each other

I was scrambling to get up and get away from Jean-Luke, who I knew would be heading straight for us. I struggled to my feet and grabbed Dave's hand. "Owww!" he complained loudly, holding a hand to his head. "Jesus, Abby! You tryin' to kill me?"

"Get up!" I yelled as I tugged at him and looked back in the direction of Jean-Luke. Just as I suspected, he was running for us, holding the gun up and taking aim. *"Move!"* I screamed at Dave as I yanked hard and pulled him to his feet.

"What the . . . ?" he began to protest but was cut short by another gunshot and the spray of small shards of siding as the bullet hit the house right next to Dave.

"Run!" I yelled and took off around the corner, with Dave hot on my heels. We crossed the length of the front of the house and rounded to the other side. Dave managed to duck around the corner just as another gunshot sounded.

"Holy shit!" he swore, "Who the hell *is* that?"

"No time to explain," I said grabbing his arm and shoving him into a row of bushes. We tumbled to the ground again and crawled through the tangle of shrubbery as I listened for the sound of running footsteps close on our heels. Just as we nestled further between the overgrown bushes, we heard Jean-Luke come pounding around the corner. He stopped short when he got to the backyard and through the tangle of branches we could see him look sharply around. He was shaking with rage, a large bloody welt on his forehead.

My heart rate was in the stratosphere and I tucked the leather pouch he was after into my inside jacket pocket, then watched Jean-Luke intently, praying that he'd head back around the front of the house again. I got my wish just a moment later when he trotted out of view and over to the opposite side of the house.

Not wasting a minute I grabbed Dave's arm again and pulled him out of the bushes. "Where are we going?" he whispered, and it was only then that I noticed the fear in his eyes.

"Into the house. We'll hide out there until he goes away, then make a run for it."

"I can't go into that house!" Dave hissed as I made my way over to the sliding glass door.

"You don't have a choice," I replied as I pulled at the handle. It slid open just as my intuition had said it would. "I must not have locked this when I let that bird out way back when. Now, come inside with me!" I whispered harshly, and with his head bowed he obliged.

I shut the door and we stood in the darkness of the kitchen, out of view, watching and waiting. After a minute I asked, "Do you have your cell phone?"

"Oh, yeah!" Dave said as he reached for the back of his pants. "I almost forgot I had it on me . . . *Son-of-a* . . . !"

"What?" I asked, alarmed.

"It's not on my belt loop. It must have come off when you tackled me."

"This day just keeps getting worse," I said as I kept my eye on the backyard. Sure enough, Jean-Luke reappeared and eyed the back door with interest. "Damn it!" I said, realizing I hadn't locked the door. I moved Dave back out of the kitchen and said, "Hurry up! He's coming inside!"

We peddled backward into the living room headed to the front door. Just as we got there we heard the back door slide open. Jean-Luke was too close for us to get out through the front door safely, if he heard us he could be through the kitchen with the gun pointed quicker than we could undo the deadbolt and get out. Thinking quickly I opened up the closet and shoved

Dave inside first but before I could follow him I heard Jean-Luke say behind me, "Ahhh, so there you are."

I shut the door on Dave's frightened face, and prayed that Jean-Luke hadn't seen me push him in there, then whipped around to face him.

"I don't have them anymore," I said.

"Where are they?" he asked leveling the gun at my head.

"If you kill me you'll never find out," I answered boldly, trying to think of a way out of this mess.

"Yes, that's true," he said, lowering the gun and taking aim at my kneecap.

My eyes got large and just before he squeezed the trigger I said, "*Wait!* Okay! I'll tell you!"

"Go on," he said, his patience at a minimum, and the gun still pointed at my knee.

"They're in the basement," I said.

"With your friend?"

I pretended to let my shoulders sag. "Yes," I answered, bowing my head in mock surrender. "He's hiding down there."

"Let's go," Jean-Luke snapped, waving the gun in a "come on" gesture.

I walked on stiff legs toward the basement, my heart thundering in my chest and my intuition on high. My guides had suggested the basement idea, and I'd almost passed on it because I felt it was a great place to get trapped and die, but at the last second I decided to trust them and so I'd gone with it. Now as I walked toward the door, I wondered how the hell they were going to get me out of this.

We turned into the kitchen and I stopped at the door. "He's down there," I said, "and he's got the diamonds."

Jean-Luke nudged me with the gun. "Open the door."

I did, and we both peered into darkness. "Tell him to come up," Jean-Luke said.

"Dave?" I called into the basement. "Dave? You'll have to come up from the basement!"

"Turn on the light," Jean-Luke ordered.

I reached forward and flipped the switch, and just as I did so a black shadow appeared to swoop out of the basement and flew right into Jean-Luke's hair. He careened backward, flapping his arms wildly, waving the gun like a party favor as something birdlike flopped about his head. Two shots went off and I ducked low putting my hands over my head. A moment later, with the acrid smell of gunpowder in the air and the little bird that had flown out of the basement still fluttering about the room, I looked up at Jean-Luke, my intuition buzzing. "You're out of bullets, fella," I said with a sneer.

Jean-Luke pointed the gun at me and fired. The empty gun clicked and he tossed the gun in the corner and stomped over to me, his face contorted in rage. Angrily he grabbed me by the collar of my coat as he hissed, "I'm going to kill you for that."

He then wrapped his hands about my throat and began to squeeze. With wild panicked motions I scratched at his hands and struggled to escape from his grip. He pulled me violently across the kitchen and shoved me into a wall, squeezing my neck as stars swam in my eyes and pain and fear drove me to kick and scratch and claw at him, but to no avail. His eyes were wild, his own breathing ragged, the rage that emanated off of him palpable.

Just as the darkness began to close around the edge of my vision I saw a necklace made of string, rosary beads and garlic loop over Jean-Luke's head, and with a violent tug, he was pulled backward and almost lifted off the ground. He let go of me immediately, and I sank to my knees clutching at my throat, my breath ragged and painful. Out of the corner of my eye I could see my handyman with a fury so intense it scared me. He had Jean-Luke by the neck, ensnared by Dave's string of garlic, pulling him about the kitchen like a puppet. Jean-Luke was now the one clutching at his own throat, nearly losing his balance every time Dave changed direction.

Dave's face never wavered in its intensity and determination, and I knew it took a hell of a lot to get him to that point. "Dave!" I called out, knowing from someplace deep inside that this wasn't going to end well. "Dave! Stop!" I called, but my voice was barely more than a harsh whisper, and it was already too late. In one final heave on the garlic necklace, Dave released Jean-Luke. He hovered on his heels at the top of the basement stairwell for a brief moment with a look of relief as the pressure from the rope about his neck abated. And then his eyes roamed right and left, and he knew he was at the edge of the stairs, tipping backward as if in slow motion. Too late his arms went wide to save himself, but there was no railing or grip that could stop his fall down the stairs.

I watched him disappear through the doorway, my hand extended out to him before he left my view, and even before we heard him hit the bottom with a sickening crunch that snapped his neck I saw Dave McKenzie's face register a look of cool satisfaction.

Chapter Fifteen

I sat in the back of the police sedan with a blanket over my shoulders and a hot cup of coffee in my hands. I was shaking with cold, even though the heater in the squad car was turned up high. I'd already been checked out by an EMT crew, and ignored their advice to visit the hospital. My neck and throat hurt something fierce, but I wasn't in the mood to deal with it.

Dutch stood in the front yard, talking with Dave and Milo, and periodically they would all glance at me. Dave told them everything that had happened, as my voice had been reduced to a harsh whisper. I'd been told by the emergency tech who'd examined me that it could be a few days before my vocal cords healed and he'd strongly advised that I take it easy on them until then.

As I sat in the car and shivered, I saw a stretcher being wheeled out of the house loaded with a blanket covering the remains of Jean-Luke, the weight of it forcing the two men pushing it to go slow. I looked from the stretcher to Dave, knowing that even though he'd felt a sense of relief when Jean-Luke tumbled backward down those stairs, soon enough it would catch up to him and I worried how that would change him.

Even now I could see him shield his expression as he watched the team load Jean-Luke into the back of the ambulance. Another ambulance was parked just a little further down, waiting for Willy.

As the doors closed on Jean-Luke, Dutch left Milo and Dave and beat a steady path to me. "Uh-oh . . ." I croaked into the silence, then regretted it as I rubbed my throat.

He stopped in front of my door and eyed me through the glass, his look a mixture of worry and fury, and all I could do was hope that the worry won out. To help him along, I rubbed at my neck a few more times, and made an extra big grimace.

Dutch rolled his eyes and opened the car door. Bending down he sighed heavily and said, "I don't know whether to kill you or hug you."

I smiled and extended my arms. "Hug please," I whispered.

The ice broke on Dutch's face as he looked at me, and with a chuckle he leaned in and gave me a bear hug that seemed to calm my shivers. After a moment he leaned back and asked, "How you doin', Edgar?"

I answered him with a so-so movement with my hand.

"You wanna get outta here?" he asked me.

I nodded furiously and he pulled me gently from the squad car. With his arm wrapped protectively around me, we walked to my SUV and just before we got in my intuition went haywire. I paused as Dutch held open the passenger side door for me and stared off into space, then looked at Dutch and said, "James," in a croaky whisper.

"You know where he is?" Dutch asked.

I nodded as the vision in my head replayed and I pointed to the car keys in his hand. Reluctantly he gave them to me and we changed places. We drove in silence and before long pulled up in front of James's house. I got out and Dutch was close on my heels. Heading to the back of the house I reached a window that allowed me to peer into the basement, and there was James, just as my vision had described, chained to a pipe and looking much the worse for wear. I backed away from the window and pointed, and Dutch moved in for a closer view. He peered through the pane and within a few seconds he had moved away from the window and headed to the basement door. With a move that combined a hard kick with a body shove the door splintered, giving way, and Dutch threw me his cell phone before he ducked through the opening. "Speed dial two," he said. "That's Milo, just whisper the address and tell him we need an ambulance."

I nodded and flipped open the phone hitting the number he'd indicated. Milo answered and I croaked out the address and said the word, "ambulance."

"Sit tight, Abby, we're on our way," Milo replied.

I closed the phone and headed into James's basement, and the scene I encountered made me come up short. James had been cruelly chained to a pipe under a sink in the basement. The skin around his wrists and ankles was bruised and bleeding. Even more disturbing was his emaciated appearance, as his clothes hung loosely on him, and I noticed with alarm that he was wearing the same clothes I'd seen him in the day I'd confronted him about his grandfather, almost a week and a half earlier.

"Is he all right?" I whispered as I came to Dutch's side.

Dutch looked over his shoulder as he continued to

try to work the chain around James's hands. "He's in rough shape. Did you call Milo?"

I nodded.

"Good. Can you head upstairs and get me a glass of water? I'm not sure he's had anything to drink in a long time, and he's barely conscious now. The water might help."

I darted up the stairs into the kitchen and stopped short, my breath catching as I gazed at a beautiful woman standing serenely at the kitchen sink. She was petite, bordering on tiny, and she wore a white gown that puddled at her feet. Her eyes were large and blue, her face a perfect heart shape and her hair a shade of platinum that was so beautiful it looked luminescent. As I watched with stunned fascination she pointed to my chest, and reflexively my hand came up to touch where she pointed. I felt the bulk of the diamonds that I'd hidden in my jacket pocket and until this moment had forgotten about. She smiled at me and mouthed, "Thank you," then simply vanished from sight. I stood there for a moment with my mouth hanging open, not quite sure I'd actually seen what I thought I'd seen.

"Abby?" I heard Dutch call from the basement. "You coming with that water?"

I shook my head to clear it and hurried forward to get the water, figuring I'd deal with that experience later. When I got back downstairs, James was coming to, and I noticed that Dutch had managed to get his hands free and was now trying to make him more comfortable by taking off his own coat and wadding it up to rest behind James's head. I extended the water to James and he took it hungrily, drinking it with shaking hands.

I accepted the empty glass he handed me and stood

up to get more from the tap above his head. I handed that glass to him and he drained most of it as well. In the distance we heard the sound of sirens approaching, and Dutch said, "Hang in there, pal. Help is on the way."

James smiled at him and nodded, then seemed to drift back into unconsciousness.

A few minutes later the cavalry arrived, and James was carted off to Beaumont Hospital. Dutch, Milo and I followed the ambulance and hung out in the waiting room while James was treated for his injuries, malnutrition and dehydration.

Behind my back, Dutch also managed to corner a doctor to take a look at my throat, and as I suspected, it was only severely bruised. The advice from the doc was the same as the EMT so I was allowed to get away with paying only a fifty-dollar co-pay for a big fat waste of time.

"You owe me fifty bucks," I whispered when I'd been released from the checkout counter and came back to sit grumpily next to Dutch.

"Let's call it even for sneaking out on me this morning at the PT's office," came his smart reply.

I decided to count my blessings and shut my mouth. Just then James's doctor appeared and said that we could go in to see him. "He's weak, so don't stay long. Take a short statement and get the rest later, okay?" the doctor warned.

"You got it," Dutch replied as we headed to James's room.

A much thinner version of the man I'd first met at the jewelry store lay propped up on pillows, his wrists bandaged and a pained expression on his face. I waved at him when we had all filed in and he gave me a small smile. His smile faded as he seemed to notice the bruise at my throat. "Did my brother do that to you?" I nodded, and James said, "I'm really sorry."

I shrugged my shoulders and smiled at him, then pointed to my throat and said, "Can't talk much," which came out barely a whisper.

"I understand," he said. Turning to Milo and Dutch, he added, "I suppose you want to know what happened?"

Milo nodded and said, "Yeah, and start about 1940 for us, would ya?"

James looked only slightly surprised, then sighed and began, "My grandfather was an evil man."

"We figured that out," Dutch said.

"You know, when I was a boy, I thought the world of him. I thought he was a hero, but then, one day when I was sixteen he came home drunk and sat down next to me and started telling me things that I wished I'd never heard.

"He said that he'd been a hero in France, an active member of the French Resistance, and was responsible for saving thousands of lives. So what if there had been sacrifices, he'd said, so what if a few had to be offered up for slaughter so that the rest could live. And then he explained how he'd acquired the inventory for his jewelry store. How he'd carefully made himself out to be a friend of the Jews, and according to him, he'd helped just enough of them to garner the community's trust. But those Jews within the diamond trade were a different story. These poor people had believed my grandfather would save them, but instead he deceived, stole from and eventually, turned them over to the Nazis.

"Realizing that his business was built on murder, I left home shortly after that. Something my brother never forgave me for," James said, pausing to massage one wrist.

"That's why you went into opals," I whispered.

James smiled painfully at me. "Yes. They were the one gem my grandfather never carried. He considered them bad luck, and refused to deal in them. When he died, and left the store to me, I considered just giving away the inventory to charity, but there was something so awful about what he did that I needed to make amends on behalf of my family for it. My father was a good man, and if he had known the truth about his own father, I'm sure he would have done the same. So I took all of my savings and began Opalescence. It took a few years, but eventually the store caught on, and I began to turn a profit."

"So that's why you donated half of your proceeds to the Holocaust Survivors' Fund."

"Yes," James said. "I couldn't take back what my grandfather had done, but at least I could try and make amends."

"So, what about Liza," Milo asked, throwing out the name to see James's reaction.

"The only thing I know about her was that she was the girlfriend of my grandfather, and one day she simply disappeared. I had already left home when she came around, and other than what my brother told me, which was some bizarre story about how she had stolen some rare diamonds from our grandfather and that he had dealt with her accordingly, I didn't know anything about her. I suppose I was just too appalled by him at that point to ask many questions. I guess I didn't want to know."

"So, you knew nothing about the puzzle box, or its contents?"

"Only what Jean-Luke told me when he showed up at my shop a week ago. I wasn't going to let him in at first, but he gave me this sad story about how he'd been living on the streets, and he looked very much the worse for it. His clothing was torn and his hair was long and matted, and his beard was overgrown. I guess I felt sorry for him, especially when he told me some awful man had beaten him with a cane when he'd begged for food on a street corner. I almost didn't believe that part until he showed me the welts on his back, and, like a fool, I let him into the shop. The moment the door was closed he went crazy, and started accusing me of giving away Grandfather's treasure. He said that the treasure had been in a box hidden in the house, and after I'd sold it I'd allowed someone else to steal our family's legacy. I tried to calm him down, talk some sense into him, but he wouldn't listen and he became so enraged he began to beat me.

"I tried to convince him that I knew nothing about any hidden treasure, that I'd sold the house because it represented a part of my past I wanted to forget. My real estate agent was one of those touchy-feely types, and she spoke about getting creeped out in the house whenever she showed it to a prospective client, but I never paid any attention to that. I'd never seen any ghost of the kind you told me about, Abby, and I guess when you showed up at my shop and began demonstrating your abilities, I knew you were for real. That's why it upset me so much when you told me my grandfather was still around, terrorizing people much like he did in real life. I'm sorry I was so rude, but when you shoved that box at me and said that my grandfather had murdered someone over it, I figured you knew the whole story and you probably wanted to blame me. At that point I just wanted to find my brother and get him back to Mashburn, and I figured I'd come clean to you later."

I nodded at him and gave him a peace sign. I knew more than most about being overprotective when it came to a sibling.

"So, what happened with you and Jean-Luke, I mean, how'd you end up chained in the basement?" Dutch asked.

"The night after the robbery I got home late, and I noticed Jean-Luke sitting out in the cold on my front stoop. He wanted to talk about turning himself back in to Mashburn, and he seemed lucid and calm, and so I stupidly invited him in out of the cold. Once inside he immediately excused himself to go the bathroom, and while I was taking my coat off, he hit me over the head with something heavy. When I woke up I was chained to a pipe in the basement. To add insult to injury, Jean-Luke was freshly showered and groomed and wearing my glasses and clothes and, to my astonishment, it was like looking in a mirror."

I nodded as he said that and thought back to my grandmother's warning about being careful of the twins. Now it made sense. James continued, "He would have left me for dead, you know," he said sadly, and I saw a tear gather in his eye and slowly leak its way down his cheek. "And the worst is that I don't know what happened to Chloe," James said as another tear gathered and fell.

"Chloe?" Dutch asked.

"My golden lab puppy. I haven't seen or heard her in two weeks, and I'm afraid of what he's done to her," he moaned.

Just then my intuition chimed in, and I grabbed the pen and paper Milo had been taking notes with. I didn't want to push my voice, and I needed to tell him about the messages in my head. On the paper I wrote, *Who's the little girl with the pink Big Wheel?*

I handed the paper to James and he read it, his brow furrowing slightly. Suddenly he looked up at me and said, "Briana Brady. She's a little girl who lives about four houses away from me. She's this little terror on her pink Big Wheel and she rides up and down the street as fast as her legs can pedal. All the neighbors think it's hilarious to watch her zoom back and forth."

I smiled as I grabbed the pad of paper back and wrote, *She's got your dog.*

When James read that he looked up at me, his eyes full of hope. "Really?" he asked.

I nodded, and gave him a thumbs-up. I knew that Chloe was safe and sound.

Just then a nurse stepped into our area and cleared her throat. "Doctor Papas would like you to let Mr. Carlier rest now," she said sternly.

We all smiled sheepishly at her; we'd clearly overstayed our welcome. Milo turned back to James and asked, "How about I come back tomorrow and talk to you a little more about your brother, okay James?"

"He's really in trouble now, isn't he?" James asked, and it dawned on all of us that he didn't yet know his brother was dead.

The nurse cleared her throat again, and gave Milo a stern look. There was some news that was best delivered when the patient was strong enough to take it, and Milo got the message. "We'll talk in the morning, James. You need to rest now."

"Okay," James said tiredly as he leaned back against his pillows and closed his eyes.

I followed the fellas out to the lobby again, and noticed the clock on the wall. I was surprised it read only two o'clock because it felt later than that. Milo turned to Dutch and asked, "So what now?"

Dutch wrapped an arm around my shoulders and pulled me close. "Now I take Abby out of Dodge and treat her to a little vacation. We'll be in Canada if you need us." And with that he walked me to the door.

*   *   *

We arrived in Windsor a little after three, and found our way to Eliza von Halpstadt's cousin, Helsa Otzeck, who resided in a lovely medium-sized Tudor on the west side of town. We walked to the door and rang the bell and after a minute it was opened by a petite woman with light blond hair and brilliant blue eyes set in a heart-shaped face. My breath caught in my throat as I looked at her because the resemblance to the ghost I'd seen in James's kitchen was remarkable.

"Miss Otzeck?" Dutch asked.

Helsa cocked her head at the two of us on her front porch, clearly at a loss as to what we wanted with her. "Oh my," she said after a moment. "You two must be here about Eliza."

I looked at Dutch and he looked at me, then we both turned back to Helsa and he said, "Yes, how did you know?"

Helsa chuckled and said, "I got the strangest e-mail yesterday from a professor at the University of Michigan. He asked me all kinds of questions about a cousin of mine who disappeared some thirty years ago, and then said that I may get a visit from the American Federal Bureau of Investigation."

Dutch smiled and flipped open his badge. "Professor Robins is an old friend of mine," he explained. "May we come in?"

"Yes, of course," she said and made room for us to pass into her front hallway.

Taking our coats her breath caught when she noticed the condition of my throat. "Oh my goodness!" she said as she leaned in to inspect the bruises forming at my neck. "Who did that to you?"

Subconsciously my hand came up to my neck and I tried to hide the bruising before Helsa made too big a deal about it. Dutch put a warm hand on my back and said, "She got that trying to protect something that belongs to you."

Helsa looked at him quizzically, then ushered us into a lovely living room where we sat on overstuffed couches and sipped iced tea, and explained to Helsa what happened to her cousin long ago.

When Dutch was done telling her what he knew, Helsa wiped her eyes, the truth of what had become of her cousin bringing her to tears. After collecting herself, she managed to fill us in on the rest of Liza's story. "Eliza found us when I was seven years old, and she was by that time, I think, around twenty. She had made her way back from Lyon to Lausanne and told my mother the whole sordid tale. One night, when her father, my uncle, had made arrangements with a local Frenchman for new identity papers, the Germans came and knocked on the door. Eliza's mother hid her in the pantry of the house where they were hiding, and before she could hide Pieter, Eliza's brother, the door burst open and her whole family was taken away and never seen again.

"As Eliza hid in the pantry, too afraid to come out, she was able to see through a crack in the door, and, as she watched, a man walked in just as her parents and brother were taken away and he began to search the small home. Eliza recognized the man as someone who had been to their home on several occasions. Her father had introduced him as someone who would ensure their safety; he had even called him a hero.

"But this man was no hero, he was a murderer. In horror and fear Eliza watched as he combed every inch of that home, twice opening the pantry. Luckily he did not see her there as she hid behind a bin of flour. He looked and looked until he found what he was searching for, my uncle's legacy, the Schwalbe Eier diamonds.

Eliza saw him take the box with the diamonds, and as he left the home, she saw him give the Germans some money, and the men laughed at their own treachery.

"Two days later a neighbor heard Eliza crying through the window and found her in the pantry. The woman took pity on her and brought her home to live with her, caring for her through the rest of the war and raising her until she was old enough to find her way back to us."

"That was one determined young lady," Dutch said.

"That was Eliza," Helsa said, her head shaking back and forth as old memories seemed to replay themselves in her head. "To this day, I don't know how she found us, because it's remarkable really that a girl so young would remember the last name of her newly married aunt. But Eliza was a bright woman, and she had a way with names and places. I remember how beautiful she was, and I wanted very much to be just like her when I grew up."

Just then a phone rang in the kitchen, and Dutch and I looked up as the sound pulled us back to the present, but Helsa ignored the distraction and continued.

"Eliza lived with us for a few years before going to university. When she graduated she moved back to Lausanne and taught school just down the street from us. Then, one day she came to my mother with news that greatly upset Mama. Eliza had discovered the whereabouts of the Frenchman who betrayed and murdered her family. She said she was leaving Switzerland for the United States to find this man and get back what he had stolen from us.

"My mother begged her not to go, she said it was too dangerous, but Eliza wouldn't listen to her and packed her bags and left. We got word from her once a month for the next three months, and then we never heard from her again.

"Years later I met and married a Canadian, and we moved here, and I tried to find out what happened to my cousin, but to no avail. Now at least I know, and a part of me can finally put Eliza to rest."

"Maybe this will help too," I croaked as I reached into my pocket and pulled out the leather pouch I'd hidden from the border guards.

Helsa took the bag and opened the top sash. Curiously, she emptied the contents into her hand, and all three of us caught our breath as three thirty-carat diamonds of near perfect cut, color and clarity tinkled together in Helsa's palm. "Schwalbe Eier," Helsa said, the words rolling off her tongue and making a beautiful sound. Just then something else tipped out of the bag, and we all looked as Helsa picked up a small folded piece of paper and pulled it open to read it.

"What's it say?" Dutch asked.

"It's the oddest thing," Helsa said as she studied the weathered parchment. "It has my uncle's name and the words 'Schwalbe Eier' along with several other names and some French acronyms for gemstones."

"The missing page of the notebook," I whispered to Dutch.

He nodded as Helsa refolded the paper and tucked it back into the pouch, then surveyed the diamonds in her hand again.

"I'm glad we could return those to their rightful owner," Dutch said, standing and grabbing my hand.

Helsa looked up at us, her eyes full of moisture as she said, "On behalf of my family, I thank you."

"Ma'am," Dutch said and gave her a small salute as he led me back to the front door, grabbing our coats along the way.

"You done good in there, Edgar," he said to me as he helped me into my coat and gave me a tender kiss on the back of my neck.

I smiled and mouthed, "Ditto," to him as we headed back to the car.

Three hours later Dutch and I were checked in to the Toronto Park Hyatt and as the hotel room door closed behind us, I'll have to admit, I was a little nervous. "Tired?" Dutch asked, taking my luggage out of my hand and placing it on the suitcase rack next to the closet.

"A little," I croaked.

"Hey," he admonished, coming up behind me and wrapping strong arms around my waist, "no talking."

I smiled as he began to nibble on my neck and answered softly with, "Then stop asking me questions."

He turned me around to face him then, and moved the collar away from my neck to examine the bruises there more closely. After a moment he cradled my face in his hands and said, "Don't ever take a chance like that again, Abby. Do you understand me?"

I nodded at him. I knew now that he wasn't trying to control me—he simply cared too much about me to let me take chances. "I mean it," he said after a minute, searching my eyes for confirmation.

I smiled wryly at him and leaned in for a kiss. He'd have to be satisfied with that.

I don't know why I thought I would need to pack so many clothes that weekend, because I sure didn't wear much. Not even the teddy. It, along with most of the rest of my clothing, stayed packed away in my suitcase, and for the next two days, pretty much the only thing I put on was tall, blond and muscular. And since I never kiss and tell, the only thing I'll admit to . . . is that it fit *purrrfectly*.

Epilogue

I waited in my car with the heater going until I saw the rental car snake its way down the street, headed in my direction. I smiled with anticipation and got out of the Mazda, shivering slightly in the crispness of the day.

Dutch and I had gotten back from Toronto a few days earlier, and my voice was slowly returning. I'd made the call when we got home, and I was happy to see that I'd received such a quick response.

The car pulled up alongside me in the driveway, and the doors opened to reveal a very pretty brunette who reminded me a lot of Sandra Bullock, and an equally handsome man with jet-black hair and ebony eyes. "M.J.?" I asked, extending my hand in greeting.

"Hi Abby, it's great to meet you," she said as she took my hand and pumped it a few times. Turning to her compatriot she said, "And this is Steven Sable. He's working on a documentary."

Steven came around the car and I smiled up at him. "Nice to meet you," I said as he took my hand and lifted it to his lips for a gentle kiss.

"Likewise," he said and I noticed the hint of an accent. "Is this the house with the dead woman at the bottom of the stairs?"

"Yeah," I said, only barely holding back the nervous giggle that wanted to erupt from my throat as I noted his accent. The combo of his baritone voice and an accent that seemed a mixture of Latin and European sounded a bit like he was melting a bite of chocolate on the back of his tongue. "This is the one."

"Come on Sable," M.J. called. "Cut the flirt and let's head inside." Steven winked at me and turned toward M.J. who was already halfway to the door. "Coming, *dear*," he said sarcastically.

I stood out on the lawn and stared after them as they disappeared through the door. I had no intention of following. I'd seen enough of the inside of that house for a while. I could only hope that whatever spirits still haunted its insides could be evicted by M.J. Holliday and her Latin sidekick.

Intuitively, I felt there was at least one less spirit haunting the house. I knew that by encountering Liza in James's home that she had at last given up guarding her family's treasure, and it meant the world to me that she had trusted me to get them safely into the hands of her cousin.

As for Jean-Paul, I figured he'd go pretty easily once he figured out the diamonds were no longer hidden on the property. The one worry I had was that his grandson, Jean-Luke, might be the newest ghostly tenant. I didn't know what ghost busting involved, but I sure hoped it worked.

Dave, Cat and I had decided that once the house was clean of all ghostly inhabitants, we'd hire a crew to do the work. I couldn't very well make Dave go back in there, especially since he'd started to develop a skin rash due to all the garlic he'd been wearing. Plus, it was unfair to expect he'd be able to work in a place where he'd killed a man. Self-defense or not, it was still a tough thing to have to live with.

Feeling chilly again I hopped back into my car and started the engine, cranking up the heat and warming my hands underneath the blower. I watched the clock and kept track of the minutes, and after about an hour the front door finally opened and M.J. came out and made her way to my car. I rolled down the window so we could talk. "I hate to tell you this, Abby, but that house is clean."

"What?"

"We've checked it from top to bottom with all our instruments, and nothing's registering. I've checked the place against my own antennae and I'm not picking up anything either. So, whatever you did to solve the mystery must have worked, 'cuz no one dead is hanging out inside."

"So I flew you guys out for nothing?" I asked, shaking my head.

" 'Fraid so. If it's any consolation, I won't charge you anything more than airfare," M.J. offered.

"That'd be great," I said, feeling relieved on a multitude of fronts. "So where's your partner?" I asked, making small talk.

"He's inside snapping some pictures. You guys gonna renovate the place and sell it?"

"Yeah," I said, smiling at her perceptiveness.

"You sure got a lot of work ahead. That place is a dump!"

"I know. It's bad isn't it?"

"And the smell," she added, scrunching up her nose. "Jesus, it's ripe in there, don't you think?"

"Ripe?" I asked, thinking perhaps she was talking about the cigarette smoke I had smelled.

"Yeah," M.J. insisted. "It's like a garlic factory in there."

I looked askance at her. "Did you say *garlic*?"

"Uh-huh," she answered. "It just reeks of raw garlic."

"You don't say," I said thoughtfully, a small grin creeping at the corners of my mouth as I remembered Dave's firm belief that a good dose of garlic would ward away any old evil spirit. Perhaps this was Liza's doing, or perhaps Jean-Paul and Jean-Luke had gotten to the pearly gates, seen the evil of their ways, and imprinted some sort of aromatic energy on the place. Whatever, I knew that the house on Fern was permanently de-ghosted.

Months later when we'd finished fixing up Fern Street and sold the house to a lovely middle-aged Italian couple, we learned that although they appreciated all the new renovations and conveniences, the thing the wife loved most, and convinced her it was the home she had to have, was that the house smelled just like her mama's kitchen back home. That, and as she told us at the closing, "The house has wonderful energy, don't you agree?"

"If you say so," I said and, just in case . . . signed those papers lickety-split.